CRAVING THE TABOO

C.L. LEDFORD

Book Cover Design by Designs by Charly

Interior Design By Designs by Charly

1st Edition 2025

❀ Formatted with Vellum

To all the thirsty sluts that need their guts rearranged with a hand
necklace wrapped around their throats.
Open those legs wide and dig those nails in deep for Daddy D.

Contents

Chapter One

DRAKE

I sat on the edge of the bed while the brunette knelt in front of me, bobbing her head over my lap. Her saliva ran down my cock and my piercings, which lined both sides of my shaft, as she gagged each time it slipped into the back of her throat. Each time I was close to spilling into her mouth, she would stop. I had half a mind to hold her head in place and fuck her face until I found my release.

She came up for air. Her makeup tracking down her cheeks. Her smirk when her eyes met with mine dwindled when I didn't reciprocate the gesture. I raised my eyebrows as she used the flat of her tongue to run from my balls to the tip of my head.

"Is there something else you would like?" Her sweet voice reached my ears while her eyes searched my face.

"Keep swallowing my cock until you feel me come in the back of your throat."

She smiled at me before covering my cock with her mouth again. My hand went into her hair while she thrust her head up and down. I grabbed my phone and took a picture of her using my cock to fuck her face. I sent the picture to TC, showing him what he was missing by staying in with some woman.

I never understood him and what he called 'flavors.' They were all blonde, so I didn't get why he called them that when he only had one type. Most of the time, I thought he was just choosing to be with blondes, but what did I know?

My balls tightened, and I gripped her hair as I spilled into her throat. She gagged but gazed up at me. Grinning, I filled her mouth with my cum. After I finished, I pulled from her mouth, and she swallowed my load. I loved it when they did that, but I hadn't found one to settle down with. At least one who wouldn't get me killed by their big brother.

She sat back on her heels and used her finger to get the little bit of cum that dripped down her chin and sucked it into her mouth. I couldn't deny that she was beautiful. The way her green eyes stared up at me, but they weren't the ones I craved.

Going to the Churchhill's for dinner once a week for the past year, TC's sister Emi had grown into her own, and it was becoming harder and harder to keep my eyes away from her.

I had taken to keeping away from her as much as I could. Other than my once-a-week torture. Emi was too young for me, but she had become an addiction in every sense of the word. Besides, TC would have killed me if I touched her, and I wouldn't want to keep that secret from my best friend, which was the only way I'd have stayed alive.

"You've gotten quiet, hun. What else can I do for you?" The naked brunette stood, her hand on my soft cock, rubbing it.

I stared at her as her tongue wet her lips with a side grin. Like I said, this woman was gorgeous, but she wasn't who I wanted. The longer she pumped my cock, the harder I was becoming. If I took her from behind, I could imagine I was with Emi. Standing, I rounded her; my hands ran down her ample hips and ass. I leaned in, and her skin prickled with chills. "On your knees. On the bed. Ass in the air."

She giggled and obeyed my direction. She wiggled as she got into position. I stroked my cock thinking about the one woman I couldn't have, who didn't even know I wanted her. Taking her beautiful dirty-blonde hair in my hand and plunging my cock deep inside her as she screamed my name. I crawled onto the mattress and pressed a finger into my partner this evening.

She moaned as I pistoned my fingers inside her, getting her ready for my cock. She made all the right sounds, and her hands clenched the covers on the bed while her cunt gripped my finger. My finger was soaked when I pulled it out. I grabbed the condom on the bed and tore it open. Rolling it on for both our benefits.

"Hun, just like I've told TC, you don't need that. I have an IUD in." She stared back at me with a grin.

Fuck. There was no way I was going to fuck someone that TC had on his list. Fuck that. If I would have known she was messing around with him, she wouldn't have even sucked me off.

"I don't fuck without one, but since you are still seeing TC, this will be the end of our night." I pulled the condom off and slid from the bed.

She flipped onto her back and glared at me. "You have got to be kidding me."

"I'm not. Get the fuck up and get dressed and be on your merry way." I grabbed my boxers and pulled them up.

Walking to the bathroom, I turned. She was still on the bed. "You have until I get out of the shower to be out of this room. If you are not, I will have security escort you out."

"You two are just the fucking same!" she yelled at me, and I chuckled while I shut the bathroom door. Locking it for good measure. I didn't need a psychopath coming in on me in the shower.

I normally never left a woman unsatisfied, but I wasn't going to fuck her when she had been fucking TC. Nope, not going to happen.

I stood in the elevator as it went up to my office. The building had been here when my grandfather first came on board. But we weren't here just because we had made it big. No, my grandfather had made a deal with Mr. Churchhill's father, and so we used the logistics company as a front while being second in command.

Laundering money through the up-and-coming company didn't make us rich, but we wanted to look more legal than the other side of the family. So when I ascended to the COO position, and TC became CEO, we implemented more of an international shipment with boats. We had doubled the income in a year and made sure to keep gaining clients.

My father had been in line to be the head of the Italian mafia but had turned it down when he met my mother. So his younger brother took it. I didn't mind. I didn't want to be heir to something that would probably get me killed one day. Hell, it probably still would. Since I was still part of the family.

After stepping out of the elevator, I headed to TC's office. He didn't answer me last night, and I didn't want him to think I was taking any of his women. TC had stayed late yesterday once his father and Mr. Emerson had shown up. All I knew was that it had to be important if Mr. Churchhill was here.

I opened the door to his office and spotted him in his chair. It used to be his old man's, and he decided to keep the thing. I would have gotten a new one, but for some reason, the bastard kept it, just like the warehouse he wouldn't get rid of.

TC glanced up at me while I made my way up to my favorite

chair. I sat down and rested my ankle on my opposite knee and waited for him to finish whatever he was doing. He seemed distracted today along with barely moving his right arm.

"So, how did the meeting go last night?" I pressed him. He stopped writing before he grunted and then continued what he was doing. "Okay, it went okay? Or you messed up again?"

"If you have to know, they have fucked me without lube. If I want to keep the company, I have to marry Aurora, *Emerson's* daughter. Which I'm not too fucking happy about." TC huffed as he sat back in his chair and stretched. I noticed that he flinched a little when he ran his hands through his hair and down his face.

"Okay, so just marry the broad. It's basically free pussy." I chuckled with a shrug.

TC glared at me, and I knew I had pushed a button that didn't need to be touched. Raising my hands in surrender, I stood and headed to the door and out of it. I was just glad that he didn't say it was about me and the looks that I was giving his sister.

"Oh, and Drake."

I turned back and glanced at him.

"Don't make any plans to get laid tonight. We have a betrothal party to attend."

I nodded and closed the door. He wasn't happy about this. If I got as much pussy as he did, I would be pissed, if I had to give it up for someone I didn't choose.

Heading back down the long hall to my office, I allowed my mind to wander. I started to question things I hadn't before. Like why did our family do what they did, and why was it that, as much as I tried, I couldn't keep Emi out of my head?

"Mr. DeLuca, your father called. He left you a message." Tiffany stood from her desk, her braids running down her back, her cleavage on display in her button down, dark green blouse. She handed out the note to me, her manicured hand slightly touching mine. I glanced at the paper before I nodded, silently suggesting she sit in her chair again.

"Thank you, Tiffany." She smiled up at me, and I entered my office.

My father's message told me exactly what TC had told me just moments before. It looked like this was going to be official. I could already tell that he didn't like the arrangement. But my father's note also informed me about a meeting with the other side of the family.

I had never met my uncle or grandfather on my dad's side. My father had kept me away from them when I was younger. But that didn't mean that my dad hadn't shown me a thing or two from that life. He still had a few things on the side that my mother didn't know about.

Once we had gotten the international shipping operational, my father talked me into adding extra things to our shipments. I didn't care, but if TC ever found out, I was sure that he would get rid of me. I hadn't known him long when we met at college. He wasn't someone I believed would be okay with my father's side business. I didn't know if Mr. Churchhill had told him about that part of my father's life.

I passed Tiffany's desk and walked into my office. The wall of windows gave more light than the fluorescent ever did. I took my seat at my desk, leaning back with a sigh. Sometimes running both businesses were tiring.

"Mr. DeLuca?" Tiffany's voice came over the intercom, bringing me out of my thoughts.

"Yes, Tiffany."

"One of the board members is here to see you." I rolled my eyes. This man had been coming to me for weeks, wanting me to talk TC into not giving the employees their yearly raise. Motherfucker was relentless. I was going to give him the go-ahead to talk about it in the board meeting just to let him get reamed by TC for even thinking about it. TC didn't just treat these people like employees; they were treated like family.

"Let him in."

The older man entered my office and strolled up to my desk. I had been fielding his calls ever since he came up to me in the elevator.

"Mr. DeLuca, thank you for seeing me. I really think with all these numbers that we shouldn't give a raise this year..."

"You know what, Frank, I think you should bring this up in the board meeting this week."

"You will back me on this? I mean, we are already overpaying some of these people. If we continue, we will go bankrupt." The excitement in his voice and facial expression told me that I was going to enjoy it when TC laid into him. Because TC wasn't one to not know things about the company. Well, other than what my father and his father had been up to. Even then I didn't think that Mr. Churchhill knew everything about all of my father's dodgy dealings.

I shrugged and leaned back in my chair as the older, balding man stood in front of me. If he took that as a yes, it was on him, not me.

"Thank you, sir. It will be much better for the company." Frank left my office and shut the door behind him.

Shaking my head, the ping of my phone brought my attention to the device in my pocket. I pulled it out and stared at it.

Father: Meet me before the party tonight. I have something to tell you.

Chapter Two

DRAKE

I was supposed to meet TC at his penthouse to head over to the Emersons' place. But after the text from my father, I wasn't going to be able to do that. When I drove into my family's estate, I noticed more guards than before. This wasn't what I expected, but being connected by blood to one of the more prominent Italian mafia clans put our lives on the line, even when we were being "good."

The guards didn't even stop me as I pulled into the drive and up to the Victorian mansion. Father must have told them I was coming. Not like they didn't know my car, but most of the time, they stopped me. Either to chitchat or be assholes, depending on their mood.

Stopping at the bottom of the cascading steps, the valet opened my door, and I stepped out. I adjusted my suit jacket and headed to the front door. The door was unlocked, and I entered, realizing that I wasn't the only one here with my father.

Male voices came from the drawing room down the hall. I made my way there, keeping my steps steady. It wasn't like I hadn't met people with my father. As I came up to the door, I realized that it was open. My father was sitting across from a man who shared his same features.

I rapped my knuckles on the door frame, and both men looked my way. My father motioned for me to come in. Entering the room, my strides brought me to them and I sat facing the other man.

Even though he shared similarities with my father, I noticed that there were things that he didn't share with him. Like the dark hair that both my father and I had. This man was blond and had blue eyes.

"Drake, I want you to finally meet your uncle, Riccardo."

"You are the spitting image of your father. At least when he was younger," my uncle chuckled.

My eyes ran over him, and I noticed the hardness in his face and the scar under one of his eyes. I wasn't just a rich playboy; I could hold my own in a knife fight. But this man, I don't think I would ever turn my back on.

"Thanks. What brings you here after not doing so for so long?" I didn't like that this man was just now coming here from wherever he came from to "visit."

"He is just like you, brother. Mouthy. I have always kept an eye on family. Especially someone I was so close with growing up. But I do have another reason for being here." Riccardo stood from his seat and walked over to the shelves that held very few books on them. "You see, nephew, I've come to bring our family back together. For our family to continue to run as one of the largest families in Italy, you need to become the head of the empire."

"And if I refuse?" I wasn't sure I wanted to be the head of this family.

"Then someone else's bastard will take over the reins, and it will no longer be run by a blood-related DeLuca." The way Riccardo's eyes cut to mine didn't instill the fear he was trying to make me feel. "If you don't take over my wife's bastard will."

"What do I need to do? I'm already running a business to launder money for you." My father had told me when he ceded the position about the arrangement that his father had with TC's grandfather.

I didn't like keeping that from the man who had become my friend and brother from another mother. There were times when I wanted to tell him, but my father had told me not to. And then there was Emi. I wanted to be with that woman, but if I was keeping a secret from her brother, how would I be honest with her?

"Until I can prove that the boy I have raised is not my heir, you will continue to run things from here. But you will have to get rid of our enemy here in LA. He is getting older and has no heir. Once he goes, things will be in a riot." My uncle came back over to the settee and sat.

"And who is this? I'm not prepared to off a man I don't know." I wasn't afraid to get my hands dirty. I had been in more gunfights than I cared to admit.

"The man's name is Jack, he's known as The Torturer. He has been running the LA crime syndicate for a long time. I have a mole in the midst, giving me information that he isn't doing so well. It is time to bring him down and take our family onto the playing field."

I nodded. It didn't bother me that I would have to kill someone. What bothered me the most was that I had heard of The Torturer. And even with him being as old as he was, I didn't think it was a good idea to take this lightly.

I pulled up with my parents to the Emersons' home. TC and Jake were already here, along with a few others. We all walked into the house, meeting up with the Churchhills. While my parents stopped with them, I headed over to TC. Who, like always, was in the middle of the crowd.

My gaze went to Emi, who was standing beside another guy. He wasn't dressed for the occasion, and I couldn't understand what she saw in him. This guy didn't even have a tux on, he wore tight pants showing that I definitely had the bigger cock. His leather jacket had chains and other shit on it. The boy was part of some cringy band.

Mrs. Emerson came in, and then Aurora. Fuck, if TC didn't get his shit together, that woman would be gone forever. But he kept bitching about the fact she had shown his mother the picture of him sniffing a line off some bimbo's stomach.

Everyone in the room stopped to watch her walk over to stand beside her parents, TC's parents, and mine. TC started moving over before his father motioned for him. Emi stayed over with her punk boyfriend as I made my way over to our parents.

Mr. Churchhill moved forward and hushed the crowd's mumbling. But I couldn't keep my eyes off Emi and the asshole she had brought with her. I couldn't believe the Churchhills would allow her to date someone like him. The way he touched her made me want to tear him limb from limb.

I realized too late that TC and Aurora were dancing. I needed to get a grip on this, and it needed to be now because, if I didn't, things would turn into chaos. I headed to the bar and did my best to flirt with the brunette bartender, but Emi continued to distract me. Now she was dancing with the neanderthal, and his gyrating against her really fucked with me.

TC joined me with Alex after Aurora had left him on the dance floor. He leaned against the bar, as he took the drink from the bartender. "We don't. This has been arranged for years."

Looking over to TC and Alex from the bartender I jumped into their conversation.

"Yeah? Well, I think it would do you some good to get away from the office for a while," I answered him, bringing his gaze over to me as I continued to try to flirt with the woman behind the bar. I grinned over at him, carrying my glass with me. "Guess that means no more women for you. I finally have a chance."

Not that I would want a chance with other women when the one I wanted the most was dancing with a Led Zeppelin wannabe.

"No, I'll still have my women. I just can't bring them out in the open anymore. I'm not going to touch Aurora." TC glared over at me, and I raised my hands in surrender. I knew when to press his buttons and when to leave the asshole alone.

"She's hot. I don't understand why you wouldn't want to fuck her?" I watched as he turned his gaze over to her. Aurora stood beside another man and her friends, who also stood beside Emi and her boyfriend. Allowing me to stare at the person I wasn't supposed to.

Part of me wanted to tell him to keep his hands off her, but what would TC say if I did? I was surprised he was letting this go on for as long as he was. Which, taking into account that he was concentrating on the party before us, I didn't think that he had noticed his sister with the punk.

The sound of a glass slamming brought my attention back to the men beside me at the bar. Ms. Brunette slid TC another drink next to his empty one. Alex stood from his hunched-over position on the bar, a chuckle leaving his mouth as he motioned with his drink to Aurora. "Because she's why he almost didn't get the company."

"Ah! So that's why Daddy Dearest stayed on for as long as he did. Didn't think he would ever let us be." I chuckled and finished my drink. Cutting my gaze back to TC who glared at me.

"Keep laughing. I'll make sure you stay overtime every night,"

TC threatened as he continued to glare at me over the rim of his glass. He turned and waved the bartender over, and she poured him another drink.

When TC became like this, it was best to leave him alone rather than mess with him further. He left our group, and Alex asked, "Where are you going, man?"

I came up to Alex and clapped him on the shoulder and shook my head. Turning back around, I realized that Emi and her new boyfriend weren't there anymore. So much for getting her away from him, and I know TC didn't realize she had brought him here.

Setting my glass on the bar, I went over to a table in the corner and sat, watching the partygoers talking and dancing. The only reason they were here was the free food and drinks. And to see what was going to happen, but both Aurora and TC handled everything perfectly with how much they hated each other.

My father was talking with some of the men who were part of the side hustle that my father now had me running. I wouldn't even call it a side hustle with as much money that was being funneled through the company. But I knew that I was going to have to talk with TC about this. Since it was *his* company now that this was going through.

The fact that TC hadn't said anything told me that he didn't know about it, and I was sure that *his* father knew. But I couldn't understand why Mr. Churchhill didn't tell him about it. Now, my uncle had come all the way from Italy and wanted me to take over the Italian mafia, the syndicate my family had built from the ground up.

That was another thing I was going to have to talk to him about. Knowing TC, he wouldn't be okay with this shit happening under his nose. And I wouldn't blame him either because he had worked very hard for what he had achieved in college. This could send that tumbling down around him.

TC walked out of the ballroom with a blonde, and I chuckled because he seemed to always have a thing for them. Even though I had a deep gut feeling that he did like dark-haired women. Especially since the other night with the brunette that he had left out to dry.

Chapter Three

DRAKE

I stood by my parents and the Churchhills, who were talking shop like always. The blonde TC had walked out with rejoined the room. Knowing TC, something wasn't right because he was never a minute man. Aurora came in, approached her friends Elizabeth and Chloe, and spoke for a little bit before they all left.

Alex had already departed from the party, but not before congratulating Matt and Laura for TC's betrothal. The guy had it bad for Elizabeth, from what TC had told me, and it took him months before she gave him her phone number. Just meant he was crazy about the girl.

After downing some more of my whiskey, I spotted TC at the door. I sat the glass down, along with some money for the bartender, and headed over to him. Whenever he gave me that look, I knew that it wasn't good. We were going to be out for a long time.

Jake was behind us as we walked out to TC's green Mercedes G-Class SUV. It was silent outside as the party continued in the house. TC hopped into the passenger side. I followed him in on the other side. Jake got into the driver seat and glanced into the rearview mirror.

"Take us to Hyde Sunset." The rough way that he ordered Jake made my suspicions even more solid.

"Damn, dude. I thought you were going to get your cock wet with that blonde." I chuckled with a glance over to him. My curiosity was piqued as I watched him.

"Yeah? Well, you thought wrong. I need some good whiskey, that shit that Mr. Emerson had wasn't hitting the spot. Besides, Aurora fucked up my chances of getting anything there." I didn't miss the wince from TC as he ran his hand down his face. Something was off with him. Normally, he would talk to me about things, but he had been quiet for the past few weeks.

The way he was talking about Mr. Emerson and Aurora, I didn't understand why he didn't talk to his father and see what else he could do other than marry someone he clearly hated. "Damn, are you really going to talk about your future father-in-law that way? His ass likes you, for some fucking reason."

I sat back in the leather seat, getting comfortable. I pulled out my phone and scrolled through my notifications. A text came through from my uncle.

> Jack is on the move. Watch what you do tonight, he is looking for his heir.

> Okay, I'm with a friend right now. But I'll keep my eyes open.

> I'll be texting soon about where I need you to go.

> Okay.

"I know he likes me, but that doesn't mean that he didn't buy shit whiskey," TC snapped at me, bringing me away from my phone as I threw up my hands. "Drake, I don't know why they want us to marry. My mother knows that Aurora intentionally showed her that picture. So I don't get why they want to make my life miserable."

"Maybe they think that she will keep you in check. I mean, that's what they thought when they left Jakey Poo with you in college." Jake glared back at me before he flipped me off. I knew that was going to get under his skin. Jake had gotten close to TC. He had done a lot for him, even when he was supposed to let Matt and Laura know about it.

Jake stopped in front of the club, and one of the valets opened our doors. We walked up to the bouncers. They let us through, and we went straight to TC's VIP space. He always had a spot at this club. It didn't matter if he came here once a year or multiple times a month.

TC dropped into the brown leather seat and one of the waitresses came up with a tray as I slid into the booth with him. They were all dressed in cosplay tonight, and ours were dressed as some anime character I had seen when I was younger. "What can I get you, Mr. Churchhill?"

"Bottle of your best whiskey and two glasses."

The waitress nodded and headed to the bar to get our order. I had to admit the place was packed tonight. The music started to seep into my muscles as I began to tap my foot to the beat. When the waitress returned with TC's bottle and two glasses, the shutter that ran the length of his body told me that he was excited for the gold-topped bottle.

She sat the bottle on the table along with the crystal glasses, before she stood. "Is there anything else I can get you? An appetizer?"

"No thanks," TC answered without even looking at her. She was trying her best to get his attention.

The waitress dipped her head and left us as TC tore the wrapper off and uncorked it. He poured both of us a heaping glass and downed his. Sipping mine, I allowed my gaze to travel around us. Since I had met with my uncle, I found myself watching over my shoulder. I spotted TC settling back into the lounge, and I grinned.

"So, I think I'm going to have a running bet with Alex."

"About what?" TC asked, eyeing me over the rim of his glass.

"To see which one of you falls first." I laughed while I stared at him over my glass and downed the rest of its contents.

"That will not happen. We hate each other," he snapped and settled back into the leather.

Reaching forward, I picked up the small yet expensive bottle and refilled his glass. TC placed an ankle over his other knee, his eyes wondering over the crowd below us. I sat back and chuckled at him. "That's what you say now. I think one of you will fall. There's no way that two people who live together will not start having some attraction to the other."

TC shook his head. I could tell what he was thinking. It was like when I first met him in college. He had been asleep in bed when I came in toying with some of the unpacked boxes.

"Damn, dude, you have a lot of shit."

The dorm was a three-bedroom to allow Jake to live with the Churchhill's son. The dirty-blond kid sat up on his forearm and shielded his eyes from the assault of the bright LEDs I had turned on.

I was curious by nature, and when I found a box that was open and half empty I took a quick peek. Starting to go through it, I reached some papers that looked like they had some writing on them. I quickly read some of the words before TC pushed me into the only part of the wall that was empty.

"Keep your hands off my shit. Who the fuck are you, and why are you in my room?"

"Ah, I forgot, we haven't met yet. I'm Drake, Drake DeLuca." I held out my hand with a mischievous grin.

TC glared at me before he took my outstretched hand and shook it. That was until I pulled him into a headlock. He grabbed hold of my hand, prying it away from his neck and pushed me out of his room as I chuckled. "We are going to be best buds!"

"Dude, I just met you. I don't know if I like you," TC told me as he folded his arms over his chest in the doorway.

I plopped onto the couch and kicked my shoes off as I rested my feet on the table. TC shook his head at me. The click of another door brought both of our attention to the dark-haired man emerging from his room, and he grinned. "Mr. DeLuca."

Figuring I would make a big deal out of this, I looked from both of them and then jumped up, heading over to Jake. Shaking his hand as he continued to smile at me.

"Jake, buddy, ol' pal. How have you been? Looks like you have to protect the Chuchhill protege, huh?" I turned my gaze over to TC and winked.

He rolled his eyes at me before he turned and walked into his room, slamming it for good measure. TC was going to have to deal with me for the six years we were going to be here, and I was going to have fun with it as well.

Those had been the best six years of my life, getting to know the man who sat beside me now. He had a level-head about him that no teen ever did. TC was calculated, and his eyes held a cruelness in them that I had never seen in someone his age.

TC took a sip of his whiskey while his eyes roamed the dance floor, and he spat out his drink while choking on what he had already swallowed. I sat forward and slapped his back a couple of times before he regained his composure.

"Dude, are you okay? You wasted a good bit of that."

"Yeah, I just saw someone I was trying to get away from." He leaned forward in his seat, and following his gaze, I spotted who he was talking about. His fiancée was here along with her two friends, Chloe and Elizabeth.

The way he was staring at her, it looked like he wanted to murder her. She had found some random guy, who was grinding on her from behind. "TC, man. Chill your face. You look like you're about to kill him."

I downed another glass of whiskey while he continued to watch her dancing. TC poured himself another drink. He had his eyes on Aurora the entire time she walked up to the bar, and another man started to flirt with her, the guy even ordered her a drink.

TC glanced back at me, and I knew that he didn't miss the lift of my lips as I took another drink. He might not know it, but I knew about the letters. I had gone into his room and read them. He was trying to apologize to the girl who he had left in the middle of the dance floor. Finding those letters was the reason I knew he and her could be something if they would let this all go.

"Are you going to come back to earth, or are you going to continue to stare at your gorgeous fiancée all night?" TC's eyes cut to me. If looks could kill, I would be six feet under.

"I'm not staring at her." He scoffed as his gaze went to the empty bottle on the table. TC motioned for the waitress to come to us.

"Yes, Mr. Churchill?"

"Can you grab me another bottle? And make sure you ask the bartender who's serving next to the woman in the green dress. Be sure to mention my name."

"Yes, sir." She scampered off and made her way to Aurora, catching the attention of the bartender for the new bottle. I watched as she turned and locked eyes with TC. He grinned and saluted her with his glass. I burst out laughing beside him because she had the same look as he did when I told him that he was staring at his fiancée.

What I didn't expect was for her to take the bottle off the waitress' tray and chug a good amount of the liquor. TC's lips were poker straight as we watched her place the bottle on the tray. With a smile she flipped him off and left the man she had been talking to.

TC slammed his glass on the table and stood, straightening his jacket. He dropped a couple of hundreds on the table for the waitress. I followed him. I couldn't keep my laughter from him as we walked out of the club.

I knew I would pay for it one day, but right now, I was having fun fucking with him. Even if I had to work overtime for a few weeks, I would.

Chapter Four

EMI

I lay in bed after what was probably the most god-awful sex, I'd had in months. My new boyfriend lay beside me, snoring. Tonight was our first night together, and it was definitely going to be the last.

Sighing, I got up from the bed in the hotel room and made my way to the bathroom. Thinking about Drake couldn't even make me come. I couldn't remember when I actually started thinking about him. But I believe it was before I started college, because of our weekly dinner with the family and him being there. I had noticed him in his jeans and tight-fitting shirt with his muscles on display.

It wasn't like I hadn't been around him most of my life. Not like he would even look my way, being my brother's best friend and coworker. Not to mention that I was nine years younger than him. He always treated me like a sister, and why wouldn't he? It was me who was becoming infatuated with him. It didn't help when he play-flirted with me either.

Besides, Drake DeLuca could have any woman he wanted. I had seen the college pictures of him and my brother. He was with a new girl every time, and most of the time, they were either brunette or red-headed.

It surprised me that he hadn't brought someone with him when he came to my brother's betrothal party. I didn't miss his glare when my gaze went to him. My brother hadn't even noticed the wannabe rocker that I had invited to be my plus one. Who was a mistake.

I didn't like that I was leaving my own hotel room, but I had to get out of this place. There was no way I would be able to live with myself if I stayed until morning. I entered the bathroom and washed my face. Coming back up I stared at my reflection, and shook my head at myself.

Finding some comfortable clothes, I slipped into them before leaving the bathroom. I grabbed my clothes that he had thrown around and my luggage bag, stuffing the items in the hard black case. Glancing around the room once more, I left him in the bed and exited the door. I didn't even look back as it shut behind me. I walked over to the elevator and pressed the button to head down. Luckily, I had driven from the Emersons' house.

I was happy that I was getting a sister, but I didn't know if this whole thing was going to work. Because with the way those two fought, I didn't think it would last. The doors to the elevator opened, and I stepped out to the valet.

"Can I help you, ma'am?"

"Yes, can you pull my car around?"

"Of course, Ms. Churchhill." The young man scampered off to get my car. It pissed me off that I was the one doing the walk of shame, but there was no way I would be able to stay in that bed with *him*. Much less walk out of that room with him in the morning.

My car arrived at the curb, and the valet jumped out and helped me with my bag. He shut the trunk of my car, while I walked around to the driver side and entered the vehicle. I closed the door and pulled away from the curb, making my way home. Mom and Dad would be there, but I highly doubted that TC would be.

Since he bought his penthouse, he never came back to the house. Unless it was for family dinners once a week. I took the right turn onto my street and noticed that an older car sat on the left. Reaching the driveway, I entered the code to get through the gate. I smudged my fingerprints from the keys before going through the now open entrance. The Oldsmobile by the curb unnerved me. I kept my eye on the rearview mirror until the metal barrier shut completely.

I stopped in front of the steps, exited the sedan, and rounded it to the steps. One of the staff came down the steps toward me, I didn't miss the worry on his face.

"Ms. Emi! Are you okay?" He wrapped a jacket around me and took my keys.

"Yes, I'm just ready to go to bed. Make sure you put the car up in the garage. Can you send security out and see if they can find out why that vehicle is sitting by the curb?" I watched out of the corner of my eye as he nodded and went to my two door sedan.

Heading up the stairs, I reached the door and entered the house. The soft lighting in the foyer gave off enough light to allow me to cross the tile floor to the stairs. They led me up to the second floor and up to my room. TC's room sat empty beside mine, other than the baseball and soccer trophies he'd won in school and college. There were times I would come and sit in his room because I missed him. It wasn't that I couldn't talk to him or see him whenever I wanted. But it made it harder since he had taken over the company.

As I entered my room, my eyes landed on my bed, and all the pent-up stress left my body. This was my comfort place, a sanctuary where I was able to be myself and not have to worry about who was watching. Sighing, I dropped the jacket the butler had given to me onto the floor and fell back on the bed.

I was over-tired and ready to sleep for the next few days.

Today was my brother's wedding day and I was hopeful it was going to be a great day. I spotted Drake and my brother walking up to the room reserved for the groom and groomsmen. Hiking up my dress, I hurried over to them before they went in.

"TC! Hold on!" Both TC and Drake turned to me and I didn't miss the way Drake's eyes took in my body.

It made my whole body flush with what I only dreamed he could do to it. I also didn't miss my chance to take in the way his tux hugged his frame. Fuck, he was gorgeous, but he was well beyond my reach.

"What's wrong, Emi?" I glanced over to TC and smiled.

"I just wanted to tell you that you look very handsome today, and I love you!" I wrapped my arms around him, and he pulled me in closer. The way he always hugged me when I was little.

"Thanks, Emi. I need to go in here." When TC's breath wafted to my nose, I could tell already he'd had one drink. He was trying to keep from showing he was nervous, but I could always tell when he was.

"It will all be over in a few moments." I smiled at him, stood on my tippy toes, and kissed his cheek before turning my eyes to Drake. "Make sure to have his back."

I stared into Drake's dark eyes. Those deep orbs made me melt each time that he locked his gaze with mine. He grinned with his eyebrow raised before he nodded. "You're not going to tell me how handsome I am?"

Fuck, his voice made me wet. Which was probably why I didn't like when my current boyfriend tried to talk dirty to me while we were fucking. TC backhanded him in the gut, making me giggle. "You're handsome, too. But not as much as my brother."

I winked at him and didn't miss his wink back while his tongue ran over his lips. Did he like me? *Naw, Emi. Pull yourself together. He wouldn't be interested in you.*

"Hey, watch yourself." I turned around just in time to see TC shoulder-barge past Drake as he smiled and shrugged.

Shaking my head, I headed to the chapel to wait with my new boyfriend. My mother hurriedly came up to me. The way she was acting made it look like she was searching for someone. "Where's your brother?"

"He and Drake just went into the groom's room."

"Why he can't just get here when I need him? Thank you, sweetheart. Go ahead and get in your seat. It's about to start." She kissed me on the forehead and hurried over to the room that both TC and Drake had gone into. I didn't want to know what she was going to do to him when she noticed the whiskey on his breath.

The chapel was decorated in red and white; the gladiolus flowers arranged in vases against the pews. Family members and friends sat in them and turned when I started to walk down the aisle to take my seat in the front row with my boyfriend.

Most of these fuckers just wanted to see whether TC was going to marry Aurora Emerson. Even if my parents and hers didn't see it, they hated each other. Yeah, there was one time I thought they liked each other but that changed at TC's introduction party.

If I had been Aurora, I would have told my parents to fuck off. Don't get me wrong, I loved my brother, but what he did all those years ago was too far. I slid onto the pew beside Keith and sighed. I felt for Aurora and what she was going through right now.

"Well, did you find your brother?" I glanced over to my left and smiled at Keith. He was good-looking, I had met him at the coffee shop the day after my walk of shame. The sex was better than the boyfriend I brought with me to the betrothal party, but it still wasn't what I wanted.

"Yes, he looks great even if he seems off." But damn, did Drake look amazing in his tux. However, I wasn't going to let him know that.

Keith sat back in his seat when the doors at the back opened. My brother advanced to the altar. His eyes straight forward, and the soft conversations about him followed him to the preacher. Some of the people here didn't like him, but there was no denying that he had done what our father and Drake's father hadn't done with the company.

The music started, and everyone turned to watch as the groomsmen and bridesmaids walked down the aisle, Drake was first with Aurora's friend Chloe. She looked pissed, and Drake was smiling. Drake strolled down the aisle the smirk permentaly on his face. When he reached the alter where my brother stood, he leaned forward and whispered something to him, making TC grin. Drake's eyes came over to me, and I didn't miss the wink that he sent my way.

Elizabeth and Alex walked behind Drake and Chloe, but they looked happier than the other two. The flower-girl and ring-bearer walked behind them. They were adorable as they came up to the wedding party. The ring-bearer stood by Drake while the flower-girl stood beside Chloe. TC scowled in my direction, but I knew his eyes weren't trained on me.

The music changed, and I was the first to stand to watch Aurora walk down the aisle, accompanied by her father, to my brother. She was beautiful, and when I glanced back to TC, he stood there frozen. I hadn't seen this look on him since he met her in the suit shop.

It was funny that it would happen again on his wedding day. Her dress was gorgeous. It showed off her curves, and the flowers brought out the smoky grey of her eyes. I would love to be as beautiful as she was on my own wedding day.

The whole ceremony was monotonous because of how Aurora and my brother recited the marriage vows. But when my brother wrapped his hand around the back of Aurora's neck and crashed his lips to hers, it was something out of one of the romance books I read. I think that was the reason I couldn't get into the sex with these guys. They weren't my book boyfriends.

TC was in a hurry when he practically dragged Aurora down the aisle. The other two couples walked behind them with the children. There were no smiles on their faces other than the two little ones.

"Well, that was depressing," my new boyfriend mumbled behind me. I turned on Keith and backhanded him. "Oof."

"That's what you get. I'd like you to keep those types of words out of your mouth."

Chapter Five

DRAKE

The wedding ceremony was torturous as I stood next to my best friend. But not from the uneasiness that TC was unknowingly exuding. No, it was from the new man that had his right hand all over Emi's left leg. But she hadn't been paying attention to him. Her eyes were on the wedding party. I couldn't take my eyes off her. Just like when I had seen her in the hallway

I wished Emi would look at me like TC did when he grabbed hold of Aurora and pulled her into a kiss. He wanted to hide the fact that he liked her. TC didn't realize that I had noticed, but I knew he wanted her to notice him for what he was capable of.

To say the kiss between TC and Aurora was hot was an understatement. That shit was burning up. I had known something was going to happen since we ran into her at the club. That woman was going to keep him on his toes, that was for sure.

I walked by Chloe with the other wedding party. To my horror, Aurora's mom had hired photographers, and I didn't miss the way TC sighed and rolled his eyes at me. Shrugging, I let the people do their job, much to the dismay of Chloe and Aurora. It didn't take too long. I thought the photographer who had Aurora and TC did a great job at positioning them. Those pictures would be amazing.

After all the photos were taken, and we entered the reception, TC took off to the bar. I didn't blame him, but he'd better hope he didn't get too wasted because they had the good stuff here tonight. I held up the bar as TC and Aurora had their first dance as a married couple. If I was being honest, they looked great together. Even if they hated each other's guts. They were well-matched. My gaze went to Emi, dancing with her new boyfriend, his hands all over her. If it wouldn't cause a scene, I'd go over there and tell him to take a hike, but that wasn't my job. That was TC's, and he was now nowhere to be seen.

Setting the empty glass on the bar. I left two hundred dollar bills under it and left. If TC wasn't here, I didn't plan on staying. I was going to find some pussy and then go home. I walked out of the main door and ran into my father.

"Drake, Riccardo wants you to go down to Vegas and meet up with a man from his syndicate." He handed my phone to me. It had been in the groom's room.

"Okay, so when do I need to leave? I will have to let TC know." He would be wondering where I was if I didn't, and I wasn't going to let him know just yet what was going on. I took my phone and began to read my messages.

"In a couple of days. Make sure you are carrying." I nodded and headed down the steps of the reception hall, stuffing my phone in my back pocket. If I was taking my gun, that meant one more person wasn't going to be staying on this earth.

The night was young as I sat in a VIP booth in, Angel Eyes, a new club that had just opened in Las Vegas, by myself. The man I was supposed to be meeting hadn't shown up yet. Which pissed me off. If I was going to come all the way to Las Vegas, he needed to be on time. A new group of people walked into the club. The two women were hot, but they had guys with them.

I sat back in my booth and continued to watch the dancers on the floor below me, scanning the crowd for the man I was meeting. Everyone danced the night away, oblivious to what was I was doing. Two women caught my eye on the dance floor below me. A blonde had caught my attention as she and her friend ground themselves on each other. She continued to glance over at me while she danced. The amount of men that were watching them intrigued me.

If I convinced them both to come back to the hotel room I had, I would be a very happy man. Well as close to happy as I could be. Since Emi was off the market for now. Being able to get rooms that were unattainable for other people was the plus side to having money. I didn't want the random women I spent the night with knowing where I lived, being as I was out of town, I had a room nonetheless.

After standing from my booth, I straightened my jacket and descended to the dance floor. I waded through the crowd, hands rubbing me while I made my way to the ladies. Once I reached them, they both turned to face me with smiles on their faces.

"Afternoon, ladies. Mind if I join?" I gave them both my best smile. The blonde licked her lips as the other woman moved forward and ran her hand down my chest.

"Sure, handsome. We haven't seen you before."

"I haven't been here. What about you and your friend here show me around?" I placed my right hand on her back.

From the corner of my eye, I noticed a tattooed guy feeling up a dark-haired woman in a red dress. She turned to the guy, trying to get away from him, when another bigger guy came up behind her and grabbed the man by the throat.

I couldn't see her rescuer's face, but I could tell from the groping man that he was afraid of the man with his hand around his throat. The man threw his hands up and backed away from the girl as much as the hand allowed him. His lips were moving, but I couldn't tell what he was saying. When the other man let him go, he quickly left the building along with his friend.

The gorgeous woman in the red dress turned and hugged the guy. Everyone on the dance floor went back to what they were doing after they left.

"The lucky bitch." The blonde huffed.

"Why's that?" I was curious since she was so enamored with the man in the suit.

"Because he's the owner of this club. He's also the wealthiest man in Las Vegas." Ah, another man with deep pockets.

"So, what about the second wealthiest man in LA?" I knew the right strategy of getting women's attention back from another man.

"Second in LA?"

My eyes caught a glimpse of who I thought was Emi. Excusing myself, I pressed through the crowd. I caught sight of Emi's face, tears running down her cheeks. She was with the guy from the wedding, and I didn't like the way he was manhandling her toward the restrooms. I finally caught up with them and pulled her into me. My fist flew into his face, and he backed into the wall, his hand going to his nose.

"Drake!" Emi's small hands grabbed my suit jacket. She had to be pulling on the back of my clothes because my jacket went taut around my shoulders. "Please, Drake! He's not worth it!"

The man scrambled away from us, blood seeping through his fingers. I had never hit a woman or made her fear me, and I wasn't going to let this motherfucker do it to Emi. Glancing over my shoulder, Emi locked eyes with me. I didn't miss the tears in her eyes.

I turned to her and scanned her body for any marks on her perfect skin. Because if he had, I was going to make him pay a slow and torturous punishment. After I was finished with that, I would kill him and make sure that no one would find him for a very long time.

"Are you okay, Emi?" She took a deep breath and then glanced down.

"Yes, I'm fine. I need to get home. TC will worry about me." I didn't want her to leave. This was the first time that I had been alone with her.

"You can stay in my room. It's too late for you to drive home." Her beautiful hazel eyes searched my face. God, she was stunning.

"Are you Drake DeLuca?" a male voice asked behind me. I turned my back on Emi and came face to face with an older man but not like my father or uncle. His hair was peppered with grey and he walked with a cane.

"Yes, that's me. Can I help you?"

"My name is Arlo. I need you to follow me." I glanced at Emi. She brought her eyes up to mine, and I sighed. Turning fully to her, I pulled out my key card from my pocket and handed it to her.

"You go straight to my room—1045—and go to bed. I'll be back soon, and we will go back to LA together." She took the room key and nodded. Her arms were covered in goosebumps as her fingers brushed against mine.

Spinning back to the older man, I motioned for him to lead, leaving Emi on the dance floor. This was going to be quick; I would make sure it was. I wanted to get back to Emi.

I rode in the passenger seat of a black two door rental, the older man driving. If my father hadn't told me to come here and talk with someone, this would have been stupid of me. To get in the vehicle of someone I didn't know wasn't my style. Especially someone from the Italian mafia. My father better be glad that I trusted him because if I didn't, I'd think that *I* was the one going to be killed.

"So you're Riccardo's nephew, huh? I'd have spotted you sooner if you hadn't been on the floor with that pretty blonde." The old man chuckled, his voice so raspy I didn't think this man breathed air anymore.

"Yeah, well, I had been in the VIP booth, like you told my uncle, for over two hours. Where are we going?" I didn't want her to be in Las Vegas on her own for very long.

"I've already got our man at the safe house."

"Okay, and what has this person done?" I wasn't a cold-blooded killer, but I protected my family and my investments.

"That is what we are having to find out. He won't talk, so we are hoping that since you are a DeLuca you will be able to get something out of him."

"So, the big, bad hitmen haven't been able to get information and you are now needing me to get it. Well, all right. What information are you wanting from him?" I glanced at the other man as he made a left-hand turn onto a dirt road.

"He is being stubborn. Mr. Riccardo wants to know how you handle interrogations. I'm one of the people who knows Riccardo's situation. So he wants to know how you handle things." He had dodged my other question, thinking that I wouldn't notice.

"Okay, you don't know what you've let loose then." He didn't know because it had been a while since I had let the beast within me out. If he wanted to know what I could do, I was going to show him.

"That's what they all say until it comes down to it." The old man chuckled as we pulled up to a small house. It looked clean from the outside, but there was no telling what it looked like on the inside.

"You'll see, old man." I smirked and let myself out of the car. Throwing the insult at him. So, this was something that my uncle wanted to test me on.

Boy, would I show him.

The old man came up the stairs with me and opened the door. The house was actually captivating. I couldn't understand why we were interrogating someone in this place. I stopped in the living room and glanced around. It was furnished with a couch and arm chair with a rug in the center of the room and side tables with lamps, just enough to make it seem comfortable.

"Are you coming, boy?"

There he was again with that boy comment. I turned to the old man and walked behind him to a door past the kitchen. We headed down a set of stairs. From the outside, it didn't look like this place had a basement. Piss and decaying flesh reached my nose, and it took everything in me to keep my composure. Arlo, Riccardo's man, turned on the light, and the sight almost made me gag.

I didn't know how they kept the smell from reaching the upstairs, but fuck, this place was fucked up. Blood was splattered everywhere, and I didn't even want to know what was in the buckets. My eyes continued around the room at all the tools hanging on the walls before resting on the man who sat bound in a chair in the middle of the room.

The chair was positioned above a drain, and it looked as if the man had pissed himself as he sat there for who knew how long. The thud of the door closing brought the man's head up. The old man stood there in front of him. "Well, it's nice that you are still alive, Harvey. Are you ready to tell us who hired you?"

"Fuck you, old man! I'm not talking to you," Harvey answered with a sorry attempt to spit at him.

I walked over and pulled the blindfold from him. His eyes closed from the attack of the light, but when he opened them, they went wide, going from defiant to scared.

"So, what have you done to get put in this position, Harvey?" I asked him as I circled him, searching for the right tool. It looked like he had been beaten and that someone had already tried taking out his fingernails.

"Fuck you, man. I'm not saying shit." I didn't miss the sound of trickling in the quiet basement room.

"You see, that's where you are wrong." I grabbed a double-bladed knife and twisted it in my hand before throwing it toward him. Slicing into his thigh enough to allow blood to run onto the floor.

"FUCK!" Harvey screamed in pain, and I picked up another one. I headed over to him and brought the knife up to his jugular.

"Did I say that you could scream?" He shook his head, and I walked away from him, laying the knife on a table, I shrugged out of my blazer and rolled up my sleeves.

"Now, what have you done to find yourself in this position?" I turned to face him with the knife in my hand again, but he shook his head. "This is how this is going to go. The longer you hold out, the more body parts will no longer be attached to you. Answer my question."

I slipped the blade down his arms and nicked his thumb where his nail should be. He didn't cry out this time, and I smirked.

"I work for Jack. That's all you will get from me. I'm loyal to my boss. But I will tell you that you better think twice about who you think your friends are."

Glancing over to the old man, he shook his head, and I sighed.

He was going to need to tell me more. I turned back around to him and drove the blade into the man's wrist. Harvey didn't scream, but I could tell his face had gone white and his breathing was getting faster. "You see, that's not good enough for me. Why is your boss watching me?"

The man shook his head and clamped his jaw shut. Taking a deep breath, I twisted the blade and felt the bones in his wrist slip. Harvey screamed out this time and started to pant, trying to stay awake as blood gushed into the drain. "He knows about the laundry you are doing through the Churchhill Logistics. Just know that family protects family, and he has a bounty on your head. Dead or alive."

I pulled the knife from his wrist, and the blood flowed faster. Harvey's lips curled in a smile. "Once he tells his heir what you are, blood will paint the streets of LA."

After pulling my gun from my holster, I shot a bullet between his eyes. He was going to die before I came here. But now I wanted to put him out of his misery.

"You have a clean-up crew? Or do I need to do that as well?" I turned to the old man, who was grinning from ear to ear.

"I've already called in the clean-up crew. They will be here tomorrow. Let's get you back to that *bellezza* you have waiting for you."

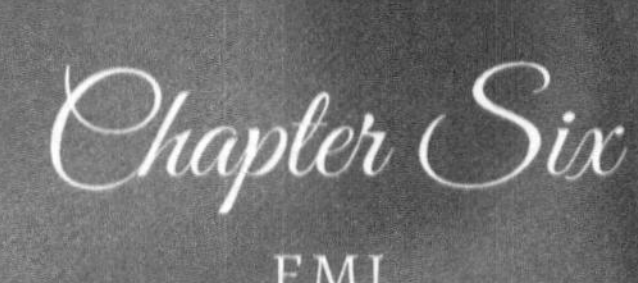

Chapter Six

EMI

D rake was the last person I'd have thought would be in Las Vegas. Keith had wanted to get away after my brother's wedding, and I was all for it. That was before he thought it would be a good idea to bring another woman into the mix. I knew most men wanted that, but I didn't know her and I wasn't about to put my health in danger.

I told him that I was leaving, which made him mad. Keith had grabbed my arm and started to drag me over to the bathrooms. If I hadn't been wearing these damn heels, I would have been able to get free.

Drake had given me his key card and told me to go up and stay there until he got back. I should have told him that I was going to go home, but he had a serious tone in his voice that made me stay. Keith had left while Drake was standing with me, so I didn't worry that he would follow me.

When I got to the room, I realized that Drake had booked the largest suite in the hotel. The place was huge, but I was used to things like this. Walking around the suite I found the kitchen and grabbed a bottle of water before slipping out of my heels.

I wondered when Drake would get back. I hadn't recognized the man who had come up to us and had taken him away from me. I stripped out of my dress in the bathroom and hopped in the shower.

The shower felt amazing after dancing and then fighting with Keith. I quickly showered and wrapped myself in one of the robes. After heading into the bedroom, I found Drake's suitcase and opened it since mine was in Keith's room.

I grabbed one of Drake's white button-downs and pulled it over my head before pulling the bedding back to climb in. He wouldn't care if I took the bed. Besides, if I was lucky he just might join me. I snuggled into the soft mattress and covered up.

I woke to the shower running and sat up. He was here. My heart fluttered in my chest. Drake always made me feel this way, and he didn't even know it. The water shut off. It was now or never. Should I make him think I was still asleep or confront him? I decided as the door opened that I was going to do the latter.

Drake walked through into the bedroom with a towel hanging low around his waist as he dried his hair. His eyes locked with mine, and I could feel the heat coming off my cheeks.

"Hey. I thought you were asleep." His husky voice went to my core like it always seemed to do.

"I heard the shower running." Drake continued to stare at me.

"Go back to sleep. I'll take the couch. We will leave in the morning." I glanced to the clock on the bedside table. It was already three in the morning.

"You can sleep here. Was everything okay? When you left with that man?" He still didn't move. I got up and walked over to him; his eyes roamed my body as I rounded the bed.

"Everything is fine. That man is nothing for you to worry about. And I can't sleep in bed with you. Your brother will kill me." He kept his hands by his sides as I ran mine up his abdomen and into the chest hair. "Emi, what are you doing?"

"I want you. I've always wanted you." I was surprised that I was being so forward with him. There was a time when I couldn't even look him in the eyes, and now here I was, telling him that I needed him.

"You don't mean that. You don't know what I am." His pupils had eclipsed his irises, making his gaze even darker .

"But I do know you. I've known you for years." I traced his jawline with my fingertips and didn't miss the soft groan that came from his lips. "I know that I'm not what you normally have on your arm, but I've been enamored with you since I came of age. I've been wanting you to look at me, but you won't."

"Emi, TC would kill me. He's my best friend. I can't lie to him." His hand came up to cover mine, and I shivered at his touch.

"He doesn't have to know."

"You know he will." I had never seen Drake hesitate before, but I knew my brother would have a fit if he found out about this.

"Drake, I need you," I answered him. When I pressed my body to his, his hardened cock brushed against my lower belly. "And apparently, you want me, too."

"You don't know what you're asking for." Drake cupped my face just before his lips locked onto mine.

He walked us back to the bed and broke the kiss. Drake picked me up under my ass; his fingertips grazing my entrance, which was already soaked. He dropped us onto the mattress and used his knees to widen my legs. The towel had slipped from his waist as he leaned back onto his feet.

Drake stroked himself as I looked at him. *Fuck!* I didn't know that he was pierced, and not only was he pierced on one side, but on the other side. Like a double Jacobs ladder. He wrapped his hand around his thick shaft and began to pump it while he stared into my eyes.

"Are you sure you want this?" I nodded and prepared for him to enter me. His fingers caressed the entrance to my pussy before he pressed them inside. They reached the right spot before he pulled them out. I groaned when he brought his fingers to his mouth and wrapped his lips around them tasting my arousal on them.

Drake tugged off my shirt and threw it onto the floor. He ran his hand that had been inside me up my belly and kneaded my breast before he pinched my nipple, eliciting a moan from me.

"Drake, please don't tease me." I arched my back, trying to get him to carry on. I needed him inside me.

"I'm not teasing you, *dolcezza*. I'm just getting you ready to take my cock. I don't want to hurt you." He leaned over me and crashed his lips onto mine just as he entered me.

Fuck! Those bars on either side of his cock rubbed against the walls of my pussy. He stretched me to the breaking point, but fuck did he feel good! My hands latched onto his back, and I dug my fingernails into his shoulder blades.

Drake took it slow, allowing me time to adjust to him. His hand went to my throat, tightening enough to allow me to breathe. Drake was nothing like the others I had been with. If we didn't get together again after this, I would have a rough time having vanilla sex.

I met him with each of his thrusts with my own. Wanting, no, needing him to go faster and deeper. "Drake, please."

He sat back on his feet and pulled me up to sit on his lap. The change in position brought a whole different feeling. Drake moved one hand to my hip and the other into my hair. "Ride me, *dolcezza*. Use this cock to make yourself come."

"Drake, you feel so fucking good. I'm going to come! Come with me?" I moaned while getting ever closer to my orgasm.

"I'll do whatever you want me to." I held on to his shoulders as I quickened my pace, needing to feel him all over inside of me. Drake's hands became vise grips on my hips as I went over the edge. He came with me. Iould feelhis cok wl just before his hot cum coated my insides.

"Fuck! Emi." Drake cursed, pulling me closer to him. My body pulsed around him as I came down from the high of my orgasm.

My heart was racing while I clung to Drake. His lips peppered kisses along my face and then down my neck. I whimpered when he went back to behind my ear, nipping and licking the sensitive skin.

"Fuck, that was great." I tried to keep myself awake but miserably failing.

Drake got off the bed and pulled me into his arms, taking me to the other side of the bed. My eyes fluttered as I tried to hold them open. "Don't let me sleep in this bed alone. I want you beside me."

"I've already fucked up. I won't leave you, *dolcezza*. We have to keep this to ourselves. But you have ruined me for any other woman."

I was already drained and falling asleep as he pulled me against him to cuddle. This was something I normally never did with a guy, but Drake was different. I just hoped that he wouldn't abandon me.

The sun shone in through the windows from the balcony, making me blink to focus on my surroundings.

I turned to my other side, and a twinge of pain ran through my core. It was like the first time being with a guy. My eyes landed on Drake, who was still sleeping.

His features were softer than when he was awake. I ran my finger along his eyebrow, noticing a small scar.

"I'm glad you're awake. It's been hard to not move and wake you." Drake's husky voice startled me, and my eyes locked with his dark brown ones. "Did you sleep well?"

"Yes." I didn't want to tell him that I was hurting. If there was a chance I could be with him again, I wasn't going to ruin my shot.

"We need to get up and get going. I'm surprised TC hasn't called me yet." Drake brushed my hair away from my face and sat up on his elbows. "Go get in the shower and clean up. I'm going to have to figure out a way to tell TC why you're with me."

"Okay, you don't want to join me?" I winked at him before turning and trying to sit up. When I tried to bend forward to stand, the pain shot into my core.

"Are you okay?" Drake's arms wrapped around me, turning me to face him.

"Yes, I just need to soak. I'll be fine." My hands went to his shoulders, and I smiled at him.

"This wasn't your first time, was it?"

I laughed and shook my head.

"No, I'm not a virgin, but I've never been with a man of your... girth?" I answered him, his hands ran over the globes of my ass. Pulling me closer to him.

"*Dolcezza*, you have to talk to me. All you had to say was I was hurting you. I like rough sex, but I won't push you into anything that you can't handle."

I pulled my lower lip into my mouth and nodded. "I can handle it. I just have to get used to you."

He was going to stop this before it got good. I glanced up into his eyes; I didn't know what he was thinking about. But I knew that my heart was racing, waiting to know if he was going to tell me this was a one-night stand.

"I can see you thinking. Tell me, *dolcezza,* what's on your mind?"

"What does that mean? Doll-chet-za?"

Drake chuckled and stood from the bed. He picked me up and carried me to the bathroom. "It means sweetness, in Italian. You know my family's Italian. We are going to have to work on your pronunciation."

Chapter Seven

DRAKE

It had been a few days since Emi and I had gotten back from Las Vegas. Today was the first time in five days that I was going to see her. I didn't think this was a good idea but once I was inside her that night it was all I could think about.

Emi was meeting me at The Ritz-Carlton in a couple of hours. I was packing some clothes and other items in my luggage. On our way back from Las Vegas, she had asked me about the other things I liked to do in bed. That night had piqued her interest and I was going to fill her in on anything that she wanted to know.

From the bed I glanced around my room to make sure I had everything before closing the luggage. Not finding anything I zipped up the suitcase and pulled it from the bed. I strolled out of my room and into the hall, heading to the stairs.

Benton was at the top waiting for me. He had been with me since I bought this place and had been a great asset. Benton reached out for the luggage and took it from me, following me down the steps.

I didn't want many of my staff to know that I was leaving for a few days. Other than my top security man and Benton. Stepping onto the tile at the bottom of the stairs we crossed the foyer to the door to the garage.

Opening the door, the automatic light turned on, revealing all the cars that I had acquired. Most of them where black but I had a few red and blue ones. My favorite one was the black with the iridescent purple in the paint. Smiling I turned to the key box and found its key.

I crossed the garage floor to my car, unlocked it and opened the trunk for Benton to place my luggage in.

"Sir, are you sure you don't want me to have one of security to go with you?"

Turning to him I placed a hand on his shoulder and smiled. "No, I'll be fine. I'm meeting someone and I'd like to keep this confidential. Okay?"

Benton nodded and stepped back away from the car. I opened the car door, slid into the leather seat and closed the door. Bringing the vehicle to life, the garage door rose allowing me to back out of the spot.

My mind was already thinking about Emi in that hotel room with me. Trying new things with her and doing the things she had mentioned on our way back. Along with some of the things that I wanted to see her in. Driving down the driveway I came to a stop before turning right and down the road to take me downtown.

I reached the hotel in record time. Stopping at the curb a valet came up to my vehicle and opened my door for me.

"Good morning, sir. Welcome to the Ritz-Carlton. My name is Avery. Do you have any bags that you would like me to grab for you?"

"Yeah, it's in the truck." I opened the hatch and Avery moved to the rear of the car to grab my luggage.

Stepping out of the running Bentley Continental GT I rounded the car to the valet who had my luggage sitting beside him as he closed the trunk. I took the bag and glanced at Avery with a smile. "Make sure you don't scratch this thing. The key is in the car."

He nodded and walked around to the driver's side and entered the car. The first time I had come here I was told from the manager himself that everyone that drove the cars were vetted for accidents.

I crossed the sidewalk and into the building. Walking over the lobby floor I headed to the front desk to check in. As I reached the desk the man behind it looked up and smiled at me.

"Good morning, sir. My name is Steve. Are you checking in?"

"Yes, it's under DeLuca."

He nodded and his fingers went to the keyboard flying over it as he started his search. Steve finally glanced up and grabbed two key cards. "Looks like you booked our Ritz-Carlton suite for two. These key cards will allow you and your guest to enter any of our amenities that you may need. Would you like breakfast sent up?"

Steve handed me the cards, waiting for my reply.

"Yes. Send everything on the breakfast menu, but have them wait to bring it for a couple of hours." He nodded and entered in my request into the computer.

I walked away from him and over to the elevator. Scanning the key cards in my hand, the elevator opened allowing me in to head up to my suite. The only two buttons on this elevator were the floors for my suite and the presidential. Pressing my button it rose to my destination.

Coming to a stop the doors opened to the suite. It was a nice size and I knew Emi would like it. I strolled over the tile floor to the back of the suite where the room was. Everything was nice and tidy ready for me to destroy with Emi.

The bed was in the middle of the room with a chair in the corner of the room. I had roughly an hour to get all this put up and down to the lobby before Emi got here. I didn't bring much but it was enough to experiment with her and to see if she would be interested in some more.

I finished putting everything away just under forty-five minutes which would give me time to go down and have a drink before Emi arrived. Taking one last look around the bedroom at my work I exited and closed the door.

Walking back through the suite to the elevator I made sure I had the key and entered the elevator to head back down. My body hummed in excitement to have her back in my arms. I pressed the button to go to the lobby floor, letting it take me the few minutes to get to the bottom floor.

The doors opened and I stepped off. Turning to the left I made my way to the Glance Lobby Bar to get a drink and find a table. I reached the bar and stood at the entrance searching for a table that I liked. After a few minutes I found the perfect table for us and strolled over to the bright red booth.

I had just sat down when a pixie cut blonde came up to me. She had a smile on her face and her small tablet in her hand. "Good morning, sir. My name is Erica. Is there a drink I can get started for you?"

"Yes, I'd like a whiskey neat please,"

"Of course sir. Any food items this morning?" She asked as she tapped on the tablet.

"No, I'm waiting for a friend."

Erica glanced up and smiled before dipping her head and going to her next table. Reaching into my pocket I pulled out my phone and tapped on Emi's name.

> Dolcezza, I'm at the Glance Lobby Bar. Meet me here and we will head up to the room.

> Okay, I'm about three minutes away.

Erica brought my drink to me and left me at my booth. Emi would be here and I couldn't wait to spend time with her. I took a sip of my drink as I watched the other patrons. Some were talking to other men and still others had a woman beside them. I wasn't one to judge a man for the woman on his arm but if I was a betting man. And I was. I would bet that some of those young women were escorts.

The table that I picked allowed me to see the entrance that way I could see when Emi arrived. Allowing my gaze to wander one more time I spotted her walking into the lobby. She had on a sundress that stopped just above her knees. Emi was gorgeous.

I raised my hand and when she spotted me her lips turned up into a smile. Emi made a beeline to my table and I stood when she reached me and pulled her into my arms. She turned her face up to me and I couldn't help but crash my lips to hers. Emi was the first to break the kiss and I helped her into the booth before I sat beside her.

Placing her luggage beside us so that we could sit for a while, I pulled her hand in mine and laid it on my thigh.

"Do you want a drink before we head up?" Emi's face turned a bright shade of scarlet as she held my gaze.

"Sure," she grabbed the small drink menu and peered over it, "How about a glass of tea?"

"Of course." Raising my hand I flagged down our server.

"Yes, sir is there something else I can get you." Her eyes cut to Emi and I didn't miss her checking her out.

"Yes, I need a glass of tea, please." She nodded, entering the drink into her table.

"I'll be right back with your drink."

I turned back to Emi and placed my arm on the back of the booth behind her.

"Do you want to talk about those interests here or in the

room?" I asked, taking another sip of my whiskey. "We will have breakfast there soon as well."

"You mean talk about what we discussed in the car a few days ago?"

"Yes, I want to know what you will allow me to do..." Erica came back with her drink and sat it down on the table. "This will be all. Apply this to my room. And here for taking up one of your tables."

"Yes, sir. Thank you, sir." She took the hundred-dollar bill from me and went to her other table.

"Are you saying I have to decide now what I want?" Emi reached for her glass and sipped it, while staring at me over the rim.

"No, but I'd like to show you some things. And see if you would be comfortable doing somethings with me." I answered, playing with her shoulder length hair.

"Okay, but I'd like to discuss this there then."

I grinned at her answer and finished off my whiskey. Scooting out of the booth I reached for her hand once I was standing. Emi's small hand slid into mine and I grabbed her suitcase with the other.

We walked through the restaurant and into the lobby. People milled around us as we made our way to the elevator. Arriving at the elevator I let go of Emi's hand and pulled out the key from my pocket and swiped it. The doors opened and we entered it as I pressed the button to our suite.

"Are you nervous?" I glanced over at her from the corner of my eye.

Her cheeks flamed as she looked up through her lashes before she pulled them back down. I lightly grabbed her chin and brought her eyes back up to me. Emi's pupils filled her irises as she searched my face. "Don't do that. I've never seen you avert your eyes from your brother. Don't you ever do that to me when you are with me."

"Okay," her breath came out as a sigh.

"Now I've order breakfast for us and I didn't know what you would like, so I got it all." She nodded and her tongue snaked out wetting her lips.

The doors opened and I turned just in time to see room service setting out all the food I had ordered on the kitchen table. Emi walked out of the elevator and stared at all the food. I chuckled and came into the suite with her suitcase.

"Thank you, this all looks great." The man smiled and went to his now empty cart. I pulled out my wallet and gave him a couple of hundreds.

"Thank you, sir. Enjoy the food." He left with his cart in the elevator.

"Drake I can't eat all of this. There's so much." Her hands were on her hips as she continued to stare at the table.

I left her suitcase by the chair and I went up and grabbed a piece of bacon before taking a seat in one of the chairs. Emi turned to me and smiled. I pulled open the top of my shirt after Emi turned to get something to eat.

I let Emi eat her fill before I stood up and walked over to her. Resting my hand on her shoulder she looked up at me. With my other hand I held it out for her to take. Emi's hand filled mine and I pulled her flush against me.

"We need to talk about what you want to try." My other hand went under her jaw, tilting it upward to me. She didn't fight me on it and I crashed my lips to hers.

The taste of strawberry jelly assaulted my taste buds as my tongue and hers fought. I couldn't get enough of her as she fisted my shirt, pulling me closer to her. After what felt like minutes, I released her and brought her to arm's length.

"I've looked up somethings on the internet. Are you wanting

me to be a submissive?" Emi stared into my eyes as her cheeks turned crimson.

"Yes and no. If you want to be then we can explore that."

"So, what are we doing today? Hashing out terms?" I chuckled at her and grabbed her hand leading her over to the bedroom.

"No, today I want it to just be you and me. I may get a little rough and if it's too much you can tell me."

"Okay."

"Strip for me down to your underwear." I watched as her confidence took over and she tugged her dress off over her head.

Emi wore a bright peach color panty and bra set, which set off the color of her skin. I could feel myself growing harder in my pants but I wasn't going to take my eyes off her. Going forward she stood still as I ran my fingers down her sides.

"Lay down on the bed. Right there in the middle of it." I watched as she leaned back on the bed and used her feet to push herself into the center of the bed. Fuck she was stunning.

I finished undoing my shirt and shrugged out of it. Emi was already breathing heavy and she eyed me from the crotch of my pants back up to my face. This is what I wanted her to do when we laid out our terms, I wanted her so ready for me that she was ready to break her role.

"Such a good girl, *dolcezza*."

Emi smiled at me before biting her lower lip and pulling it between her teeth. She was fucking sexy when she did that with her pupils eclipsing her irises. I leaned over to get on the bed leaving my pants on for the moment.

"Are you ready?" I crawled up her body kissing every few inches.

Her body shivered when I reached her hip. I made sure not to go to her pussy, saving it for last once I made her wet enough.

Using the flat of my tongue I ran it up her panty line to underneath her bra. Emi arched and reached for me.

I grabbed her hands and held them above her head. Shaking my head I grinned at her before latching onto the top of her breast and sucking it into my mouth.

"Drake, please!"

"Please what *dolcezza*?" I asked popping off her and staring into her eyes. If I didn't know that her eyes were hazel, I would have sworn her eyes were black.

"Please... I need you inside me."

"You will get me after I get done playing with you. And you can't touch me while I am."

"Okay, Sir," Emi answered with a grin.

That three-letter word did something to me that nothing else had ever done. I released her wrists and sat back on her thighs, running my eyes over her body. Reaching to her bra I grabbed it and ripped it from her body.

"Drake! I loved that one!"

"I'll buy you a new set." I answered while sliding down and dipping my fingers in her waist band.

Pulling them down her legs Emi lifted her ass helping me to get them off. Emi had shaved her gorgeous pussy and I felt my mouth watering. I lifted her ass up and crashed my lips to her pussy.

Her legs shook each time I applied pressure to her clit. Emi's thighs tighten against my head as she ground herself against my face. She tasted so fucking good.

"Drake! You're going to make me come!"

I didn't let up on her and continued my assault, making her come over my tongue and chin.

Chapter Eight

DRAKE

I stood at the corner, watching the older man get out of the limo and head into one of the gentlemen's clubs that he had been frequenting since I found him. My uncle wasn't lying when he said the man was old, but I didn't expect him to be this elderly.

What else I couldn't understand was why he didn't at least have a bastard child from the many women that he had been with. I had done my research, and he had been one of the top playboys in our world. Along with being the most gruesome. He didn't get his nickname for just sitting around. This man once tortured someone to within an inch of his life and had him treated before doing it all over again.

Jack the Torturer wasn't a man to mess around and even if he was older now. I still wasn't going to go in half-cocked. He was the head of the LA mafia, and I knew that even if his men weren't like him, they could still be very deadly.

Part of me thought I had seen this man before when he was younger, but I hadn't known about Jack until my uncle had told me about him. I mean, he could have been on the TV like other criminals in this area had been, but something was gnawing at me.

The man didn't look over his shoulder, but who would when they were like him? Besides, he had ten men around him at all times. I didn't know how I was going to get to him with his protection. Another car came up behind the limo, an old beater.

Three men got out and noticed one of them was red-headed. He looked like the leader of the group as two goons flanked him. He was lanky and looked like he had missed a few meals. The redhead looked over his shoulder, and I didn't miss that his nose had been broken recently. He wasn't like Jack, that was for sure.

Sighing, I turned and walked the two blocks back to my vehicle. I needed to get some sleep. But between staking out Jack and my mind running with the thoughts of Emi wrapped around my cock again kept me awake. I was surprised that TC hadn't noticed I wasn't at my best. But he had his own shit to handle at the moment.

I had told him that one of them was going to fall, and I was pretty sure it would be him. He talked a big game, but I knew he wasn't getting any from his "flavors." TC had been in one hellacious mood since he'd married Aurora.

TC had taken to working later than normal and then coming in earlier. If he didn't slow down, he was going to crash, and then I would have to deal with the company on top of what my uncle wanted. I just couldn't understand why my uncle had beef with a mobster in LA. Reaching my vehicle, I opened my door and slid into the leather seat of my midnight-black Rolls-Royce Wraith, bringing it to life. As I put the car in gear, it purred, and I peeled off the curb. I had to make sure I didn't stand out in this part of town. For as many mobsters as there were here, they all drove expensive cars, other than the redhead.

I passed the limo and the old beater car as I made my way back to my home. Unlike TC, I had bought a home out in Beverly

Crest. He wanted to be closer to the company, so I needed to be a little further away. To be able to have the optimal property I had paid a pretty penny. The house I built on the property had a state-of-the-art security system, which my father encouraged me to have.

The only thing that was missing was Emi in my bed, waiting for me. Every time I was near TC, I thought he sensed that I had done something. But he never said anything. The fact that I was now keeping two secrets from him fucked with me. Either of the secrets could get me killed.

My phone vibrated in the seat as I pulled up to my gate. I glanced over and grabbed it from the leather and opened the message, I smiled. Emi had sent me a photo, and not just any photo, but of something that she wanted to try. I had never pegged her to be into things like this, but fuck if I wasn't going to let her try them with me.

This particular one had her tied up. Just thinking about it made my cock hard. To see her strung up, sopping wet, had my imagination going crazy.

If that is what you want, dolcezza, I will get it for you. But I'll tell you right now, you will need a safe word with that.

Really?

And what if I don't give you a safe word?

Yes, and we need to talk about other things.

You don't know what you are saying.
You need to think of one. If not, I will
think of one myself.

hmm.... Pineapples?

If that is what you can remember when
you can't take any more. But we still
need to talk about things.

That sounds delightful. ok.

I shook my head as I pulled my car into the garage and sat back when I killed the engine. Unzipping my slacks, I tugged out my cock and ran my hand over the bars and head, making it hard. I snapped a picture of my hand teasing the tip before sending it to Emi.

What a nice thick cock. What I
wouldn't do to have that inside me
right now.

All you have to do is bring that ass of
yours to my place.

I can't, I'm shopping, and I plan on
going to this sex shop to browse.

Then tell them you have a tab and
want it sent to my house. I have a
room where we can try anything your
heart desires. Along with the things
that you buy.

You promise?

> With my life.

> :)

After tucking my cock back in my slacks, I exited the car to take a long, cold shower. Emi had a habit of texting me with things she thought would make me cringe. But she didn't believe that I would do anything to satisfy her. I'd kill for her and then fuck her as the person died in front of us. Whatever she wanted, I'd do.

I stripped out of my clothes, phone in hand, and headed into my bathroom. Fuck, with the picture that she sent and then what she said, I was rock hard. My phone buzzed again with a text.

> What do you think about this outfit?

A picture came seconds later, and God-fucking-damn! It was leather and had chains hanging off the neckline and belly button. Straps wrapped around her neck and met in the middle of her breastbone to a metal ring, which tied onto the straps holding the top on her shoulders. Leather cords ran down her legs and connected to those that circled her thick thighs. Her tits billowed over the little coverage the top offered, and I was sure that the panties were crotchless.

> What are you trying to do to me, dolcezza? I'm going to be hard until I see you again.

> You like it? You don't think it's too much?

> Fuck no. You better get that one. I want to see you in it on your knees before me.

I don't know if I want to be on my
knees.

Listen, you start being a brat I'll show
you what happens to you.

You won't do anything. ;)

She was definitely a brat. I stepped into the shower just as my phone buzzed again. Placing the device on to the holder I clicked the message and Emi's picture came up. Fuck this woman knew what she was doing. They were crotchless. Emi was sitting on the bench with her legs wide open with a finger inside her delectable cunt.

How much do you want my cock in
that cunt?

So much!

Show me…

I fisted my cock as the video call rang through. She wasn't playing. I answered the call and smiled at her. Emi's movement in that fucking lingerie made my hand slowly move along my cock as I watched her move over to the bench. She had earbuds in; Emi knew what she was doing.

"Dolcezza, did you have this planned?" I grinned at her when she pulled her bottom lip into her mouth and nodded. "Don't be shy now. Show me how much you want me. Let the whole store know what you are doing in there."

"People will hear." Her eyes widened as she stared back at me. "My friends will hear. They are in the stalls beside me."

"You started this, *dolcezza*; now you have to finish it. The only way you are going to finish it is when I'm painting this shower with my cum."

Emi swallowed and got comfortable. She sunk two fingers inside her wet cunt, and with the other hand, she played with her clit. I grabbed some body wash and squirted some in my hand to help me slide over my cock.

With the way she was using her fingers and spreading it open for me to see the pink flesh underneath those beautiful lips, I would be coming first. I tightened my grip on the head to keep my orgasm at bay while I watched her.

Emi was panting, and she trained those fuck-me eyes on me as she came for the first time. She didn't make too much noise but if someone were listening closely enough, they would hear her.

"I want another before I get off, and I want my name on your lips, *dolcezza*."

"They don't know about us."

"There are plenty of Drakes in the world. Let them know who you come for."

Emi doubled her efforts, adding a third finger. After a few seconds, her mouth dropped, and she began to pant again. The little whimper that escaped her lips almost made me bust the nut I was holding in. I needed to hear my name.

Her chest was heaving, and her fingers were thrusting faster. I let go of my head and pumped my cock with the same aggression.

"You're almost there, Emi. Say my name, let everyone in that store know what you're doing in their dressing room."

"Drake! I'm coming!" When her eyes snapped open and landed on mine, I could see the glossy film over her orbs. The squirt that came from her did me in.

"Fuck, Emi!" I sprayed my shower with cum but wished I was painting her walls with it instead. "You did such a good job, *dolcezza*. Get that lingerie. I want to be able to touch you."

The redness that raced across her cheeks brought a grin to my lips.

"What's wrong, Emi?"

"I can't believe I just peed on this floor. I've never peed on myself." She turned her back on the phone.

"Emi, have you never squirted before?" She glanced over her shoulder and shook her head. "Fuck, what kind of men have you been with?"

"None like you." Her bottom lip had slipped in between her teeth.

"That's okay. Because you won't be embarrassed about that again. Clean yourself up and buy it. I'll find some way to have you again with that on." Emi nodded and stripped out of the lingerie. Fuck, this woman didn't know what she did to me.

Emi dressed quickly and grabbed her phone and the lingerie along with her purse. She looked down at the phone, and a small grin graced those pouty lips.

"I have to let you go," she whispered. Her lips moved in the camera's view.

"I know, *dolcezza*. Be safe, and I'll see you soon."

Emi smiled and ended the video call.

Chapter Nine

EMI

I took a deep breath and wiped away the tears that had left my eyes as I came. When I opened the door, I ran into my two friends. Their arms crossed over their chests, and their hips cocked as they stood in front of me in the lingerie they had picked out.

"What?" I tried to push past them, but they held their ground.

"What? You come out of that stall, and the only thing that you say is, 'What?' No, ma'am. What the fuck was that all about?"

"And who is Drake? I thought you were dating Keith?" Hannah raised an eyebrow and stole a glance at Summer.

"I ended it with him after the wedding. He wanted to have a threesome with some random girl. I wasn't down with that." My heart was still pounding from what Drake had suggested that I do. I mean, was I embarrassed by what I had done? Hell yeah. Would I do it again? Yes, especially if Drake asked me to.

Because part of me wanted to know more about what his sex life was like. Because of what I had already experienced with him, he wasn't vanilla. Both Hannah and Summer rolled their eyes and held their ground. More people were starting to stare at us. Which was causing me to get more nervous about the puddle on the changing room floor.

"Look, I need to buy this. You both look great, okay, but do you mind if get past you so I can sort this out?"

"Fine, but we want the deets on your new man," Summer threw over her shoulder as they went back into their changing rooms to change.

I walked out of the area that housed the actual changing rooms. The other patrons stared at me as I went up to the counter. I mean, they were in a sex shop, too, so I didn't understand. Well, I did understand why they were staring, but hell, it could have been a movie, right?

The woman behind the counter gave me a curious look before ringing up not only my lingerie but the other items that I had gotten.

"That will be $654.39. Will you be using cash or card?"

"Um, they will go on Mr. DeLuca's tab. And can you have the bigger items sent to his place?" I told her as I leaned in. I didn't need him to buy these, but if he was going to, I wasn't about to say no.

"Okay. Then you are ready to go." She placed all my items in two bags and handed them back to me with a smile.

Holding my head up high, I walked out of the store and ran right into Heath, my bodyguard. He had wanted to come in and scope the place out, but I didn't want any more attention on myself. And bringing a bodyguard into this store would have done just that.

But I had brought just as much, if not more, attention on myself with what I had done with Drake in the changing room. Heath took my bags and placed them in the blacked-out SUV, and I got in the back to wait for Summer and Hannah. I was pretty sure that Summer had the hots for Heath. Not that I was yucking it, but he wasn't my type.

He was on the skinnier side, not too skinny but not as bulky as the others. The only thing he had on them was his height. His blond hair whipped around in the wind as I waited on Summer and Hannah to come out of the store. Heath had a good jawline and looked good in the suit that TC made him wear. But there was just something about a tall, muscular man, and Drake was that man for me.

Hannah and Summer came out of the store, and Heath opened the door to let them in the SUV. He closed the door behind Summer, heading to the passenger side of the vehicle. He got in, and my driver pulled away from the curb.

"So, are you going to tell us who Drake is?" Summer's voice brought my attention to her. The fact that Heath was in the vehicle made me nervous. Would he know who they were talking about? And would he tell my brother?

"He's just someone I met at the club in Las Vegas." I giggle, trying to think if either of them would know why Drake was in Las Vegas.

"Come on, girl. Give us the information. Not any person can make someone do what you did in that changing room," Hannah interjected herself into the conversation as she popped the dick sucker out of her mouth.

"How about we have this conversation at the house? There are guys in the vehicle with us." I didn't want to talk about this with Heath in the front seat. His loyalty was to my brother.

"Girl, you said you'd tell us in the SUV."

I cocked my head at them and motioned with my eyes to Heath. The driver I didn't care about, but Heath I didn't trust. My brother didn't need to know about my sex life.

"Fine," Summer huffed, crossing her arms while sitting back in the seat.

Usually, I told these two everything, and I would tell them about Drake when I was safely at home with them, in the privacy of my own room. Ever since TC had the whole family fitted with bodyguards it had ruined any of my chances of having my own place. Not that I hadn't gotten away from my bodyguard a few times. One of those times while I went to Las Vegas with Keith.

He had basically told me that I wasn't to be alone at any point unless I was going to the bathroom. But damn it. After Las Vegas with Drake, I wanted to be able to have more of him, even if the phone calls and sexting were hot as fuck.

They were nothing like being with him, but I couldn't bring him to my parents' house. Even if they had let me move further down the hall. It would be weird to have him in my room with my parents downstairs.

I glanced out the window and noticed the same car parked a couple of blocks down from my parents' house again. Leaning up, I grabbed the driver's shoulder, bringing his attention to me. "Make sure you wipe off your fingerprints please. Heath, can you call the guards and see if they can take a look at that car down the road?"

Heath looked to where I was pointing and nodded before he grabbed his phone and pressed a button.

"Jake, we may have a problem at the Churchhill residence. Do you know if Dave or Chad can meet me here to check out a car?" Heath nodded to the inaudible voice of TC's bodyguard. "Roger that, sir. I'll get the girls in the house and grab Dave and Seth since they are here."

"Of course, sir. We can take care of this, no reason to bother the boss." Heath hung up as we went through the gate. Turning on me, he looked each of us in the eye, "When we get to the house, you three get inside and lock the door. Mr. and Mrs. Churchhill are not here, so head for the bunker."

"What the fuck do you mean the bunker? What bunker?" I had never known about this part of the house. When was that put in?

Heath sighed and brought his phone up again to his ear. "Brian, need you at the front door to take the girls to the bunker."

He quickly hung up and was out of the vehicle before it stopped. He opened the back door, grabbing and pulling me from the SUV. Heath pushed me up the stairs while Summer and Hannah followed behind me. Brian met me at the door, pulling me into the house.

Brian's grip on my elbow was tight as he walked me down the hall and into the basement. We went up to the south side wall, and Brian pressed into the wall. It opened into a room. "Don't come out of here until Heath or I come back to get you."

I couldn't say anything to the man I had known most of my life. He stepped out of the room and left us. They didn't act like this when I mentioned the car down the street. Whatever Jake told them must have put a fire under their ass.

"What's up with your bodyguard?" Hannah huffed as she plopped down on the seat.

I still couldn't figure out when this was put in because it had never been here before. And it couldn't have been anytime recently since I hadn't lived at the dorm in some months.

"I don't know. But I've seen the car on the street twice now."

"Fuck, girl, they did this over a car down the road. People park on the road," Summer groaned and walked around the small room.

"Look, I didn't say anything. But my brother put Heath with me because, apparently, he pissed off some people. And that car isn't something that would be in this neighborhood," I told her. If it had been a newer car, I probably wouldn't have said anything, but it was the same car as last time.

"What did he do to piss someone off? Fuck the wrong woman?" Hannah giggled and elbowed Summer.

"Hey! My brother isn't that bad."

"Oookkay. Whatever you say, girl. I've seen the tabloids. TC's got a new woman on his arm every week. I mean, I would love to be underneath that hunky flesh of your brother."

"Oh my God, Hannah! I don't need to know this!" I knew my brother had his women, but now that he was married, I hoped she would keep him out of the tabloids. "He's married now. So you won't be getting anything from him."

"I know, and that sucks."

I rolled my eyes and continued to pace the room. Glancing at my watch, there had only been ten minutes since Heath left. I grabbed my phone and sent a text to Heath to find out what was happening. But he didn't respond. Did something happen to them?

Fuck, would something happen to us since there were no bodyguards? I glanced around the room and couldn't find anything to help protect us. Why wouldn't they leave something here to fight with?

The door opened, and my heart raced before I noticed that it was Heath coming in. I didn't miss the blood that had stained his once-white shirt. "Let's go, the coast is clear."

He opened the door further, allowing us to exit. I stopped and turned, watching the door return to a wall. To the untrained eye, you wouldn't know that it was there. Heath came up to me, and I stared back at him. "What happened?"

"They won't be bothering you or your parents anymore." He steered me out of the basement and up the stairs.

"Whose blood is this?" I needed to know whether the guys all came back okay.

"It's Brian's, but he's going to make it." I nodded and made my way up the rest of the stairs.

"Your bags and the other girls' bags are in your room. The butler brought them up for you." Heath's voice made me spin at the top.

I nodded and stepped through the basement door into the

kitchen. Everything was quiet as I followed my friends up to the second floor to my bedroom. Entering my room I came face to face with my two friends.

"Okay, we need answers. First is what happened in the sex store?" Hannah questioned as she plopped onto the bed.

"Two, who is Drake?" Summer cocked her head as her gaze went from me to Hannah.

Rolling my eyes, I sat down beside Hannah and motioned for Summer to get the door. "This is going to take a while."

Chapter Ten

DRAKE

TC was distracted by his wife. I had noticed that when he would sit at his desk and pretend to be signing things. Today was one of those days and he was carrying his Glock. I had been carrying mine for a while, too, ever since I noticed some punk hanging around the garage entrance.

My phone pinged on my desk, bringing my attention to my watch, and I grinned.

I want you.

I want you too, but you know we can't get caught.

I know, but you're always working. :(

The phone on my desk rang, and I picked it up.

"DeLuca."

"Drake, I'm taking the rest of the day off. You're in charge," TC replied. I was silent for a moment before I glanced back at my phone.

"Okay, you know I got you, man." My mind went to the text messages from his sister, and I couldn't help but think about a rendezvous with her here. It was a risk to bring her here, but fuck, she was right, and I needed her just as bad.

"Thank you, I'll see you tomorrow."

"You're welcome. Get some sleep, man."

> Get your ass to my work.

> Yes, sir. ;)

Fuck, those two words went straight to my cock, making me hard under my desk. I pressed the intercom button and waited for Tiffany to answer.

"Yes, Mr. DeLuca?"

"I have a visitor. Please let her in my office when she gets here."

"Of course,"

Tiffany wouldn't tell TC. Besides, my office was further away from TC's. By the time Emi got here, he would be gone.

It wasn't long before Emi came through the doors. I held her gaze, and she smiled and locked the door. She was wearing a skirt and a shirt, which was tight enough to show me that she wasn't wearing a bra.

"I'm here. What do you want to do with me?" She licked her lips and, with a sultry look, strolled over to my desk.

"You know where I want you, but we need to have a conversation." My cock strained at my zipper, and my hand went to my lap to try to quell my hard-on.

Emi came around the desk and pushed my laptop closed before sitting in front of me. She opened her legs and fuck, she wasn't wearing any panties. I leaned forward, but she placed her foot in the center of my chest. I cocked an eyebrow, amused that she thought she could come in here and act like she was in charge.

She wasn't completely aware of her role, but she would be learning. However, the sight of her bare pussy made me forget about the conversation we needed to have.

"Not yet. I'm not wet enough." I grabbed her heel and slipped it off, bringing her foot to my lips. I placed a few kisses on the top of it before giving her a warning look and a reminder.

"You've overstepped, *dolcezza*. This will be your only free pass. You're lucky you have me hard and wanting; otherwise, I'd turn you over my knee and punish that gorgeous ass of yours. Now, how do you want me to make you wetter, *dolcezza?*" I ran my tongue up her leg. She shivered, and her pupils widened in excitement.

"I want your mouth on my pussy." Her fingers went to her clit, and she used them to rub around her nub while she dipped her left hand's fingers into her slick cunt.

Fuck! She was making me so fucking hard, and all I wanted was to release my cock and get balls deep inside her pussy. I shoved her hands away and told her another rule. "Don't touch my pussy unless I tell you to."

I widened her legs and placed them on my shoulders before pulling myself closer to her. Shimmying her skirt farther up her thighs, I took a moment to absorb the sight of Emi's perfect pussy. I brought my lips to her clit and pulled it into my mouth, my eyes locked on hers.

Emi moaned and leaned back against the desk. My laptop crashed to the floor as she stretched out. She was going to get me into trouble with her brother, but that was the last thing on my mind as I slipped two fingers inside her tight cunt.

"Yes! Drake right there!" she cried out and arched her back off the desk. I didn't stop her because who was going to stop me? Not anyone in this building, that was for sure.

I reached down and unzipped my slacks, pulling them off with my other hand. One thing I couldn't have was her pussy juice on them, but I wanted her all over me right now.

I pulled off her clit with a pop and looked into her eclipsed gaze. Fuck, she was beautiful. "I think you're ready. Are you ready for my cock?"

Emi nodded, and I stood, positioning my cock at her entrance. Moving slowly so that she could adjust to my size this time, I felt the ripple of her pussy along the bars that lined my dick. Emi arched her back, and her hands went into her hair. "Are you good?"

"Yes..." The sigh that accompanied her answer sent chills through my body. I grabbed her hips to steady myself before I rocked inside her.

Watching my cock slide in and out of her tight cunt had my climax building further. Seeing it disappear and then remerge was amazing. Emi's eyes never left mine as I quickened my pace. She was wetter than she had ever been, making it easier to slide in.

I moved my thumb over to her clit and began rubbing circles and pinching it, bringing her ever closer to the edge of her orgasm. My phone began to ring, and I didn't miss the smile on her face as she sat up and pulled off her shirt.

"You gonna get that?"

"Fuck... DeLuca!" I didn't want to get the phone. What I wanted to do was to latch onto one of those perky nipples that were now in my face.

"Mr. DeLuca, I was wondering if..."

"Not now, Frank!" I hung up on him and took hold of one of Emi's nipples. Her fingers wove into my hair and pulled me closer while the walls of her cunt clutched at me.

"Drake, right there! Don't fucking stop! Fuck, I'm coming."

Emi's body tightened, and it felt like she was spasming as she came around my cock. I followed her, holding her against me as I sat back in my chair with her on my lap. Something wet landed on my shoulder, and as soon as I gave her my last drop, I pulled her away to look at her.

"Are you okay? Did I hurt you again?" I asked while wiping away the droplets of tears from her cheeks.

"No, you didn't hurt me. I've never had an orgasm like that before."

"So, what are you telling me, it was so good you teared up?" I chuckled and kissed her lips, hoping she would let me taste her. She opened her mouth and deepened the kiss, using her tongue to fight with mine.

"I want more than this." Emi broke the kiss and stared at me.

"I do, too, but how would that work? I can't just come over to your parents' house."

"Then I'll move in with you." Her eyebrow twitched up with the corner of her lip.

"You sure you want to do that? TC would find out, you know."

"That's true since he has a guard tailing me constantly. You are going to the Gala, right?"

"Why does he have a guard tailing you?" I asked, ignoring her question.

"Apparently, some gang members from his past have shown up and now have a hit on his family." She shrugged. Why didn't he tell me about this?

"How long has this been going on?" I released Emi as she got up and grabbed some tissues from my desk and started to clean herself up. I had half a mind to tell her to stop, but then I didn't want her to bump into anyone who would be nosy on her way out.

"Before the wedding, I'm sure." She bent down and grabbed her shirt from the floor, pulling it over her head.

"How did you find out about this?" I asked, watching her fix her hair.

"I may have over heard him talking on the phone one time with Jake. He's always either on his phone with you or him." Emi shrugged again with a roll of her eyes.

That was when he started carrying the Glock. I wonder if he had seen the kid I saw, too, lurking around the garage. Standing, I pulled my pants up, zipping and buttoning them, then tucking in my shirt. It was the first time I had fucked someone at work.

I sat back in my chair and watched Emi run her hands through her hair to fix it. She glanced back over to me, and I patted my lap. We still needed to have that conversation about her safe word. Emi shook her head and giggled as she came up to me. I pulled her into my lap so we were facing each other.

"We have to talk about your safe word." I moved her hair out of her face so that I could see her eyes.

"I thought we already did?"

"Not quite, *dolcezza*. We established what your safe word was. Now I need to know how you use it."

"Drake, I'm not stupid. I know that I use it if I can't take whatever you are doing." She crossed her arms over her chest, making her breasts press into my face.

"I didn't call you stupid, Emi. I need you to tell me that you know what it is used for because this is how you trust me. You have to be able to know your limits and tell me when that happens. Because, at that moment, whatever is happening stops until we've had this conversation. Okay?" I held her gaze as I tried to reiterate what I was saying. There was nothing I wouldn't do for this woman, but that also meant I needed to establish her consent, too.

Emi nodded, and her cheeks brightened with whatever she was thinking. As much as I would love to discuss her limits right now, it wasn't the time to do that. Emi placed her hands on my face and then brought her lips to mine, brushing them softly before deepening it.

"I have to get out of here. I'm sure my guard has noticed I'm not in the store anymore," she said as she pulled away.

"Don't ever ditch your guard again. I'll pay him off if I have to, but don't you ever leave him. Do you hear me?" I grabbed her jaw to make sure she continued to look at me. I knew about things like this. One slip up and she would be gone.

"Okay, but I'm fine. Nothing is going to happen."

"You say that, but you don't know these people. They will take you and do horrible things to you just to get to your brother. So, don't go anywhere without your bodyguard. Do you understand me?" Emi nodded, and I pulled her into me, crashing my lips to hers.

If those fuckwads did anything to her, I would kill them one by one. TC wouldn't even have to lift a finger. I would burn this city to the ground until she was back at my side.

"You're worse than my brother." Emi pushed away from me. "I have to go."

"Get out of here and tell that bodyguard he better not lose you again." I let her off my lap and slapped her ass as she made her way back out of my office.

I went around the desk and picked up my laptop and all the papers that Emi had shoved off it when she laid back. Scanning over the papers, I rolled them up. I had been trying to convince TC to let me take the warehouse off his hands. That way, I could use it to help move the items my uncle wanted through.

Turning away from my desk I strolled over to my door, I opened it and turned left. Emi's scent permeated the hallway. When I turned the corner, TC and Jake walked into his office. I was pretty sure he'd told me he wouldn't be returning today.

I strolled in behind them and froze as my eyes landed on Emi sitting on the couch. Jake sat down in one of the high-backed chairs near the door like he always did. *Fuck, why was Emi with TC? Did he know?* I put on my best smile and walked forward to his desk with the rolled-up papers I was going to place on his desk in my hands.

"Well, looks like someone couldn't stay gone today." I plopped down in one of the chairs in front of TCs desk and propped my leg on my knee. I could feel Emi's eyes on me.

"What do you need, Drake?" TC looked aggravated. I wondered if it was Aurora that made him this way.

"I was thinking about talking to you about that old warehouse by the coast..." TC held up his hand at me and shook his head. Maybe this wasn't the best time to talk to him about it.

"I told you I'm not selling it. It will rot until I figure out what I need it for."

Part of me wondered if I told him who my family was and what his grandfather had done, he would be more than willing to run this together. My uncle wanted me to keep this in the family, but TC was part of my family. I hated keeping this away from him.

Chapter Eleven

DRAKE

My phone dinged one after another. TC had already headed to the waiting SUV to meet Ms. Petticort, our new potential client. My father held me on the phone, keeping me from walking with him. After locking the drawer with the money laundering business in it, I grabbed my phone and made my way down.

TC was already pissed since I hadn't gotten down there yet, and this was starting to wear on me. I groaned as another ding of my phone sounded. Pulling my phone out of my pocket, I glanced at the screen and smiled.

I walked out of my office, waving to Tiffany as I went down

the hallway into the elevator. My attention solely on the phone in my hand.

Idk what color dress are you going to be wearing?

I was thinking… gold?

Ok, I'll make sure to match my tie and cufflinks. Think I could get a selfie?

Stepping into the elevator, I pressed the button for the first floor. My phone lit up as her picture appeared. Fuck, Emi was gorgeous in that glittery gold dress. It was strapless and dipped all the way to the lower part of her back. If she wanted me to match her, I would.

Fuck, Emi you're gorgeous. If you wear that at the Gala, there is no way I'm going to be able to keep my hands off you. And your brother might end up noticing.

I was hoping you would say that. I hope he doesn't. I'm getting this. See you at the Gala.

The elevator sang, and I stepped into the lobby. It was busy today, with people heading in and out of the other elevators beside mine. The employees who walked past me greeted me with either a nod or a wave. Most of these people didn't even know me other than the giant picture over the elevators with TC's.

I've been thinking about you.

Have you now?

> Yes, what does a girl have to do to see you again?

> I'll see what I can do after this meeting. I'm getting in the car with your brother. So we need to be careful.

I opened the Mercedes SUV's door and got in. Glancing over to TC, he was glaring at me, but I gave him a grin. Jake cleared his throat, bringing TC's and my attention to him.

"Head on out, Jake, now that Mr. DeLuca has decided to grace us with his presence." I knew I had pissed him off. I couldn't tell him about the laundering that was going on. At least, not yet. And with how he had been tense these past few weeks, I couldn't tell if it was from the gang that I now knew about or if it was something else.

"Look, when an employee has a question. You have to answer it." I laughed, trying to make light of the situation as I straightened my suit jacket and sat back.

"If it wasn't more important than this new client, you should have had her email you," he snapped.

All right, he wasn't in the mood for my shit, but now that I had started, I couldn't stop.

"Touchy, touchy. I didn't think those types of emails were permitted through work email. I'll let her know in the future." I winked at him. Knowing full well I wasn't talking about a woman. If he wanted to assume it was, then I would allow it.

We sat in silence, and I glanced at Emi's reply since I had entered the vehicle.

> I thought you put a blocking screen protector on your phone?

Did you get caught by my brother?

You did, didn't you?

We didn't get caught. And yes, I got the incognito screen protector. I'm in the SUV with your brother, and he is already pissed.

What did you do now?

I was late in getting to the car.

Then I will let you be then. But we still need to figure something out. I need you.

Of course, dolcezza.

Jake stopped the vehicle at the front of our client's building, and we exited the SUV. I stretched once I got out of the Mercedes. Most of the time, I wished TC would get a bigger car than this one, but for some reason, he liked it.

I reached back in and grabbed the suitcase that TC had so neglectfully left in the back seat and widened my strides to catch back up to him.

Entering the lobby, I noticed the building was being renovated as we walked up to the reception desk. Mr. Petticort had almost let the building become neglected. I was glad to see his daughter was doing something with it.

A cute redhead was sitting at the desk and glanced up as we approached. She smiled before standing. "Hello, I'm Cassandra. Assistant to Ms. Petticort. She requested I wait down here to bring you to her office. She is expecting you both."

TC nodded, and Cassandra led us to the elevator. From what I had seen while growing up in this world, not many women would take over their family's company. But this one had made it known that she had done what a lot of her gender hadn't been able to. She was brutal in some ways, but only to the men who thought she was ignorant. And this woman wasn't ignorant. She was at the top of her class in college, and she didn't stop there.

The doors opened, and TC and I entered the elevator, with Cassandra taking her place in front of us. My eyes wandered to her backside, and I nudged TC. Even though, in my head, I was in a relationship with his sister, I couldn't change what I would normally do. TC cocked an eyebrow up at me. He was still not in the mood for my shenanigans.

Cassandra entered the code to get us to her boss' floor and stood in front of us with a confident air. Even with us in the elevator, she was very relaxed. When the elevator dinged, Cassandra stepped to the side, and a scrawny man stood in the opening.

"Here we are. Jay will show you the rest of the way." Cassandra held the door open. Giving a wink to Casandra as I followed TC out of the elevator, she smiled and shook her head at me before allowing the doors to close.

Jay quickly made his way away from the elevator, making TC and I follow him at a quick pace. His hair was gelled back, giving him a greasy look rather than a well-groomed one. And I didn't miss the glare that he sent back to me and TC when he turned to lead us to Ms. Petticort. TC had stiffened since the elevator, and I was ready for anything to pop off if it did.

He stopped and knocked on Ms. Petticort's office and entered without waiting for her to invite us in. Jay moved to the side and let us in the room. This room had been renovated, too, because the desk and floor gleamed in the sun's rays.

Ms. Petticort sat behind her desk like the queen she was. Softly curled blonde hair and natural makeup graced her features. This woman knew she had power and wasn't about to relinquish it. Her eyes locked with TC's before she smiled.

The woman stood from her desk. She rounded the furniture and held out her hand to TC. Her tight-fitting dress hugged her body like a second skin. The crimson fabric brought out her skin color. "Mr. Churchhill, thank you for meeting with me here. I know it takes you away from your business, but I figured it would be good to get you out of your building."

"You're welcome, Ms. Petticort. This is my COO, Drake DeLuca." TC released her hand, and she crossed her arms as she allowed her eyes to roam my physique. She clearly didn't want to shake my hand.

"Yes. Now, why don't we get down to business?" She motioned to the chairs in front of her desk and then sat in her seat.

TC and I took the chairs offered to us and waited for her to continue. Ms. Petticort leaned forward and threaded her fingers under her chin. She looked between both of us and then grabbed a folder that was to her right.

"So, I was thinking about getting into international shipping, but to be honest, this is new to me, and I wanted the best to export my products." She handed TC the folder, then sat back and crossed her legs.

TC opened the file and took his time reading. With how he was reading it, it looked as if we would be negotiating what she wanted. I opened the briefcase and pulled out the small laptop to begin a new document.

Since Lindsey wasn't there, it was up to me to keep up with what was being said and what had been agreed upon. I wasn't as fast at typing as her, but I could remember enough to make this work.

After typing for the length of the three-hour negotiations I was glad that they had come to an agreement about price. Ms.

Petticort would be one woman I would never want to negotiate with again for the rest of my life.

I didn't know how TC was able to stand it, but he was the CEO. After standing from my seat with TC, we exited the office and headed back down to the elevator. Cassandra was sitting at the reception desk and smiled as we walked out. Jake and Sam had already returned the SUV to the front of the building, waiting for us.

"She was gorgeous. But fuck, she was intense. I don't think I've seen a woman like her before," I rambled to TC in the car.

He rubbed his temples before he took a deep breath and continued down the back of his neck. "Can you just shut up?"

"You need to get laid. You're too uptight," I countered as I pulled out my phone and scrolled through social media.

Emi was posting about her day. Which was dangerous, given that the gang was after TC's family. I wondered if he had a guard with Aurora because they didn't know whether he was in love with her or not. Exiting the app, I glanced over to TC from the corner of my eye. He looked tired. I really wanted to ask him about the gang and why he didn't tell me about them. But then I would have to tell him how I knew, and I wasn't ready to let him kill me.

When I opened my text messages, I noticed that my father and uncle had messaged me. But I wasn't ready to answer them just yet. I clicked on my conversation with Emi and typed.

> Tell that bodyguard of yours to bring you to my house. And make sure you pack that lingerie. I'm fixing to buy him off.

> Okay. You sure you don't want me wearing it to meet you?

Dolcezza, you can do whatever you want. Just get to my house, because I'm leaving once we get back.

;)

If TC was keeping his family safe, I was going to have her at my place because she would be even more protected there than anywhere else. But if I knew TC like I know I do, he probably had a state-of-the-art security system at his parents' home.

Chapter Twelve

EMI

After Drake's text, I hurried and put on the lingerie. Pulling a dress over my head to cover the lingerie, I packed a suitcase with all my makeup and extra clothes. If I could, I was going to stay with Drake. As long as he was able to pay off Heath.

I grabbed my phone and charger and stuffed it in my purse, before I stepped over to my suitcase

I hated when he said that; it made me feel old. Even though I knew he was being respectful, it still got under my skin. Grabbing my suitcase, I walked the short distance from my bed to the door, opening it I exited the room. I made it down the hallway and the stairs before Heath got to the front door with the car.

Ever since the other night when Heath had Brian rush me to the basement, I never went out at night, much to Hannah and

Summer's dismay. And then Drake telling me not to leave my bodyguard made me even more scared to go out at night. I didn't understand what my brother had done to piss a gang off and why he didn't just go to the police.

Heath pulled up and jumped out of the car to grab my suitcase. He placed it in the trunk and then opened the back door for me to get in. Sliding into the leather seats, I texted Drake back.

> I need your address, sir. ;)

> I sent you a pin. We are almost done at the office and then I'll be leaving.

> Okay.

"This is where we need to go." I showed Heath the address and sat back.

"Drake's house?" Heath looked at me in the rearview mirror with his eyebrow quirked up.

I didn't presume that he would know where Drake lived, and that made me nervous. Maybe I should've had the butler take me to his house. But then again, Drake still needed to talk to Heath.

"Yes, did I stutter?" I didn't like that he was questioning me. I was hoping he didn't see the lines of my outfit underneath.

"No, ma'am." He put the car in drive and headed out of the driveway.

I could hear my heart in my ears now that we were on our way. It didn't sit well with me that Heath knew how to get to Drake's house without having to use the GPS. Had he been there before with TC? He was part of TC's security team. Did he know the addresses of my friends, too?

We pulled up to Drake's gate, and he pressed the call button, and the gate opened. Heath drove up the driveway and stopped at the front door. He got out and retrieved my suitcase before opening my door.

The door to the house opened, and a gentleman in black pants, white shirt and a black vest, walked down the steps. Heath waited with me as he stopped in front of us. I could tell that the man was older and that he was possibly part of Drake's staff.

"Good evening, Ms. Churchhill. So nice of you to visit. My name is Benton. Mr. DeLuca will be here shortly." He smiled at me and then turned his gaze to Heath. "Mr. DeLuca will meet you in the drawing room."

I smiled at Benton, and he took my suitcase while we followed him. I never would have thought that Drake would have a place like this. It was very modern and didn't look as if it was a bachelor's home.

The doors shut behind Heath, and the electronic locks clicked behind me. Drake had really spent some money on this place. Benton led us down one hallway and then stopped at a closed door. He opened it and motioned for Heath to head in.

Heath walked in, and Benton shut the doors before he gestured for me to follow him. He took me back up the hallway and up to the second story of the home. Benton brought me to a door, which he opened for me. "This is Mr. DeLuca's room. He told me to tell you to make yourself comfortable. I will have dinner sent up in a couple of hours."

The older man then bowed and made his way back down the stairs. I pulled my suitcase into the room and glanced around the space. It could easily hold three of my rooms in it. In my mind, I knew that Drake would have a big room because he hadn't been in a small hotel room in Las Vegas.

I placed my suitcase by the closet and continued to roam around the room. The bed was a king, sitting in the middle of the wall. The windows were on the left side of the bed, allowing a view of the mountain range. I walked over to them, staring out as the sun slid behind the range.

"You know, I always thought one day I would find you here staring out that window."

Drake's voice made me turn. He was leaning up against the doorway with his hands in his pockets and a smile on his face.

"Yeah? Have you been thinking of me that long?" I crossed my arms over my chest. Waiting for him to come to me.

"I'm not a predator if that's what you are asking. I didn't really start looking at you like this until a few months ago, and even then, I tried to keep my hands to myself. You are my best friend's sister." The way he stalked up to me had me shivering. I pulled my bottom lip between my teeth when he reached me.

Drake's hand came up to my face, and his thumb softly pulled my bottom lip, freeing it from my teeth. I didn't hesitate to run my hands up his torso while his other arm snaked around my back.

"I still need to go talk to Heath. When I get back, I don't want this dress on since you decided to wear the lingerie. Okay?" I nodded, Drake's words making me wetter the deeper his tone got. Drake's gaze flickered over to the bed before bringing his attention back to me. "I want you on that bed. Those gorgeous legs spread open, showing me that ravishing pussy."

I nodded again, and Drake crashed his lips to mine in a punishing kiss. He broke the kiss and turned away from me. Leaving me in his room to do what he had instructed. I pulled the dress over my head and laid it on the chair.

Crawling over the bed, I rearranged the pillows into the middle of the headboard and laid down, rubbing on my clit. My fingers were just not his; ever since he had brought me to climax, it was harder making myself come. I hurried off the bed and went to my suitcase and grabbed my clit vibrator.

I got back in bed and turned on my toy to the lowest setting.

Touching it to my clit, my legs spasmed with each vibration. The door opened, and Drake entered the room. His head cocked to the side, watching me. "You're such a good girl being on that bed for me, and God damn, do you look luscious in that lingerie."

Drake shed his tie and shirt before he reached the bed. He was undoing his belt at the foot of the bed, watching me play with my pussy. Drake came around to my side and sat down. "Do you trust me?"

"Yes," I whimpered as he kissed me.

Drake stood and then reached for something under the bed. He grabbed my left ankle and attached a soft cuff to it before going to the other side and attached another to the other ankle. His fingers lightly ran up my inner leg, causing goosebumps to race along my skin. Drake took my right hand and put another cuff on my wrist.

"I'll take over with this in a moment. I need this hand." I dropped the toy, and it buzzed on the bed between my legs as I extended my hand to him.

Drake tightened the restraints to where I couldn't move. My heart was racing while he released his cock from his pants. He kneeled between my spread legs and picked up the toy. "Don't take your eyes off me, *dolcezza*. I want to see that lust in your eyes."

He turned the toy up a couple of notches and put it in his mouth to wet it before he touched it lightly to my clit. The intensity of the vibration made me try to arch, but the restraints kept me from moving. The grin that crossed Drake's face caused heat to my face.

"What's wrong? Can you not take it?" He chuckled as I pulled on the restraints.

"Drake, please, I feel like I'm going to pee again."

Drake pulled the vibrator from my clit and leaned over me. His breath blew over my face as his tongue traced my jawline. "Oh, *dolcezza* that's called squirting. And if you squirt on me like you did in that changing room, you will make me one happy man."

He kissed my forehead and replaced the vibrator on my clit, sinking two fingers inside me. The way he pushed and pulled them out of me had me on the edge. As much as I tried to hold back, he was coaxing me to come.

"Drake, I'm so close!"

"Not yet dolcezza. I want you to squirt on me." He pulled out of me and laid down on his stomach. Drake replaced the vibrator, but it was even more intense while his mouth and the flat of his tongue lapped at my entrance.

Fuck, if he continued this, I just might. My lower muscles tightened and relaxed at the vibration and his tongue. Fuck me. There was never going to be another man who could make me feel like this. I tried my best to keep from letting what he called 'squirt' go, but I couldn't any longer.

I groaned as it exploded from me and onto his face. The gush and his moans caused my body to heat again. With as many men as I had been with, none of them had even thought about doing something like this. I had one who didn't even want his cock sucked.

Drake lifted his head, and his tongue whipped out and ran over his lips. He groaned as he pulled it back in his mouth. "Fuck, you taste good."

He sat back on his feet, his cock standing at attention. Its silver barbells caught the little bit of light that came through the wall of windows. I bucked my hips, wanting him inside of me. I needed him to fill me with not only his cum but to stretch me with that thick cock.

"Drake," I whimpered when his lips latched onto one of my exposed nipples.

His other hand went to the other nipple, twisting and pinching at it, making it harder. My hips continued to buck against him. Searching for the head of his cock so I could try to slip it in.

"Is my dolcezza wanting Daddy's thick cock?" His eyebrow raised while he stared at me with my nipple near his mouth.

"Yes," I whimpered with another buck of my hips when I felt his cock at my entrance.

"I'm not sure you want this as badly as you think you do." He chuckled, dipping in the head a little before taking it back out.

"Drake, please! Fuck me with that huge fucking cock," I moaned out, and his hand that had been teasing my nipple wrapped around my throat. Squeezing gently as he went back to teasing my nipple with the tip of his tongue and the head of his cock teasing my entrance.

God, I needed him inside me, filling me to the brim with his cum. It was a good thing that I was on birth control. Otherwise, I'd have been pregnant long before now. Drake slowly slipped his cock further inside of me as I struggled to get him to go faster.

Chapter Thirteen

DRAKE

Emi was a moaning, wet mess as I teased her pussy and her nipple. I tightened my grip on her throat, looking for her consent to continue. From what she had told me, she had never had sex like I'd slowly been showing her. .

"Is this okay? I need you to talk to me." I loosened my grip to allow her to speak.

"Yes. I want to know what it's like."

"Then we need that safe word. Do you remember it?" I pulled out of her, and she groaned with the loss.

"Pineapples." She smiled at me, her eyes begging me to fuck her, and I tightened my grip again.

"Remember that, okay?" I kissed her face and then swiftly entered her again.

Her mouth fell open, and her brows knitted together as I held my position inside her. I slowly pulled out, but her eyes never left mine as I pushed back inside of her. The whimper that escaped her was forced as I hit her G-spot.

Emi arched her back, trying to use what little of her body she could since I had her restrained. She pulled on the cuffs with each moan. Her cunt gripped me like it didn't want me to leave.

"Fuck, *dolcezza*, you feel so good wrapped around my cock. Are you going to come for me?" I grunted as I rocked inside of her, releasing her throat to cage her body.

"Yes, please!"

I crashed my lips to hers and pushed deeper inside her. I wrapped my arms up under her arms and pulled her closer to me. Pressing her face into my shoulder, she bit down, and I groaned. Fuck, the pain from her bite and then the pleasure of her pussy wrapped around me, were competing with the receptors in my brain.

"Drake, I'm almost there. Right there, please, right there!" Emi's body became tense as her pussy clamped around me, milking me as I held her tighter, spilling my release inside her.

"*Dolcezza*," I whispered in her ear as everything wound down.

I sat up and undid her restraints. Emi's eyes fluttered open, and a smile spread on her face. "That was so good."

"If you think that was good, wait until I show you what else we can do." I grinned back at her before sliding off the bed and taking her with me. The swing had been up since she got here, and I didn't think she had seen it while she was getting ready for me. "I need you to stand for a moment."

I positioned her in front of the swing before picking her up and sitting her in the contraption. She glanced at the straps and then locked her gaze with mine. Grinning at her, I pulled her legs through the stirrups to the underside of her knees before resting her lower back on the bottom half and then pushing the other two to her upper back, on her shoulder blades, and finally the other one under her neck, allowing her to lie back.

Adjusting the stirrups to let her legs hang without using her muscles, her hands rested on the straps above her head. I ran my fingers along the inner part of her legs and down to her dripping cunt that was already ready for me. "Fuck, *dolcezza*you look gorgeous strung up for me."

Emi glanced up at me as I moved to her head. Her tongue snaked out and ran over her bottom lip. The lust in her eyes as I returned to between her legs had me hard and ready for the next round.

"Drake, stop teasing me," Emi moaned as I rubbed one of my fingers along her entrance and to her clit.

"Oh, *dolcezza*, I'm not. I'm just making sure you are ready for me again. I don't want to hurt you." I knelt on the small footstool and grabbed Emi's hips, bringing her pussy to my mouth. My tongue darted out and flicked her clit, making her arch in the swing.

I sucked her pussy lips into my mouth while I used my tongue inside her cunt. Standing, I spat in my hand and covered my cock in it before positioning the head at her entrance. I pushed in slowly, watching as I disappeared inside her. I stood still as I let the swing do all the work. Emi's tits bounced with each swing.

The echo of our bodies slapping against each other and the squelch of her soaked pussy, as I thrust into her, sounded in my ears. Fuck she felt so good. I would fuck her every minute of every day if I could.

"Drake, you're going to make me come again!"

"Then come for me, come all over me." I pulled her close and continued to thrust in and out of her and wrapped my arms around her thighs. My middle finger rubbing on her clit made her legs spasm as I pressed inside her over and over again.

"Drake, you're going to make me squirt!"

I doubled my efforts in bringing her closer to my favorite thing that she could do. When her body became taut she moaned and then let it go. The sound as she let go and drenched my lower body, had me losing my load inside of her.

Pulling her from the swing, I laid her limp body on the bed

and went into the bathroom. I grabbed a clean washcloth and wet it before returning to clean Emi off. Emi hissed at the warmth of the cloth as it touched her sensitive sex. Finishing cleaning her up, I tossed the cloth in the hamper. I got into bed and pulled her in against me while bringing up the satin sheet.

Emi was asleep before I even had time to look at her. Her body was spent. Having two orgasms back-to-back. The longer she stayed with me, the more her body would get used to those multiple orgasms.

As much as I wanted her to sleep. We had to have the conversation about her limits. I had been taking it slowly in being rough with her. But if she was wanting to be my sub then she was going to have to tell me what I couldn't and could do to her and her body.

I had never had a permanent sub before. Even though I had been with countless women each one had her limits on what I could do to her. With Emi I was going to make her permanent and so we would learn together what her limits were going to be.

"Emi. Wake up. We need to talk before anything else happens. We've waited too long and I'm afraid that things might get out of hand."

Emi groaned and tossed over to her side facing me. I pulled her close and kissed the top of her head. "Come on Emi. When we are done talking you can go back to sleep. Because I have to go to the office."

"Uh... Fine."

I chuckled and slid out of bed.

Emi stretched with a yawn as she swung her leg out from the bed. I led her over to the small table and chairs in my room and sat her down. Pulling up the other chair beside her I grabbed the paper that I had printed before she got here.

"Look over these things and tell me what is a no and what is a yes."

"And what if some are a maybe?"

"That's fine too."

I watched as she slowly read through the list of things on the paper. Sometimes I noticed her reading back through some and squeezing her legs. She was intrigued and I was going to make sure that whatever she wanted to do or try was done.

Once she was finished reading the limits she went down to the terms. Some of them she had already learned that she wasn't supposed to do but there were others. I even added her calling me sir to it because she said it so seductively in my office.

Emi looked up at me, her eyes wide with her mouth open. I cocked an eyebrow and she returned her eyes back on the paper.

"Would you really use a toy on me at a restaurant?"

"Yes, dolcezza. Because watching you trying to hold back would bring me so much joy."

"Okay, I want to do this. Where's a pen?"

"Are you sure?"

"Yes." I handed her the pen that was laying on the table and she marked each one of her hard and soft limits. This was another reason she was going to live with me.

I sat at the board table with TC at the head of the large surface. He had been out of it this morning as the board members each said their piece. Granted, he didn't look tired, but he was definitely not in the mindset for this meeting. Luckily, Lindsey was taking notes like she always was in our meetings.

"Mr. Churchhill?"

TC looked up from the graph that Mr. Dunn had given him at the beginning of the meeting. His expression made me grin and cock an eyebrow at TC before bringing him up to speed, "Mr. Dunn was just saying that you made a good call on the expansion to ship internationally. Profits have been higher in the past three years than the past decade."

"Good, and the projections?" TC sat back, more confident than a few seconds ago. As much shit as I gave him, I would never let him look bad in front of the board members. He surveyed the men, waiting for one of them to answer him.

"Sir, we expect them to keep rising," Lindsey said from her position behind TC. She had been reading ahead of the meeting and wasn't afraid her boss.

TC nodded in acknowledgment and stood, straightening his jacket, "Perfect, this meeting is adjourned."

Everyone dipped their heads and stood before they left. Lindsey went with them. I, however, stayed behind, waiting for TC to tell me what he had been thinking about. I was hoping that he finally got laid so that he would stop being an ass to everyone.

"What has you all smiles today?" he asked me while heading over to the windows and looking out over LA. I followed behind him, knowing he was going over there to think, as he always did.

"Seems like you need to get laid. You were spaced out badly during the meeting. And that's not you. Let's go to the club. Find some girls." I clapped TC's shoulder with a chuckle.

"No, I need to make arrangements for the Gala." I didn't miss the quick flick of his eyes in the window.

"I thought you already had your tux?"

TC turned to me, as if about to tell me something, but his face hardened, and when this happened, there was no getting anything out of him.

"I don't think you need to know everything about my life," he hurled back at me with a glare.

I raised my hands in surrender and continued to smirk as I walked out of the boardroom. He was getting some pussy otherwise; he wouldn't be acting like he was now. But he normally told me about them, and the only person I could think of was his wife.

As I walked down the hall, my phone went off in my pants. Fishing the device out of my pocket, I took a deep breath before answering my father's call. "Ciao, Papa."

"Ciao, figlio. Your uncle wants to have another meeting. He will be in tonight. He said that he has someone who has integrated into Jack's mafia. We need to start finding ways to take him out before he gets wind of your uncle being stateside." I waved at Tiffany as I passed her desk and entered my office.

"What do you mean? And why is Uncle Riccardo having an issue with this man? Where are we meeting?" Sitting in my chair, I turned it to face the window. TC wasn't the only one with a view of the city that held millions of secrets.

"Once you meet up with your uncle tonight, you will know why. He wants to meet at my house. I will see you there." He hung up the phone as I heard my mother's voice on the other end.

I didn't think that she knew about this side of the family. She had met my uncle many years ago. But I'm sure that with the way things were going now, she didn't know that he had been in town.

Part of me didn't want to take over the family business. I didn't want to move to Italy and leave the life I had built with my best friend, and soon my life with his sister. Talking to Heath that night in my house had been complicated. He didn't want to keep things from TC, but I had offered to pay him double his salary if he kept quiet about Emi staying with me.

She was safer there at my house than anywhere else. Not only because of the security system, but because I had guards around the place. The thought of a gang taking Emi boiled my blood. So, she was going to stay with me. Emi would still have Heath watching over her when she went out.

Picking up the paperwork that I had wanted to talk to TC about, I put it in my desk drawer and locked it again. I needed to talk to him about the warehouse. If he wasn't going to sell it, I was going to have to tell him about what was going on and what his grandfather and my family had come to an agreement about. But right now wasn't the time.

I pulled into the drive at my childhood home and parked in front of the steps. The need to get this over with quickly so I could get back to Emi was the only thing on my mind. Walking up the steps, the butler let me in the doors, and I headed down the hall to my father's drawing room.

My father's and my uncle's voices carried into the hall before I pushed open the doors. Their quick movements told me that they had both been trained to be aware of their surroundings. Something that my father continued to do even though he was no longer in the game.

"Father, Uncle. What is so urgent this time?" I strolled in and sat on the couch.

Fuck it, they could come to me this time. If he wanted to make me the head of the family, I was going to act like it until he told me otherwise.

"Drake, it's nice to see you. I like the way you dealt with the Harvey problem. You have it in you to lead. But we need to talk about how we are going to get rid of Jack. Aldo told me about the statement from the prisoner before you shot him."

"Yeah, apparently, I have a bounty on my head. Dead or Alive. But I have yet to have anyone come after me. Besides, I'd have them lying in a pool of their own blood before they got close to me." I chuckled as they both sat on the opposite couch.

"That's the thing, son. They have people on you. The informant says that he is one of them and has been trying to keep them off you, but they are getting wary of him. We need to act quickly to keep you safe." My father leaned forward before looking at his brother.

"Look, I've been doing my own research." This man has at least ten men around him at all times. The motherfucker looks like he will be dead within the month. If he doesn't have an heir, why worry about him? I think you have outdated information because according to the guy you had Aldo and me get information from, he does." I glanced between them and didn't miss the stiffening from my uncle.

"Technically, he doesn't have one. But we have been looking into this and think that he actually does. However, I don't think he knows yet. We don't need him to find this son because if he does, then his family name will continue." My uncle pulled out a piece of paper from his suit jacket and handed it to me over the table. "That there is, unfortunately, a poor quality photo of who we think the heir is. If he's anything like his father, things in LA could get bad again. Jack cannot find this boy."

When he said this photo was bad, he wasn't lying. This was the most awful thing I had ever seen. The boy in the picture was covered in what I could only assume was blood. The picture looked old in itself. If this boy was still alive, and that was a big if, he would have to be in his twenties now.

"Even with how terrible this photo is. This thing looks old. *IF* this boy is still alive, you know he has to be older now," I told them and dropped the photo on the table.

"We know that the woman that was his mother is dead. She died when he was a young child. He's been on his own ever since. The only way he was in this picture was that he's in a gang."

"How do you know this? And where did you get this photo?" I shook my head and glared at my uncle.

"This was found when we found Harvey. We wanted to know if this picture was of Jack's heir. They must have been on his trail for a while, keeping an eye on him."

"So, what do you want me to do? If they found him and killed the only one who knew of him being the heir, how do you think we are going to find him? This city is massive, and what's not to say that this boy might be dead already."

"We need to keep an eye out for him. If we find him, he needs to be killed with his father." My uncle's stern gaze made me realize that this was a territory grab. He wasn't going to share.

Chapter Fourteen

EMI

I woke up in total bliss. Even though he had woken me up at the crack of dawn. The things that man did to me had ruined me for any other man. I could never go back to vanilla sex again.

He had awoken a deep need buried inside of me. Something I had been needing for a very long time. Drake's scent enveloped me, making me wet. My eyes landed on the swing and the ties that hung from the ceiling and the bed.

Being suspended was a whole new sensation. Drake had me all tied up and at his mercy, but I'd do it again if he would let me. Sitting up, my body screamed at me, and I smiled. I had never used those muscles before in my life, and I wanted more.

I reached over and grabbed my phone. Drake had left early this morning to go to the office. After pushing back the covers, I opened my camera app and took a picture for him. I wanted him to be desperate for me when he came home, even though he usually was for me.

Woman. Why would you send me this?
I'm going to slide you over my cock
and make you scream my name.

I'm already wet for you. When will you
be home?

As soon as I finish with my father. I'll
be there to make you come all over my
cock.

I can't wait.

Oh, dolcezza, you are going to eat
those words.

I smirked and got up from the bed, walking up to the swing. I ran my fingers over the straps and cuffs. They weren't like I imagined. I didn't think it would hold me, but it did. I couldn't wait to use this again.

Sighing I turned on my heal and padded over to the bathroom to relieve myself, I made sure to look around at the ensuite room. Drake had good tastes in color palettes, which was suprising for a bachelor. The entire house was immaculate and up to date.

The shower was tiled in a soft white with dual waterfall shower heads. It didn't have a shower door; instead, it had a glass wall. I never would have thought he would have this in his bathroom.

I went over to the sink to wash my hands and walked back into the bedroom. While pulling one of Drake's T-shirts over my head, I went out of the bedroom. Drake's cardio routine kept me going the entire night, so now my stomach was telling me it needed some food.

The house was quiet other than my steps on the hardwood

floor. The kitchen was just as stylish as the rest of the house. I opened the fridge and looked through it, pulling out Tupperwares of leftovers.

Drake's staff kept the place tidy and the kitchen stocked with food was a miracle, since there were so many security personnel around the place. Venting the lid, I placed the Shrimp Scampi in the microwave.

I glanced out of the windows before I grabbed a glass bottle of Coke and opened it from a mounted bottle opener. The sound of a sliding door grabbed my attention before the beeping of the microwave.

"Oh! Ms. Churchhill. If you would have told me you were hungry, I could have made you lunch." Her accent was thick with a Spanish twang.

"It's okay. I just need something small right now. What is your name?" I smiled at her and pulled out my food. The steam wafted up and around my hand scorched the pad of my thumb. "Fuck, that's hot."

"Are you okay?" She rushed over to me as I sat the Tupperware on the counter. "It's Elsa. My name."

"I'm fine. The steam just got me. I'll be okay." I smiled back at her as she continued to look at the scald on my hand.

"Come, run this under the cool water." She pulled me over to the sink and placed my hand under the cool running water. "There, it should be okay. If it continues to burn, run it back under the water."

"Okay." I smiled at her and nodded before drying my hands.

I went back over to the bowl and sat down with it at the small table overlooking the lawn. Drake really outdid himself with this house. It was comfortable and easy to want to stay.

I finished the food and placed the container and fork in the sink. Elsa was humming in the pantry as she pulled out the ingredients for the evening meal. I couldn't help but grin as I headed back up to Drake's room. All the things that we could do in this room were exciting, and Drake had only pulled out a few things from his other walk-in closet.

Drake had allowed me to go in to look and touch the equipment. Don't get me wrong, I had seen some of these things, but I had *never* used anything like this. I remembered when I brought in a toy during sex, and the guy I had been with was disgusted with me. Safe to say, I never saw him again.

I strolled into the closet to see what else I could take out and play with while Drake watched. At least, that was what I wanted to convince him to do. Him watching me play with myself was something I wanted to do, to feel like I was in control. I spotted different plugs, and my heart raced as I grabbed one that I thought would be a good size before I brought it over to the dresser.

Glancing around the room, I tried to figure out the best place for Drake to sit while I made him watch. If I *could* make him. Because I don't think that he would be fond of being tied up. I giggled at the thought of him bound in ropes and not being able to touch me.

"*Dolcezza*, is there something that you want to tell me?"

My eyes widened, and I turned to face him in the doorway. In my daydream state, I didn't hear him come up behind me. Drake's eyebrow cocked up, and that handsome smile made my heart race as I tried to think of something to say. He was leaning against the door frame, his tie pulled down and the top three shirt buttons undone, showing off some of his chest hair.

"Well, I was thinking that maybe we could try some more toys. What do you think?" I asked him, putting my arms around my back.

Drake pushed off from the doorway and stalked up to me. Just the way he stared at me had me clenching my thighs to stave off the need to jump into his arms.

"And what is it that you would like to try out?" Drake's eyes went behind me, and a smile graced his lips.

"Um. Whatever you think I would enjoy. I've never had a guy want to use toys in bed before."

"Really? They must be very emasculated by a fake cock then." Fuck, his voice when he let it get that low.

"Yeah, they must have been." I didn't want to sound so needy, but that was exactly how it came out.

"Since there is a plug on the dresser, do you want to try it out?" My heart raced from his question. I'd played with toys before by myself, but the men before Drake had never wanted to use them. And I hadn't even thought about a plug before. "If it's too much, all you have to do is use your safe word."

I nodded, and Drake's hands went to the hem of the shirt, pulling it up and away from my body. Goosebumps chased his hands as they rubbed down my sides and into my panties, slipping them down my legs. The growl that came from him had my eyes locked on his as he lifted me into his arms. I didn't miss the subtle scent of cigars on him.

Drake carried me to the bed and set me on the unmade covers. I didn't miss the bulge in his slacks as he went over to the dresser, grabbed the plug, and then went back into the closet with all the toys. He came back out with a bottle and a different plug; the only reason I knew it was different was the color and size. Drake placed the plug and the bottle beside me as I lay there, squirming for him to touch me.

"You forgot one thing, *dolcezza*. Well, two. As much as I would love to use that plug on you, you are not ready for that one, and you will need lube." Fuck, I didn't think the one I had chosen was that big, but what did I know?

"Oh." I pulled my bottom lip between my teeth and watched as he kneeled between my legs. The smirk on his lips made me cock an eyebrow before he wrapped his arms around me and flipped me to my stomach.

"Ass up and pull those gorgeous cheeks apart, *dolcezza*."

I did as he said. The cool substance ran over a hole I had never used before. My heart continued to speed up along with my breathing. I didn't know if I was ready for this.

"Calm yourself."

"I don't know if I can do this."

"*Dolcezza*, all you have to do is say your safeword and all of this ends."

My mind was racing. Did I want to stop? No. Did I want to try something new with a man who rocked my world and I trusted with my life? Hell fucking yes. I shook my head and calmed myself just as I felt the tip of the plug.

I tensed until I felt his finger on my clit. Drake leaned over my back, and his breath hit the lobe of my ear. "That's my good girl, *dolcezza*."

He traced his lips into the crook where my shoulder met my neck. Drake bit into that spot as he pushed the plug into me. A slight pressure in the beginning had me almost second guessing my decision but his finger on my clit held my attention on the pleasure it was bringing me. "Fuck! Drake."

"Do you feel good right now?"

"Yes, but I want you inside me," I moaned as his fingers continued to play with my clit and his teeth raked across my shoulder.

"Stay right there. Don't move." I turned my head and watched him get off the bed and back into the closet. When he reappeared, I didn't see anything other than his fist clenched and a smirk on his lips. "I'm going to rock your world, *dolcezza*, even more than in that swing."

I heard the click, and then a soft buzzing sound reached my ears. My core tensed with the thought of it touching my body. I didn't know what it was, but my body hummed in anticipation. When the soft silicone touched my clit, it took everything in me to stay in position.

"Does that feel good?"

I nodded into the bed, my hands fisting the sheets. My body spasmed as I got closer to my orgasm, but when Drake entered me, it was all downhill from there. The way I was stretched in both holes and the bullet on my clit, there was no way I was going to not keep my orgasm away.

"Drake! I'm going to come!" He chuckled as he continued to thrust in and out, urgently commanding that my body gave him what he wanted.

Drake's other hand went into my hair and pulled me up into his toned body. His lips pressed against my ear. "Then come, *dolcezza*. Let the whole world know that I make you like this."

His hand in my hair unraveled from the strands and wrapped around my throat. His thrusts became slow and hard as he pummeled my pussy. With the plug in my ass, his hand around my throat, and the vibrator on my clit, my climax crashed around him. Drake came with me. His deep, throaty growl sent shivers down my spine.

Sweat dropped onto my shoulder as he dipped his head to run his tongue up my neck and along my ear. "Fuck, I don't know what I'd do if I ever lost you."

I giggled at his comment. I leaned against him as the last of my climax faded. Our breathing was in sync as Drake pulled out of me and turned off the bullet. I stayed on my knees and watched him walk into the bathroom. He was the only man to actually help me clean up after sex.

When he had done it the first time, I was a little embarrassed, but now it was the norm for us. Drake came out of the bathroom and motioned for me to turn. I grinned at him and turned, laying back on the bed at the edge.

"You're such a good girl." The warm cloth touched my pussy, and I groaned as he used his other hand to take the plug out. "Now tell me, did you really enjoy being filled?"

"Yes, I've never come so fast."

"Well, this is the only way you will experience it. I don't share." His hard gaze had my body burning with desire.

"I don't want to be."

Drake nodded and headed back into the bathroom with both toys.

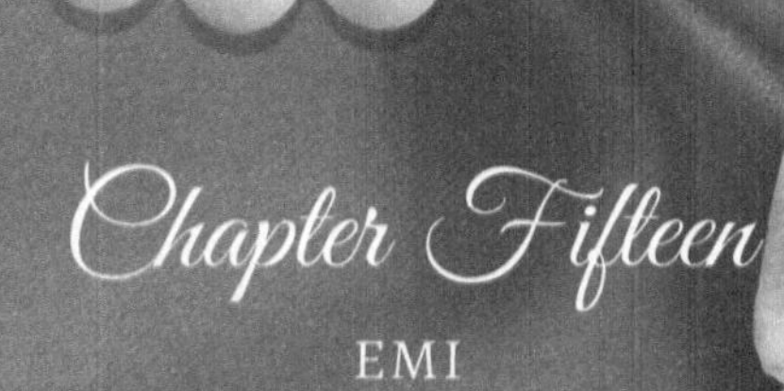

Chapter Fifteen

EMI

Drake left a few hours before me. He had to be with my brother at the start of the gala. I was staring at myself in the floor length mirror, admiring the glittering gold dress that hugged all my curves. The nude heels went perfectly with the dress and showed off my French-painted toes. My smoky eyelids drew even myself into my hazel eyes. I didn't put too much makeup on because I had noticed that Drake didn't like it much.

I was wearing the necklace that Drake insisted on buying me. The thought of trying to keep TC from noticing it or even my mother made me nervous. Drake had yet to tell TC that we... well, I didn't really know what we were. If we were just friends with benefits, then I was fine with that, but I needed to know.

Walking away from the mirror. I made my way out of Drake's room, I turned to the right in the hallway coming to the top of the stairs. I paused before going down the steps. I found Heath waiting for me at the bottom of the stairs. He didn't like keeping things from my brother, but he wasn't going to turn down the money Drake was offering him.

"Let's go. I don't want to be any later," I told him as I strolled past.

"Mrs. Churchhill wants to meet up with us at the front of the gala."

I rolled my eyes and stopped at the door. Turning on my heel, I placed my hands on my hips, "Okay, so why are you still standing there?"

Heath stalked out of the house to the SUV. I shook my head and followed him. He made it known with his subtle actions that he didn't like the fact that I subjected myself to Drake. He didn't like that I was with Drake. But that wasn't up to him.

He opened the back door and let me in. Heath snapped the door shut and hopped into the driver's seat. I stared out the window as we made our way to the gala. The palms became less prominent and gave way to buildings before Heath cleared his throat. I glanced to the front to see him watching me in the rearview mirror.

"Emi, you know that Drake is a playboy and one of the most eligible bachelors in LA. Right now, you are just an easy lay for him. Please, put an end to this before you get hurt."

"Thank you for your concern, but what if I'm okay with that?" I sent a glare in his direction.

"There's no way you could be okay with this. I've seen what he has done before you."

"I don't see you talking about my brother the way you talk about the man who has doubled your salary," I shot back at him.

"He makes your brother look like a saint," Heath threw over his shoulder before bringing his eyes back to the road. "And what about the times you don't hear from him? Or he doesn't come home?"

I didn't care what Drake did before me because I knew that he was only with me. But then there were times when he wouldn't call me back or answer my phone calls. He would only text me.

Was he with another woman? Someone more experienced than me?

Taking a deep breath, I tried to calm myself and take my thoughts out of my head. I mean, what could he possibly be doing? He had a day job that he had to get to, but what about other times?

The Land Rover stopped at the steps and a valet opened my door. My mother stood at the top of the steps with her bodyguard just a few feet away from her. She was gorgeous in her off-white gown with lace running down the skirt.

Walking up the steps, I knew Heath would be behind me as I went to my mother. The face-splitting smile on her face caused me to smile back at her. It had been a few weeks since I had moved out of my parents' house and into Drake's. My parents didn't even know where I had moved, since I had taken very little with me, and I wanted to keep that from them.

"Emerald, you look amazing! Is your date going to be here?" My mother pulled me into a hug, and I melted into her arms.

"Thank you, Mom, I don't have a date." If she looked close enough, she would notice that Drake and I matched.

"That's too bad. I was really hoping to see you with the man you moved in with." My mother wrapped her arm through mine, and we went into the building.

My eyes adjusted to the lights from the ballroom before they locked onto Drake with TC and some other men. The lights glinted off the gold cufflinks, and I saw a man grab his tie and laugh. They were making fun of him.

The lights above the tables hung down, making it seem as if buildings rose from the circular furniture. Spotlights of blue, purple, yellow, and red gave the room a darker feel, but it was illuminated enough to see each person. The tables had already been placed with silverware, wine glasses, plates, and napkins.

Drake's eyes glanced at the stairs as my mother and I

descended them. His tongue came out and wet his lips before he grinned at me and winked. Even if I didn't know what this was, he made sure to show me affection.

"I swear that man could seduce any woman in this room if he wanted to." my mother chuckled while she steered me over to a group of younger people. I was hoping that she would bring us over to Drake's group. Though it didn't stop me from glancing over my shoulder at his group.

They were talking about God only knew what. My brother had a whiskey in his hand looked up at the door each time it opened. Like he was searching for someone. Drake laughed, but his eyes were always on me. My father, Drake's, and Aurora's continued to stand in the middle of the room with him and TC as others came up to them to introduce someone or talk to them.

"Hey, Emi. You are looking gorgeous tonight." I glanced over to my left and noticed a guy from college beside me.

Sandy-brown hair and a white smile. Ethan was the quarterback at my college, and he made sure to let everyone know. I'd had a fling with him back then, and that was when I realized that I wasn't really into him.

"Hi, Ethan. How did you get into this party?" He wasn't that rich since he didn't get his dream of becoming an NFL player.

"I was invited by a board member from your father's company." Ethan gave me what he thought was an alluring smile, but it just gave me the creeps.

"Oh, you mean my brother's company? Well, isn't that nice. I hope you enjoy the party." I tried to walk away when my mother threaded her arm back into mine. Glancing over to her, I furrowed my brows and then shook my head.

"I'm sure Ethan here would like a dance. What do you say, Emi?" I couldn't believe she was trying to match me to this asshole.

They were not going to arrange my marriage. Not like they

had done with TC. I mean, they didn't choose wrong by choosing Aurora, but I wasn't going to go along with this. There was nothing I wanted to keep bad enough to allow them to make me.

"Maybe some other time, Mother. I have to go to the bathroom." I broke away from her arm and headed to the bathroom. My feet couldn't get me away from him quick enough as I wove through the crowd of richly dressed people.

Entering the restroom, I glanced at my reflection in the mirror. The gold of my dress brought out the color of my hair, but the fire in my eyes had me breathing rapidly. I just needed to be able to chill out so that I could go back out to the party.

"Hey girl, are you okay?" Summer's voice brought my eyes to the mirror.

"Yeah, just trying to get away from that jock my mother seems to be trying to set me up with."

"Do you really think that she would do that?" Summer came up closer and leaned against the counter.

"I wouldn't put it past her since she and my father arranged TC and Aurora."

"Well, before I came in here to find you. I saw your brother kiss Aurora in front of everyone. That means everyone in that big room knows she's his," Summer chuckled as she turned to gaze at me in the mirror this time. "So, let's go and flirt and dance with some hot guys."

I shook my head and followed her out of the bathroom and back into the throng of people. Part of me knew they would start to develop an attraction to each other. I mean, hell, that fucking kiss at the wedding was breathtaking. My gaze shifted to Drake and the group he had been with since I arrived. Now Aurora was there along with some other woman who was hanging all over Drake.

My stomach dropped. He wasn't really mine. I had been fooling myself into believing that I was okay with how things were. I turned away from them and continued to follow Summer to Hannah. She was talking to another group that was more our age.

One of the other guys in our group switched positions with Summer and stood beside me with his hand on my lower back. I stiffened, thinking that I shouldn't allow him to do this. But Drake had a woman all over him, so what the hell! Another man joined our group, standing on my other side.

I turned and locked eyes with Drake, and he shook his head. My lips pulled into a tight smile before turning back to the people I was with. I tried to make myself flirt with the people in front of me.

The guy on the left leaned in and ran his nose up my neck and along my jaw. I playfully pushed him away and continued my conversation with Summer. He whispered in my ear, "Gorgeous, I want you around my cock."

"I don't think that will happen." I giggled, not missing the subtle hint of alcohol on his breath. I knew that some of the younger attendees would drink before since they were given bands to wear.I pushed him away again to give myself some room when I felt fingers brush against my ass.

I spotted Drake over my shoulder, and he flicked his eyes to the elevator and then disappeared. I excused myself and started for the elevator With Heath behind me.

I didn't know why I had done what he wanted. The doors opened, and Heath and I stepped inside when Drake squeezed himself between the doors. His arm wrapped around my waist, and I glanced up before wiggling myself out of his hold. His gaze was on Heath before he said, "If you don't want to hear things you'd rather not hear. I suggest you get out."

Heath left the elevator, and Drake pressed the button.

Chapter Sixteen

DRAKE

Standing in the circle with TC, our fathers, and Mr. Emerson, I tried to keep tabs on where Emi was at all times. TC wasn't doing very well in trying to hide what he was doing, and I internally laughed at him.

"Looking for someone?" I nudged him in the arm, almost spilling his drink.

"No."

"Looks like Lyla is here. She has been staring at you this entire time." TC had warned me about this one.

She wanted more and he didn't. The blonde was still pining over him. The doors opened, and TC's attention went to them as his wife entered. If he wasn't fucking that goddess, she needed to divorce him. Every man and woman in the room stared at her as she stood at the top of the stairs, surveying the crowd.

The skin-tight black dress flowed with her body and the neckline was cut at least three inches below her tits. Two slits ran up to her hip bones, letting every person in the room know she wasn't wearing anything underneath. Aurora was halfway down the stairs when two men went up to her. Each one took her hands and kissed the back of them.

TC's body went rigid, and I could tell that he was trying not to make a scene. When she smirked at him and then kissed the two men on the cheek as she continued to flirt with them. She was a spitfire, a woman who TC needed to put him in his place. TC finished his drink and thrust it into my hand and stormed through the crowd.

I couldn't help but laugh out loud, bringing our fathers' gazes to me. She had him hook, line, and sinker. I glanced over to my vixen in her gold dress and itched to go to her. Emi had ridden with Heath so we could keep TC none the wiser about where she was living at the moment.

But the fact that there were so many men flirting with her had me acting like TC internally. If I did anything about it in front of TC and her father, they would know something was going on with us. And I couldn't let them know just yet.

Lyla slipped into our group when I wasn't looking and threaded her arm into mine. I glared down at her, and she smiled up at me. When I glanced back up at Emi, we locked eyes and I shook my head. Emi smiled loosely and continued to talk with her group. Heath was a few feet away from her, like always.

Mr. Emerson left the group and headed to TC and Aurora. I didn't like that Lyla was all over me. Anything that I said made her laugh, and I was about to leave her there when TC and Aurora joined the group.

"Oh! TC, I didn't see you! How have you been?" Lyla's voice brought TC's gaze to her, and I didn't miss the conniving grin on his lips. I rolled my eyes and nodded at her.

"Lyla. Have you met my wife, Aurora?" TC brought her hand up to his lips, and Lyla stiffened.

"No, I didn't know that you had gotten married." Her voice dropped an octave as she pulled her arm from mine.

"I'm surprised you didn't. It was announced to the world," TC quipped and then turned to Aurora. "Would you like to dance?"

"Sure, it was nice to meet you, Lyla." Aurora gave Lyla a small smile before they walked away from the group.

Before Lyla could turn back to me, I slipped into the crowd to head over to Emi. I placed the empty glass of whiskey on a waiter's tray and used him to get closer to my target. Walking behind her, I ran the tips of my fingers over her ass and flicked my eyes over to the elevators.

I had waited long enough to get her in the hotel room I had reserved. Emi nodded and excused herself from her group while making her way up to the elevators. I moved my gaze to the dance floor and noticed that TC was still dancing with Aurora, giving me plenty of time to get to the elevator with Emi. Just before the doors closed, I pressed inside, wrapped my arm around Emi's waist, and turned to Heath.

"If you don't want to hear things you'd rather not hear, I suggest you get out." Heath rolled his eyes and stepped out of the elevator.

The doors closed, and I turned back to Emi. She had her bottom lip between her teeth and was leaning against the back wall. I pressed the button to our floor before caging her.

"Drake..." I hadn't even touched her yet and her eyes were hooded.

"I love it when you moan my name, *dolcezza*." I ran my nose up her neck, and she whimpered in my ear.

"Drake, I need to know what this is. Are we just friends with benefits? Or something more? What is this?" Emi looked up at me. I could see the hurt in her eyes. Even though I tried to let her know that I wasn't into Lyla.

"I thought we were together? I haven't told TC yet, which is why I didn't come to you as soon as you walked in. I need to tell him, but I don't know what he will do." I pressed my forehead against hers and pushed her against the wall.

"You were letting that woman drape herself all over you. So I didn't know. I…" Emi shook her head and placed her hands on my chest while she gazed up at me.

"Emi, I'm telling you now. I want you and only you. I was just letting the others think I was still available. That is, until you want me to tell your mom and dad that we're together." Emi grinned before fully smiling.

"You mean you want me? Not just as a booty call?"

"I want us to be official, but I have to talk to TC. I'm hoping he won't kill me for fucking his sister behind his back." I shouldn't be surprised that she thought that I only wanted her as a booty call.

The way I had been acting in public wouldn't exactly show her that I wanted to make this work. And that was on me, because she hadn't been around any man since the club in Las Vegas. I pulled her closer and pressed her into the elevator wall.

"You're all I've ever wanted," I whispered against her lips before I crashed mine into them. Her hands ran under my jacket and paused before she broke our kiss.

"What is this?" she questioned as she pulled open my suit jacket.

I had forgotten to take it out when I got here. But it looked like my mistake was going to force me to tell Emi about this before I wanted to. I sighed and ran my hands through my hair. "It's a gun. I have it for protection. There are things I need to tell you before you decide that you really want to be with me."

Emi's eyebrows furrowed, and she looked up at me while she cocked her head. I pushed back some hair that had fallen on her face. A couple entered the elevator, and I pulled Emi close to my side.

I didn't like that I had made her feel like she was a booty call.

Because she was anything but that. I glanced down, and she was staring at her feet. Slipping a finger under her chin, I lifted her head to look at me.

"Don't ever lower your gaze, you are not weak. I want you to hold your head up high. Do you hear me?" I stared into her hazel eyes until she nodded.

Grinning, I pressed a soft kiss to her lips, "I love you, Emi."

Emi pulled her bottom lip into her mouth, there was a blush on her cheeks as she smiled up at me. The elevator stopped, allowing the other couple to get off, and then continued to our floor. My heart was racing. I didn't know how much I could or should tell her. If she knew everything and was ever taken, they'd be able to push her in ways I didn't want to think about. .

The elevator opened, and I placed my hand on the lower part of her back as we walked down the hallway. Even though we had a lot to talk about, part of my mind kept imagining other things that I wanted to do to her. The movement of her lower back muscles slid under my fingertips, making them ache to dig into those cords in her back.

We stopped at the room door, and I pressed my fingerprint to the scanner, opening the lock. I allowed Emi to go inside first, following after her. When she looked over her shoulder and smirked, the whole talk went out the window.

"Emi, what are you doing?" I questioned while loosening my tie.

The only thing I could think about was tying her up in the bedroom and not letting her go until I was done with that beautiful body of hers. Her hands ran down her body, and she gripped the end of her dress before pulling it up to show more of her legs. The swell in my slacks told me we wouldn't be having this conversation until after I had taken her.

"I've been wanting you ever since I got here. I think you should give me that big Italian cock."

I couldn't take my eyes off her as she continued to walk backward, lifting her dress even further. My chest rose and fell in quick movements as I felt my heart racing, waiting for what she was going to do next. Because since we had that first night together, she had been showing me what she has been yearning for in a man.

"Oh, *dolcezza* you are going to have this and then some," I growled out as she hit the arm of the couch, landing on her back. Her black panties showed underneath.

"Is that so? You haven't shown me anything yet." She winked and inched backward on the couch.

Unbuckling my belt, I slid it out of the loops with a snap before dropping it to the floor, the buckle bouncing off the polished wood floor with a clink. Slowly, I began to unbutton my shirt and walk toward her.

Emi's fingers slipped into her panties and worked them down her shapely thighs. When she got them to her feet, she kicked them my way. I caught them and pressed them to my nose. Fuck, her smell when she was wet and horny drove me over the edge. Pulling them away from my face, I glanced down and saw her finger deep in her pussy.

Shrugging off my shirt, I dropped it on the ground next to my belt. I stuffed the lace into my mouth, tasting her on them, as I undid the button and zipper of my slacks. My cock stood at attention and I dropped to my knees and grabbed hold of Emi's ankles. I pulled her to my face, dropping the panties from my mouth, and grinned at her before I dove into her pussy.

Chapter Seventeen

EMI

When Drake knelt by the couch my heart fluttered. I loved it when he took control of things, and when he clamped down on my pussy it was hard enough to hold back fisting his hair, much less the moan that escaped my lungs.

"Fuck, Drake! Don't stop!" My first orgasm was building as he continued to change the pressure on my clit.

I knew I was stalling by not talking with him about the gun. But I wanted to be with him before I learned what the reason was. I knew that my brother was packing, too. Could it be that Drake was also carrying because of the same gang?

The nip on my thigh brought my attention back between my legs. Drake's eyebrows were raised as he looked up at me. I knew he had caught me thinking of other things while he was trying to make me come.

"Am I not doing a good enough job to keep your attention, *dolcezza*?" The shimmer on his lips made me wetter.

"Sorry, I was just thinking. But, you know, I love it when you go down on me." I smirked when he glanced back down.

"Then I need to do better at making your mind think of nothing but me," Drake said, the corner of his lip lifting, and my heart started to race. I knew when that corner lifted, I was in for a fun night.

Drake stood and motioned with both of his index fingers for me to stand. When I got to my feet, the smile on Drake's face made it to his eyes. "Take the dress off."

I did as I was told and slipped the dress below my breasts and allowed it pool at my feet. With the dress off, I was naked in front of him, and I didn't miss his tongue that ran across his lips.

Before he could say anything, I knelt and grabbed the base of his cock with one hand and used the other to cup his balls. Drake's hands went into my hair, and I locked my gaze on him. Doing this would have him punishing me later, but I wanted this. I used the flat of my tongue over the tip of his cock before swirling it around, making him groan and tighten his grip on my hair.

I loved to tease him before swallowing him into my mouth. Drake shuddered and tightened his grip again, pushing himself further into my mouth. He slipped the head of his cock down my throat, the bars of his double Jacob's ladder stretching my throat.

"Breathe through your nose, *dolcezza*." he groaned.

When my eyes locked with his, his eyes were eclipsed by his pupils. His mouth opened as he breathed through his nose. The rope of muscle in his neck pulsed as I sucked and twirled my tongue around his girthy cock.

I could feel the dribble running down my chin, and I knew it was coating his thighs when he pushed his cock all the way down my throat. Fuck, he felt amazing as he fucked my face. My pussy was dripping onto the wooden floor.

"Your throat feels so good wrapped around my cock, *dolcezza*. You take me so well, like the good girl you are. Even though you did this without asking." Drake tensed and I knew he was fixing to come. I moved my hands from his cock and balls to his ass.

Digging my nails in his globes as warm cum shot down my throat. Drake pulled out slowly, and I sucked every last drop from him until a pop sounded as the head exited my mouth.

"Don't drop a single morsel. I want you to savor that present and I want you to swallow it."

I never broke his gaze as I wiped my lips with my fingers and then scooped the little cum that had leaked onto my chin between my lips. The growl that he emitted as I pulled my fingers from my mouth made my pussy clinch, and I swallowed the salty seed.

Drake squatted down and picked me up by the back of my thighs. I wrapped my legs around his waist as he walked us to the bedroom in the suite. My hands played with the hair at the nape of his neck while his arms pulled me closer.

"Fuck, woman. I have never been as obsessed with someone like this." Drake's husky tone ran right through me while he took us to the bed and dropped me on the soft mattress.

"Then why are you not inside me yet?" I had to be careful what I said since we had talked about our dynamic. I had already sucked him off without him telling me that was what he wanted.

The crook of his eyebrow, along with the lift of the corner of his lip, had me biting my bottom lip. My eyes roamed his body and the length of his pierced cock. Drake's body made me squirm, thinking about how moved inside of me.

He used his knee to open my legs, and he grabbed my thighs, pushing me to the middle as he kneeled between my legs. Drake's cock had hardened, and it stood at attention while I stared. Of all the men that I had been with, I had never thought a cock could be beautiful, but his, with the light bouncing off the jewelry, had me mesmerized.

"*Dolcezza*, as much as I loved your mouth around my cock. You did that without permission." The lust in his eyes told me that he wasn't as upset as I thought he was. "You won't be coming this time. Do you understand?"

"Yes, Sir." I pulled my bottom lip between my teeth and tried to tighten my thighs around him to pull him inside me.

Drake placed my calves on his shoulders, and his hands wrapped around my hips. He lined me up with his head and thrust inside. My hands went to his forearms, and my back arched as I moaned out so loud that I knew the room beside us had to hear me. And yet, I didn't care; it didn't matter what everyone else heard or saw as long as it was with Drake.

Our eyes held each other before he clenched his teeth and glanced down, watching as his cock appeared and reappeared. The rope of tendons and veins jutted out as he continued to pummel me.

My pussy clenched around him, and he stopped. Drake's fingers dug into my skin. "Don't come *dolcezza*. I told you that you couldn't."

I nodded and tried to think about something other than how full I felt. Fuck, this was going to be hard. I dug my fingernails deep into his skin as he began to move again inside of me. Drake leaned down, pulling my knees to my shoulders.

"Fuck, *dolcezza* you feel so good. Tell me how much I make you feel good."

"Drake. Why do this when you told me that I couldn't come?" I panted as the sweat from his brow dripped onto me. I felt his right hand pull away from my hip and wrap around my throat.

"If things get to be too much, use your safeword." I nodded. Drake tightened his grip on me, and it took everything in me to keep myself from coming.

The way he used his hands, his cock, but most of all, his voice is what made my body react. I wanted him to fuck me and let me come all over him. I couldn't pull my eyes away from him, and when I glanced up, I noticed the mirror above the bed.

I couldn't pull my eyes away from the motion. My toes curled and uncurled as he thrust into me. The muscles in his back loosened and tightened as his ass kept a smooth rhythm.

My body begged to come, but I had to keep myself from doing it. If I did, Drake would make this punishment last longer. I removed my hands from his forearms and reached up, wrapping them in my hair.

"Fuck, I'm not going to last much longer." My eyes met his just as I was about to pass out. "Fuck!"

Drake loosened his grip on my neck as he sat up on his knees. His hands went to my thighs, and he smiled at me before glancing further down. "This pussy looks gorgeous with my cum inside it."

His compliment heated my skin. My whole life, I had been told that I was beautiful and gorgeous, but the way he said those words cemented inside me that they were true. He used one finger inside of me to push the cum back in. "I want to stretch this pussy. I want to put my whole hand inside this."

"Your hand can't fit inside of me."

"Wanna bet? A baby can come out of it. Why can't my hand?" My mind was spinning as he pushed two more fingers inside, "But we won't be doing it tonight."

Drake pulled his fingers out of me and allowed my legs to rest on the bed. He got up and reached out his hand. He pulled me close to him and pushed my hair out of my face.

"I didn't forget about the gun. So, don't try any more tactics to avoid our conversation." I pulled back and looked at him.

"I won't hide anything from you, *dolcezza*. I want you to be by my side for the rest of my life."

"What are you asking me?"

"I'll get to that later. But I will be asking you to marry me," he chuckled as he pulled me into the bathroom.

"So, the gun? Why are you carrying it? Is it the same gang?" Drake turned from me and started the shower before facing me again.

"Yes and no. I noticed the same kid that TC did. So, I started carrying. But then my uncle came from Italy and told me that he wanted me to take over the family."

"That's a good thing though. Right?" I searched his face, trying to find out if I was missing something.

"Not really, Emi." Drake pulled me into the shower with him and continued, "My family has ties to the Italian mafia. If you don't want to be with me after learning this, I understand."

I stood there in his arms, under the spray of the water. Drake was part of the mafia, and if I married him that would put me in that family, too. But why would he only tell us now ? I mean me? Because he has been like family to me and TC since my brother came into the family.

"TC knows, right?" I watched as his face shifted through multiple expressions, "Drake, does TC know?"

"No, he doesn't. But I will be telling him when I can. Right now, I have to find a man for my uncle."

"Who is this man?"

"A very dangerous man. They call him Jack The Torturer, and, apparently, my family and he have had beef for a very long time."

I shivered under the water. The closer I got to Drake, the more I was being pulled into this mafia life, and I didn't think I was all that afraid of it.

Chapter Eighteen

DRAKE

TC had been drumming his fingers on the boardroom table since we sat down an hour ago. These types of meeting tended to last for a few hours. I didn't think that he had been paying attention to anything that these fuckers were saying. He was definitely in serious thought about a woman because he had a far-off look that I had never seen on him before.

When Frank stood up to talk, I figured TC would be paying attention since Frank was in charge of finance. But TC hadn't even budged from his position; something or *someone* had his attention.

"I vote that we do not give a raise this year."

TC's gaze rose, and he stared at him before shifting his sight to the other men around the table. Each one shook his head and glanced at the table. None of them could hold his unwavering stare. The look in TC's eyes as they returned to Frank were cold and calculated.

"And why is that, Frank?" Frank's eyes widened. TC's voice only went that deep when he was ready to dominate the room.

"Well, we are overspending..." Frank stammered as he played with the papers in his hands.

He relaxed a little when TC nodded and became a little more confident that he was going to get the vote from the CEO. But I knew TC; he was lulling Frank in a false sense of security before he attacked. "So then, if you want to cut wages, why don't I cut yours instead? You have two incomes, right?"

"Mr. Churchhill, sir. I have a family, too."

I had to hold back the smile that was threatening to creep onto my lips.

"So do the people you want to withhold a raise from. My father has always treated every employee here like family, and that is what I intend to do." TC stood, making Frank sit as he walked around the table. At this point, I couldn't hold back the grin that was spreading on my face.

"Just because I'm the owner and CEO does not mean I know nothing about the financial side of this company. I know that we have billions in the savings account. I also know that what you are telling me about the outgoing money is bullshit. I didn't go to school to have you and anyone else run all over me." TC stalked behind Frank and patted his shoulders. Leaning over his shoulder, TC held the gaze of every man at the table. Part of me thought he was also talking about me.

"So, when you want to bring up not giving the employees a raise like they have been given every year, just remember that I can cut yours in half to let you see how they live."

Frank was nodding by the end of TC's words and pulled the rest of his papers together. TC could be brutal at times in this room with these men who hadn't gone hungry. Which was another reason that he continued to give the employees raises, and they weren't small.

"This meeting is adjourned. Have a wonderful day, gentlemen." He pulled away from Frank and walked over to the floor-to-ceiling window. Men stood from their seats and staggered out like dogs with their tails between their legs.

After the last of them exited the room, I stood and came up beside TC with my hands in my pockets. I didn't know if now would be the best time to tell him everything. Hell, he probably already knew and was waiting for me to say something, "You really had it in for him today, bud."

I decided that I would bring that up for now, but there was something else that I wanted to see what he thought about. The smile on my face couldn't be helped, knowing that Emi was at my house probably still in bed exhausted from the night before.

"What's up? Is there something on your mind?" TC turned to me, and I quickly stopped grinning.

"What do you think about Emi dating?" It was the only way I could find out what he thought without giving myself away.

"She's old enough to date. But he better not hurt her 'cause I'll put him in an unmarked grave if he does." TC locked his steely ice-blue gaze on me before continuing, "Is she dating someone?"

I shrugged before punching him in the arm. "You know I'm right there with you."

It was a bad time to talk to him about Emi and me. I could feel it, and I didn't want to be pushed out that big-ass window and plummet to my death.

"I'm going to head out early. Are you good here?"

"You know I have you, man. I saw you with the wife. You looked good together. Looks like I'll finally have my way with the ladies."

"Go for it, but make sure you keep your eyes open. The people from my past are watching you too." TC clapped me on my shoulder and left the room. That wasn't like him. He had it bad for Aurora just like I told him he would.

I couldn't help but grin. He had gone down the rabbit hole with the woman he swore he hated. But it was the first time that he had mentioned his past. I didn't like that he had been keeping this from me, since he normally told me everything.

Then again, I couldn't say anything because I had to tell him about me and his sister. But keeping this from me was something bigger, it could cause something bad to happen to either of our families. And I wasn't going to let that happen because he was my brother, even if we were not blood.

For all the bravado that he was showing everyone else, something was weighing him down, and it was getting to me. My uncle still wanted me to find Jack the Torturers' heir, but I still thought he was dead. There was no way the kid was still alive, from the way he looked in the picture he was way too skinny and looked like he hadn't been taken care of properly for a long time.

Leaving the boardroom myself, I boarded the elevator and headed down to my car. I needed to do some more recon on Jack. In the back of my mind, I was sure that my uncle wanted me to off the LA mob's leader. To show that I had it in me to lead our family.

When I reached my car, I entered it and started the engine. I tore out of the garage and pulled out into traffic as I made my way to the places that Jack frequented. The building loomed in front of me as I parked and sat. Jack was like clockwork, he never deviated from his schedule.

So when I saw the black SUV park in front of the building, I grinned. I didn't know how this man had survived as long as he had. Anyone could have taken him out long before now. The bodyguards filed out and let Jack out of the vehicle, but another man came out with him.

He was about the same age as Jack, maybe a few years older. The only thing different about the man was that he was glancing around him. He was definitely someone who was used to living on the streets.

Jack, however, walked with his guards into the building

without a worry in the world. The more I watched him, the more his mannerisms started to become more familiar. I continued to sit and watch for the next four hours, waiting for Jack to come back out.

This time, I was thinking about following him to see if there was a way to find out where this man lived. I needed more information so that I could get my uncle off my back. My phone pinged, and I glanced down. Emi had sent me a picture of her lying by the pool topless. Fuck, she liked to tease me when I wasn't around to spank her ass.

But I wasn't going to let her get away with this. I chuckled and shook my head as she sent me more pictures with her fingers in her mouth and her eyes closed.

> Dolcezza if you continue to send me these. I'll make sure you get the punishment that you deserve.

> Ooo, you say those things and it makes me wet. ;p

> Marmocchia, you keep saying those things and I will string you up in that swing and make you stay there as I watch you leak with arousal for me to take you.

> Then hurry home.

I chuckled again and placed my phone in the passenger seat, turning my attention back to the building I had been staking out. I watched the door until the older man emerged from the building. He pulled out a small box and put the cigarette in his mouth. Pocketing the box, he lit the cigarette and took a drag of it.

Quickly, I pulled out my phone and took a picture of the man. He had to have some worth if he was around Jack. He didn't have just anyone around him. The man with the lit cigarette took another drag from it before he looked my way. I stared back, and he smiled back at me.

I was going to have to switch cars next time. I moved my Glock to my lap, just in case the man wanted to approach the car. But he just threw the butt onto the sidewalk and used the ball of his foot to snuff out the embers.

He turned on his heel and walked away from the building. I sat there, still waiting for Jack to come back. He never stayed long here. Which was why I decided that I was going to follow him this time. I wanted to know where he lived so that I could know more about the men he surrounded himself with.

I didn't have to wait much longer when he left the building with his entourage. The way he looked at my car told me that he had noticed me sitting out there. Jack nodded to me before climbing into the SUV.

"Well, guess I won't be following him today." From my car, I watched them drive away. I was definitely going to need to change cars.

As I turned over the car and put it in drive, someone knocked on my window. I glanced over and noticed a man with dark brown hair and green eyes. He motioned for me to roll down my window, which I did.

"Can I help you?"

"Yes, if I see you here again, you won't drive away the next time." The kid—I call him a kid because he was younger than me —had big balls on him.

"I'll see what I can do about that."

I rolled up the window and sped off. Glancing behind me, I noticed that he had hopped on a crotch rocket and raced away in the opposite direction. I was going to have to be more careful now that Jack, the older man, and now the kid knew I was watching this building.

Chapter Nineteen

EMI

Drake had been working longer hours at the company. TC hadn't answered my calls or texts over the last couple of weeks, which wasn't like him. I was worried because I knew that the only reason Drake was working these longer hours was because TC wasn't there. Something was wrong.

I was standing beside a vendor at the farmers' market when someone came up beside me. At a quick glance, I thought he was my father, but with a second, I realized that the older man just looked like him. They could pass as siblings, and the craziest thing was he looked like an older version of TC.

When he turned to me, I quickly returned my gaze to the items on the table.

"You turned out to be a beautiful woman."

"Excuse me?" I looked at the man fully, and that's when I realized that I knew him somehow. But it had been years since I had seen him.

"Make sure that Italian takes care of you." His blue eyes held mine. They were just as icy as TC's. If I didn't know any better, I'd go as far as them being closely related.

"Do I know you?" I took a step back to give myself more room.

He was wearing a suit, but it didn't look like one that my father or TC would wear. Not to mention something that Drake would wear. It had pinstripes down the pants, and even though it was a darker suit, you could tell that it had been washed a lot.

"You would if I had been more in your life. Just make sure that Italian takes care of you as well as TC." His brows knitted together as he stared behind me. "Make sure you stay safe, little one."

He turned and walked away from me, which was when I saw the other men in street clothes move with him down the street. It was like they just appeared out of thin air. When I looked behind me, I noticed Heath was rushing up the street. I had told him that I needed a few minutes to myself, and he had allowed it as long as I was still visible.

"Who was that?" Heath panted as he came to a stop in front of me and scanned me.

"I have no idea. I think we need to tell Drake about this, though. He mentioned that Drake needed to take care of me twice." I looked at the disappearing figure with his bodyguards. He had to be important with the number of men he had.

"Fuck, Drake and TC are going to kill me."

I sighed and rolled my eyes before leaving the table. Whoever that man was, he had to know my family, and it made me wonder whether it was because of TC's past or if it was something that had happened with my parents.

Heath stayed close to me as we made our way back to the car. I pulled out my cell phone and brought up Drake's text messages. I didn't try to hide them from Heath, if he looked, that was on him.

> Hey babe. Are you at home?

> I'm heading home now.

> K we need to talk when you get there.

After I sent that text, I freaked out a bit because I didn't want him to think that it was something bad.

> It's nothing bad…

> HAHA. I didn't think it would be.

> K see you soon.

Heath opened the rear door, and I entered the vehicle and settled into the seat as he shut the door and rounded the back of the car to the driver's side. He looked into the rearview mirror before checking the other mirrors and pulling into the street.

"Head home, Heath. Drake and I have to talk about what just happened."

"I think you need to keep it to yourself." Heath was sweating. I was sure he thought he was going to be in some shit about leaving me alone. Again.

"Are you afraid that you might lose a hand?" I giggled as he huffed in the front seat.

Did I think that Drake was going to be pissed? Yes. But if he found out I didn't tell him about what had happened, he would be even more pissed. So whatever happened to him after my talk with Drake, he would have to deal with.

Heath sighed and continued to drive. I couldn't believe that I was now calling Drake's place home. I still went out on lunch dates with my mother, which were always in restaurants that weren't full. But I still enjoyed those outings.

We pulled up to the house, and Heath stopped, turning off the car. He got out and opened my door to let me out. I walked up to the front doors just as Drake turned into the driveway. Heath stiffened when he saw the car, but he didn't say anything.

Waiting at the top of the steps, I smiled as he came up to me, matching my smile. Drake leaned in and placed a chaste kiss on my lips before wrapping his arm around my waist, and we walked into the house together.

"So. What do you have to tell me, *dolcezza*?"

"I think we need to talk in your office?"

Drake nodded and led me there. I noticed that Heath had stayed outside with the cars. He didn't want to be on Drake's war path after I told him what had happened. I walked up to the sofa and sat down as Drake shut the door before sitting beside me.

I turned to face him and took one of his hands. "So you know I go to the farmers' market, right?"

Drake nodded with an eyebrow raised.

"Well, some man came up to me and told me that, and I quote, 'make sure that Italian takes care of you.' I've never seen this man, but he looks like my father and even more like TC."

Drake's smile dropped and his face turned dark. He stood and began to pace in front of me. I had never seen him like this. "Drake?"

"Where was Heath when this man was talking to you?"

I sighed; I knew this would come up.

"I had asked him to stand back and watch. I was trying to find something to give you for your birthday. I didn't want him to know what I got you."

"That was still a bad choice. This man—how old do you think he is?"

"I don't know. My dad's age? Who was he?" Now I was scared. Who was this man, and how did he know me? And not only me but my brother and Drake.

"I don't care if you are shopping for dildos or lingerie, Heath better be with you. I'm not playing, Emi." Drake squatted in front of me and held my hands. I could tell that he was upset, but he was trying to keep his emotions in check as he looked at me.

"Okay. but who was he?" Something told me that Drake knew about this man, and I wanted to know the same.

"Remember when I told you about the man I was after for my uncle?" I nodded, trying to search his eyes. "Well, I'm sure that the man who came up to you was Jack. So that is why you need to be careful and always have Heath with you. I can't lose you, *dolcezza.*"

Drake pulled my hands up to his mouth and placed two kisses each to the back of them. Well it looked like until Drake dealt with this man, I would be having Heath at my side at all times.

I woke up the next morning like I normally did. Reaching for my phone, I checked the time. Drake had been at the company for a few hours now, and it was almost time for lunch. I smiled and jumped out of bed. Normally, I would never go to the company, but I was today.

Surprising Drake at lunch would be good for the both of us, and maybe I would be able to see TC. That way, I could see why he has been ignoring me. I got dressed in a skirt and a flowy blouse comfortable and texted Heath to have the car around the front.

I didn't put on much makeup. Just enough to highlight my eyes. A nice neutral brown with a little bit of white to accent my hazel eyes. After one last look in the mirror, I left the room and went downstairs to wait for Heath.

Getting to the bottom of the stairs I crossed the foyer to the front doors. Benton opened them for me and I exited them just as Heath brought the car up to the front steps. I walked down the stairs and entered the open door on the sedan. Heath closed the door and got back in the vehicle.

"Kenny will be with us today. Where would you like to go?" Kenny was one of the new hires that Drake had gotten since I moved in, and I wasn't as close to him as I was with some of the others.

"I want to go see Drake. So, we need to go to Chuchhill Logistics," I told him and Kenny as I stared at him in the rearview mirror. They both nodded, and Heath shut my door and entered his.

The drive was quiet, and I could tell that Heath didn't like that he wasn't driving. I didn't like that it being so quiet in the car, either. When it was just me and Heath, it didn't stay quiet long, but I didn't know how to even start a conversation with Kenny in the car.

Grabbing my phone, I decided to text Drake and let him know that I was close to the company and coming to see him. If he were busy, he wouldn't see the text, but he couldn't say I hadn't let him know.

When I saw the office building, my heart began to flutter. Did I want him to take me on his desk again? Hell fucking yes! But would he? I wouldn't put it past him. Kenny stopped the car in front of the building, and Heath got out to open my door.

"Kenny, take the car to the garage and wait there until I text you." Kenny nodded and left when Heath shut the door.

"So, why do I have two of you now?" I asked when Heath held the door open to the office.

"Because, apparently, the man who came up to you was someone that Drake has been tailing, and he doesn't want just one person with you in case the man has other ideas." Heath followed close behind me as we made our way to the elevator.

The first office I would be going to was my brother's. He was about to get in trouble for not answering me. He knew better than to leave me on read. When the elevator opened, I noticed Lindsey was at her desk typing away.

So if she was here working, that meant my brother was, too. I walked up to his office and pushed my way in. The typing behind me stopped. It was empty and cold. Nothing was out of place, but you could tell that TC hadn't been there for a long time. "Where's my brother?" I asked Lindsey after leaving the office

"Emi, he hasn't been here in a couple of weeks. I've been receiving tasks from him via email."

"Then why wouldn't he be answering my texts?"

"I don't know, ma'am. But I know Drake has been handling most of Mr. Churchhill's job since he has been gone. The board members are not happy that he isn't in the meetings." Lindsey sat back in her chair and grabbed her water bottle, taking a sip out of it.

"That's not like him. Does my father know?"

"I don't believe so, ma'am. Drake has been doing really well."

I nodded to her and left her desk. Drake had been hiding this from me, and I didn't like that. I knew that he had other things than the company to worry about, but he should have said that TC hadn't been working. I nodded at Tiffany, who returned the gesture before heading into Drake's office to give him a piece of my mind.

I stopped in my tracks when I realized that Drake wasn't alone. A blond man, who I didn't recognize, was in front of Drake's desk and then there was the man who had come up to Drake in Las Vegas.

Drake's gaze left the men and came to me before he motioned for me to come forward.

Chapter Twenty

DRAKE

I heard the doors open before I turned my gaze to the door. Tiffany wouldn't have come in since I told her I had this meeting with my uncle and his second-in-command. When my eyes locked on Emi, I knew it was too late to have her go and sit with Tiffany.

Motioning for her to come to me, she heeded my command without hesitation. Riccardo looked behind him as she approached me. I didn't like that he glared at her as if she was interrupting something. In a sense, she was, but she knew about my family ties now. I wasn't going to keep her in the dark any more than I had.

"*Dolcezza*, what a pleasant surprise." I pulled her into my lap and kissed her.

I was letting him know that she was mine and that if he got any crazy ideas, he might not make it to his next birthday. Because if he thought he was going to use her to get to me, he was even more crazy than I thought. I would kill him for her and TC if he did anything.

"*Dolcezza*, this is my Uncle Riccardo and his friend Aldo.

Uncle, this is Emerald, my fiancé." I didn't miss the look that he sent over to Aldo.

"Fiancé? When did this happen?"

"Well, since I'm my own person and this is my life, I decide who I wanted to spend the rest of my life with   ."

My uncle sat in the chair he had been in before Emi came in. I pulled her closer to me and ran my hand up her thigh, causing her to shiver.

"Now, what is the issue? I have given you all the information that your insiders couldn't. So, what else do you want from me?" I made sure to run my nose up Emi's neck, and I chuckled when she stifled her moan.

"You haven't dispatched him nor his heir. You haven't even found his heir yet," my uncle growled as he stared at me and Emi.

"No, I haven't found him yet, but you have all the information you need. So I don't get why I have to take him out when you are the one who wants him gone," I answered as I continued to play with Emi.

"I told you when I came over that you had to take him out. If you did, you would get the Italian mafia." He sat back and steepled his fingers.

If this was how it was going to be, I wasn't going through with this. Emi had been sitting here in my lap, trying to keep quiet. I was going to have to reward her.

"Well, I will have to see what I can do, but if you want to continue to push my timetable then you can take over," I snarled at him. I wasn't one to be treated like his underlings.

"When you find the heir and have killed the mob boss, call me." My uncle and Aldo got up and walked out of my office.

When the office doors closed, I stood up and placed Emi on the desk in front of me. I widened her thighs and grabbed her hair. "What are you doing coming to see me? Huh?"

"I thought it would be nice to come have lunch with you. I

didn't know you had a meeting, or I would have waited," Emi moaned, and I pulled her hair harder.

"*Dolcezza,* you never have to wait for anything. If you wanted me to fuck you, I would have sent them out and had you again on this desk." I didn't think having her sit on my lap during the meeting would have as much of an effect on me, but fuck if it did.

"I wouldn't mind being fucked again. But I really did come to have lunch with you. Along with asking you about TC. He hasn't messaged me in a couple of weeks."

Well, fuck. I didn't think to tell her that he wasn't here. I knew by the look in her eyes that she had gone into TC's office and noticed that he hadn't been there in some time. When he messaged me and told me he needed a few days away from the company, I didn't even think twice about it. Because I knew that if it were the other way around, he would do the same for me.

I let go of her hair and allowed her to sit straight while staying between her thighs. Her pupils were wide as she gazed back at me. "With everything that was going on, I forgot to tell you about him not being here. But when I get the time, I will reach out to him and see what he is up to."

Emi nodded and then put her hands on my chest. I stepped back and allowed her to jump off the desk. She stepped up to me and placed a quick kiss on my lips. "Thank you. Now, if you don't mind, I would like to get something to eat, Mr. Deluca."

"Of course, *dolcezza.* You pick whatever you want." I smiled back at her. When I had told my uncle she was my fiancé, she didn't even question it, and she still wasn't.

It had been a few days since I had heard from TC, so I decided to call him. I had been keeping the board members at bay. They didn't like that they hadn't been able to get in contact with TC, but there wasn't anything I wouldn't do for that man. He was practically my brother.

"Hey, man, it's been a minute. Are you doing okay?"

"Yes, it has been a while and I'm sorry. I should've called you, but I have to get to bed. I'm hoping things go my way tomorrow." TC hesitated, which had me wondering.

"What's happening tomorrow?" I stood from my desk and went to the gun case in the corner.

"I've kept things from you, and they've come back to haunt me. I've placed everyone that I care about in danger. I have to take care of this to keep everyone safe. They took Aurora, so if I don't make it back. I need you to take over the company." I paused at the defeat in his voice and the words that he uttered. Something I had never heard before.

"Who took her? How long has she been gone?" I paused while pulling out my Glocks.

"My old gang. She left me a couple of weeks ago, but Marcus has had her for the last three days." There it was again, the defeat, fuck, he fell hard for Aurora.

"What can I do to help? You know I'm here." TC chuckled and then sighed.

"Drake, I can't pull you into this…"

I cut him off before he could say anything else. "TC, I've not been truthful with you either. My family has ties with the Italian mafia. I can help you rescue Aurora. I'm not afraid to get my hands bloody."

"The Italian mafia?"

"Yes, my uncle is the Capo in Italy. But my father runs underground gambling rings, and since he and your father started

Churchhill Logistics..." Fuck, this was hard. I'd had to keep this secret from him.

"Since my father and yours started the company?" There was that tone—the tone of a CEO.

"We have been laundering money through the company. To move it from the gambling rings to bank accounts."

"You what? And my father knows about this?" I didn't want to tell him about this over the phone, but if this was the only way to get him to let me help, I would do it.

"Yes, and I have been keeping this quiet until your father told you. He apparently forgot about it." I didn't like throwing Mr. Churchhill under the bus, but dammit, he was supposed to tell TC.

"Yeah, apparently. Later, we need to talk about this, but if you want to help, I won't say no."

"Good. When and where do I need to be?" I loaded the gun, and it pushed a bullet into the chamber.

I need you to go to the warehouse that you've been bothering me about and enter through the back door. Marcus will come through the side door with Aurora. I know he will be bringing someone, but I don't know how many. Jake and Sam will be coming with me." TC's confidence was back as he instructed me.

"I got you, dude. I'll be there."

"Thank you, Drake."

"No problem," I placed the gun back in the safe and locked it. Tomorrow, I was going to make sure my best friend got his wife back.

I turned as I was making the last knot in the concrete barrel. Jake was pulling Marcus over to me near the water. He was the man I had seen walking in the building with Jack. I was one hundred percent certain that he was, and if TC was part of this gang, then he must have met Jack before.

"You shot him in front of her, didn't you?" I asked him with a grin. His eyes snapped to mine as he pulled off his jacket. He had that look of someone who had killed and hadn't batted an eye.

"Yes, he did. I tried to stop him. But he did it anyway." Jake glared over at TC before grabbing hold of the man's legs and bringing him closer to the edge.

"How did she react?" I was curious because I knew for certain that Mr. Emerson had never looked at a gun before.

"She didn't even budge," TC grunted as he squatted down to help me tie the rope around his ankles.

"Then she will be fine with your past. You need to let her know sooner rather than later." TC and I pushed the concrete barrel into the water, and it pulled the corpse of Marcus down into its depths. I stood with TC and looked between him and Jake, "We need to talk as well. Once we make sure Aurora will be okay, of course."

"We will. We have to make sure we are on a united front from here on out."

I nodded to TC before he turned and returned to the car Aurora was in. When I saw her tied to that chair with the man at her back, I could tell she hadn't been taken very good care of. TC was a madman when he arrived at the warehouse, ready to burn it all to the ground.

Aurora had washed herself, but you could tell that she hadn't been allowed to have a shower the entire time that she was there. Not to mention, there were varying stages of bruising on her wrists.

Emi was impatiently waiting for me to tell her that Aurora and TC were both safe. As I walked to my car, I pulled out my phone to call her.

Chapter Twenty-One

DRAKE

After I helped dispose of the body, I realized the person TC had killed was one I had seen going into the building with Jack. It made me wonder if TC knew Jack because he was in the gang with Marcus. I needed to find out if he was aware of the LA mafia boss. If he did, we needed to have another conversation.

I headed into the hospital to check-in with TC and see how Aurora was doing. The lobby was busy, but I made sure to look at the signs to find my way. As I walked into the elevator to head up to the VIP floor, I leaned up against the back wall when two nurses stepped on with me. TC had made sure that he had a whole floor just for his family and friends.

The nurses exited the elevator on the fourth floor, and it took me up to the top floor. Emi had come yesterday to spend time with her brother and family. I still hadn't talked to him about her and me, so I planned to say something today. Did I think I was going to die? I wouldn't put it past him.

The door to the elevator opened and I exited the elevator to the immaculate grey-and-white hall, I strolled past the busy nurse station and to Aurora's room. The door was open and I walked in before an auburn-haired nurse stopped me in my tracks. She didn't have much makeup on, but that didn't take away from her beauty; the stern look on her face made me stay where I was. "Who are you?"

"Well, sweetheart, I would be the best friend of that big fucker over there," I teased her, but she didn't smile or even move from in front of me.

"He's fine. That lughead is my friend." The nurse stepped around me, and I didn't miss the side eye that she gave me, which made me chuckle internally as I walked in.

"Hey, man. How's things going over here?" I picked up a chair and put it beside TC.

"She's still sleeping. The doctor thinks her body is exhausted from the whole ordeal. So, since it has been twenty-four hours, we are going to put a feeding tube in."

I gave him a look because everything that had happened was non-coincidental. I hated seeing him like this. He had even called me yesterday to talk about the company, but I knew he was using it as an excuse to get out of the hospital room. "Well, at least she's getting rest. You know you can take as much time as you need. I'll take care of the company while you handle this," I told him, and I meant it.

"I know. It's just hard to know what she is going to do once she wakes up. Those guys really did a number on her," TC answered.

TC didn't realize who I was until I told him about the gambling ring my father had in downtown LA. Apparently, he used to go there for Marcus to get his money from some of the men there. We had been linked for years and didn't know it.

I didn't want him to do this alone, even if he had Jake and Sam with him. They didn't know how to lose their morals to do what was necessary with these people. Come to think of it, I probably went a little overboard when Marcus ran; just as the shots started, I followed him along the catwalk above him. Finding a metal chain, I swung down and pushed him onto the concrete floor with my feet. Marcus landed face-first and broke his nose. I turned him around while I brought out my knife.

Cutting the side of his face with it, as I grinned at him, his eyes flew open when he recognized me before TC caught up with him. I knew then that he was the man who had been going in with Jack. I pulled Marcus up and shoved him against the wall. We had both gone to town on this fucker, and when we stopped, we pulled him up off the wall and took him to the front of the warehouse.

TC told me he wanted him to apologize to Aurora, so I hung back to get things done at the water's edge. I couldn't tell you how many people I had submerged in this calm channel. But it was more than I could count on both hands.

"I can believe it. Like I said, I have your back—now and always." I ran my hand through my hair; it was a tick I had when I tried to figure out if I should ask a question. "What would you think if I told you I was dating Emi?"

"I'd tell you just like I told you in my office—if you hurt her, no one will find your body." TC snapped his eyes to me. I knew he was protective of her, and I knew I was never going to hurt her. Because I needed her by my side in this.

"I can promise you that. It has taken me a long time to work up the courage to ask you. I love her." I stared back at him and knew that he was thinking about something to say to me.

"I believe you, Drake, and I will happily call you my brother. But like I said, don't hurt her."

I noticed that Aurora's hand moved, which brought TC's attention to his wife. I stayed still, watching to see if she was waking up. Aurora's eyes slowly fluttered open, and she looked around before she locked her gaze on my best friend.

"Are you okay? Are you hurting? Are you hungry?" TC rambled before he stood and sat on the bed with her.

"I'll go get the nurse." TC barely acknowledged me as I left the room. They needed their space, and she also needed that headstrong nurse who was in her room when I got here.

I spotted her at the nurses' station with a doctor. Heading up to her from TC's room,I made myself known with the rap of my knuckles.

"Excuse me. I just wanted to let you know that Mrs. Churchhill just woke up. You might want to go in there." The nurse looked up at me, and that's when I saw her badge. Her name was Kali.

"Thank you. Dr. Simmons, would you come with me? It looks like we won't need that feeding tube." She stood, and they both hurried to the room at the end of the hall.

I followed them and entered the room, leaning against the wall by the windows. I wanted to be there for my friend, but I also wanted to stay out of the way. TC kissed the back of her hand and moved away to allow the doctor and Kali room to work.

"Aurora, follow the light. How are you feeling? Anything hurting?" Dr. Simmons asked, flicking the small light from one eye to the other.

"I'm hungry, and I'm sore, but I'm not in pain."

Kali was taking her blood pressure before checking her heart rate manually, even though Aurora was connected to a monitor.

"Kali, get Mrs. Churchhill something small and easy to swallow. I don't want her to throw anything up."

"Okay, Dr. Simmons." Kail left and was back with some Jello within minutes. She sat the cup on the tray table and turned back to the doctor.

"Try this, and if you keep that down, we will get you something else, okay? Just call Kali. She will get you whatever you want." The doctor patted Aurora's arm and walked out of the room.

Kali stayed to enter things into the computer. While TC went back to Aurora and grabbed the cup of Jello with the spoon. He opened it, scooped out some of the orange dessert, and fed it to his wife slowly.

I stood from the wall and went to the foot of the bed. The way Aurora gazed up at him each time told me that she wouldn't leave him. TC didn't have to worry about that. "TC, do you want me to inform your parents so they can let the Emersons know?"

"No, I'll call them in the morning. They can come visit her then." I grinned at my friend. He had tried his best to keep from falling in love with this woman, but in the end, he'd failed.

"Okay, well, I'll let you both have some alone time. Well, as much alone time as you can have here." I laughed as I headed back out of the door.

I had to throw that comment in because if I didn't, it wouldn't be me, and TC would probably think I was sick or something. I passed the nurses' station again and waved to them.

I was going home to my own woman that I had fallen head over heels for. I left the building and got into the car that had been waiting for me. Sometimes, I couldn't believe how much clout we actually had in this city.

I pulled away from the curb and headed to Churchhill Logistics. TC needed time to deal with what had happened, which I was going to let him do. They both needed time, that was for sure. My phone rang in my cup holder, and I answered it from my car's touch screen.

"Hello,"

"Drake, it's Riccardo. I need to meet with you."

"I'm heading over to the office. I can meet you there if that is okay."

"That's fine, I'll be there in twenty. We have a few things to discuss, and I'm sure you know some things that need to be shared." He hung up without so much of a fuck you or goodbye. Not that I expected it, but hell.

I pulled up to the company's private garage, entered my code in the pad and went to my parking spot. I killed the engine and sat in the car for a moment before exiting and heading to the elevator. Part of me wanted to tell him to shove it. I didn't want any part in this.

I needed to know who the heir was to the LA mafia boss. The more I thought about it, and the more I watched Jack's haunts, the more I realized that I was closer than I thought.

The elevator doors opened at the top floor, and I stepped out onto my floor and headed to my office. Lindsey glanced up from her desk as I passed. I nodded to her and continued to Tiffany. She glanced up with a smile.

"I have family coming to meet me. Make sure to bring them straight to my office."

"Of course, sir." She nodded before I walked through the doors of my office.

Chapter Twenty-Two

DRAKE

I was sitting at my desk when Riccardo and Aldo came in and walked up to me. My uncle's face told me he wasn't in a good mood. Which, after our last meeting, I didn't think I would hear from him again until I found Jack's heir.

At this point, I didn't believe that the boy in the picture was still alive; if he was, he was long gone from LA. I wouldn't blame him either. Being homeless here wouldn't let you make anything of yourself.

"What do I owe the pleasure?"

"Aldo has found the boy. He is the CEO of this company. I think you've known that this whole time and didn't want to tell us." He slammed his hands on my desk, and I stood quickly. I didn't like that he had come in here to boss me around. That wasn't going to happen.

Rounding the desk, I grabbed my uncle by the throat and pushed him into the bookcase. Books fell around us when he hit the shelves. Aldo came up behind me, and I pulled my Glock from the inside of my suit jacket, leveling it at the old man and cocking it.

"Try me, old man, and I'll put a bullet between your eyes," I growled and glared at him from the corner of my eye. I tightened my grip on my uncle. Turning back to the man I had against the bookcase, I snarled, "What do you mean the boy in the picture is my best friend?"

"Just what I said. I had my tech people do some facial recognition." My uncle ground out through his restricted throat. His eyes were starting to turn red and pop blood vessels.

I loosened my grip on him but didn't let him move. He took in a deep breath with the release, and the desire to take his life was overwhelming. Thinking about what Emi had said made me start thinking about how closely Jack and TC resembled each other. And how he fit in perfectly with the Churchhills. Fuck, was TC really Jack's heir? And if he was, what was I going to do about that? I couldn't just off him; he was one of the biggest names in this industry. Besides, he was my brother, and I wasn't going to hurt him or Emi.

"He must be dealt with. You have to kill him and his father." My uncle pressed as the thoughts swirled around my head.

"No. That man has been my brother through all of this. I will not kill him on a hunch."

My uncle choked out a chuckle as I held him. I would not do his bidding. The Churchhills had been my family since I was born. When they adopted TC, I became even closer to them.

"You think he wouldn't kill you if he knew that you were related to me?"

" I know that he wouldn't because he knows I have ties to the Italian mafia. When I told him, he didn't bat an eye. So, let me tell you one thing. If you even try to hurt my best friend, I will kill you and any man loyal to you. Which will allow the bastard child your wife currently has in your home to take over."

"Drake, there's no need for the threats," Aldo answered from behind me. I turned on him again.

"It wasn't a threat; it's a promise. So, like I said before, try me, old man." I let go of my uncle and stepped back. He rubbed his neck as he glared at me. "Now, if you try to tell me that the man I have been running this company with is my enemy, you just became enemy number one. Get the fuck out of my sight."

Aldo came up to my uncle and pulled him toward the door, Riccardo then turned back to me. "I hope you know the mess you have made for yourself and your father."

"If you can threaten your own brother like that, then you were just using me and him to make sure some bastard didn't take over. And if you try to hurt anyone else like my parents, I will tell the little wifey that you are looking to replace her because of her adultery."

My uncle glared at me and left with Aldo. I might have made an enemy out of my uncle, but if what he said about TC was true, he would want to know who his father was. And Jack would want to know about his son.

I just needed to figure out how I was going to get them together.

I was back outside of the building I'd seen Jack at for the past few months. I knew he wouldn't be here, but I hoped the old man would be. I needed to know if he knew TC. Because if my hunch was correct, he knew everything that went on down here. I just needed him to show up and give him this number.

My car door opened, and the young man on the bike got in. I turned to the kid and grinned.

"I thought I told you not to come back here, or you wouldn't be leaving?"

"Yeah, well, I just couldn't get your pretty-boy face out of my mind, so I had to come see you." I laughed out loud with his expression. "I'm joking, kid. I need to see the old man who smokes. Can you tell me where to find him?"

"Why do you need to talk to Leo?" He seemed guarded, which he should be hell, my uncle wanted his boss dead.

"Because I have information that your boss needs to hear." The kid glared at me and exited my vehicle as he dialed a number, leaving the door open.

After a few moments he got back in and turned to me. "We're going to pick him up at Lakewood." The kid pointed ahead of him, and I pulled off the curb.

"What about your wheels?" I looked back at the multicolored bike that seemed to have been pieced together.

"No one steals my shit. They know better." He was confident that no one was going to touch it, so I headed for Lakewood. Did I think this kid was going to off me? Probably, if he was told to. Would I just let him? Fuck, no.

I turned left down the road, passing more buildings that were older than me. Which was probably why Jack liked to hang out around here. I took a right, making my way further to the outskirts of downtown.

Coming around the newer shops, the kid motioned to the man standing by the bus stop nonchalantly. I pulled over, and Leo got in the car. Once he was settled, we left to find somewhere to talk.

The guy looked like he hadn't had a shower in days, and he smelled like it, too. I was going to have to get the car detailed when I dropped them both off. Or sell it. "So, Riker says you have information for the boss?"

I nodded and pulled into a parking lot, shutting off the car, and turned. Pulling out my phone, I found the boy's picture and showed it to the old man. Something about his body language told me he knew things.

"Riker, why don't you find you something to do for a while?" Leo turned his gaze to the kid, then brought it back to the phone.

Riker, hopped out of the car and walked away. With a level voice, Leo asked, "Where did you find that?"

"It doesn't matter where I found it. This kid, you know him, right?" I questioned, and he nodded. "Who is he? And don't lie."

"I hadn't seen that boy in a long time until a few weeks ago when he took Nick with him. He apparently needed information. But he was sticking out like a sore thumb," Leo answered as he sat back. "With his fancy new blue jeans and T-shirt."

"What kind of information?" If he was looking for information, maybe he already knew Jack was his father? But that would be around the time he had asked me to hold down the fort at the company.

"Don't know. He found Nick and took him. Haven't seen him since." Leo shrugged and looked out the window.

"Tell me his name."

The smirk that graced his lips told me that was what he wanted me to ask. "You should know his name. He's the CEO of your company."

Fuck! The kid in this picture was TC. So, did that mean Jack knew he was still alive? And if so, why did he allow him to live on the streets and be adopted by the Churchhills?

"Then you need to tell your boss, Jack, that the head of the Italian mafia is after him."

"Are you not part of that family?"

"Yes, I am. But TC is my family more than the man searching for him. I will protect TC with my life."

"I'll let the boss know." Leo went to exit before I grabbed his sleeve.

"Here, give him this." I handed him one of TC's business

cards with his cell phone number on the back. "Does Jack know about TC?"

"Not until his mother told him on her deathbed. He has been trying to find him since. When he did, the kid was about to go to jail. So, instead of bringing him into the fold, Jack had family take him in to give him a better life." Leo opened the back door and then stuck his head back into the vehicle. I'll give this to him, and since you're a friend, I'll see if we can take the hit off you."

I nodded. I didn't know what to say. TC had always thought that his parents left him, but in reality, his father didn't even know he was alive until his mother died. And even then, his mother died when he was young, so there was nothing that he could have done. I couldn't believe he made it that long without any help, but I could see how Marcus could take him and change his outlook.

The more I learned about my friend the more I couldn't believe how he survived the years on the street. It had to be his tough exterior and the unwillingness to give up. From what I saw in the picture, he was everything his biological father was and then some.

Leo shut the door and nodded to Riker, who got back in the car so I could get him back to his bike. The need to get back to Emi was strong. I didn't know how to start to tell her about this.

As I stayed in thought during my drive, I came to the conclusion that I wouldn't tell Emi about this until I could get TC and Jack together. Again, that was if Jack wanted to have a relationship with his son. Something told me that he would want to.

Chapter Twenty-Three

DRAKE

TC called me the day after I had given his number to Leo. Someone connected to Jack must have called him. Was I wrong for choosing a man who wasn't blood over my uncle? I didn't think so because once I married his sister, I would be part of the family.

My phone rang on the counter, and I grinned. "Hey, man, what's up?"

"I'm going to need you to help me get my family out of here for the next two weeks." The concern in his voice brought me back to when he lost Aurora.

"Okay... What's wrong?" Maybe I was wrong about Jack and I had gotten my best friend in a whole lot of trouble.

"The main boss Marcus was under had his underboss call me. He wants to meet me in two weeks. I need to make sure that he isn't going to off my family." Fuck, my stomach was doing flips, but if he wanted to kill TC and his family, he would want to get this done quickly.

"Dude, I doubt sending them anywhere is going to help. If he wants to off you all, he will find them. On the day you meet him, take Jake and Sam. If I go, you might be killed. I'll keep the others safe." I would do anything for TC and his sister.

Emi came into the bedroom and closed the door. She had been laying by the pool topless.

"I should have been thinking. If I had been, I would have gone to him first to get the go-ahead to take Marcus out. It wasn't like he was making the boss any money." Something banged on the other side of the phone, and the only thing that I could think had happened was that TC had punched something.

"But that's not the issue, though, is it? And we don't know what the issue *is* right now." Emi sidled up to me and began to rub her hands up and down my body. She always liked to tease me when I was having a serious conversation.

"Okay, we just need to have them all in one spot. I guess we'll have dinner at your place so they won't think anything about it. The boss doesn't know about you..." I internally chuckled because the boss knew me *very* well. And I'm sure that if I weren't helping him get to see TC, I would have been dead by now.

"That's fine. I'll invite my parents too. Is that okay?" Emi giggled as she pulled me over to the bed. I couldn't be doing this with her brother on the phone. I put my finger to my lips and shook my head. "Shhh."

But it only made her giggle more. I placed my hand over the mouthpiece of the phone and growled, "It's your brother. Shhh!"

"... you think they won't get hurt." I pushed Emi onto the bed, and she sat with a smirk.

Emi reached for my slacks and removed my belt before unbuttoning them. She looked up and waited with her fingers on the zipper, ready to pull it down when I gave her the go-ahead. Her pleading look had my mind in a different place than where it should have been. I nodded, and she unzipped them and pulled out my cock.

"Did you forget who my family is?" I mean, my mother

didn't know anything about what my father was into but TC didn't need to know that. Besides, he had other things to worry about.

"No, but I don't want to cause anyone to lose their lives." Emi wrapped her lips around the tip of my cock, and I had to hold back a moan and hiss so as not to alert TC to what was happening right now.

He knew I was dating his sister, but he didn't need to know that she was sucking my cock while I was talking to him. Emi hollowed her cheeks and then pulled me farther into her mouth. I almost groaned when she took me into her throat.

"They will be fine. I have tons of security around my place." I managed to answer as Emi stroked my cock with her tongue, and her hand played with my balls.

"All right, we will talk more. I'm sure Aurora is out of the shower by now."

"Okay, boss. See you Monday?" I was trying my best to get off the phone with him. I shouldn't have given her the go-ahead.

"Yeah." The line cut out, and I threw the phone onto the bed as Emi worked over my cock.

She had gained confidence that she didn't have when we got together. The sounds she made when she sucked my cock had me blowing my cum in her mouth before I wanted.

"Fuck, *dolcezza*. You are getting so good at that." Emi popped off and swallowed every last drop.

"I learned from the best." Emi stood to her feet and kissed me.

No other woman would be able to do this to me ever. I was going to have to put a ring on her finger before anything else happened. I just might have done it when TC was meeting his biological father.

That would give the jeweler plenty of time to size and make what I wanted for her. There was no way I would give her something that wasn't unique.

"That you do. So, what do you think about going out to dinner tonight?"

"Sure, where do you want to go?"

"How about I take you to Vyanna's? After that blow job, I need a nice juicy steak."

Emi giggled and sashayed into the bathroom. Fuck I loved this woman. I was going to make her my wife and then put DeLuca babies inside her. I glanced down and realized that she had left me with my pants around my ankles.

Shaking my head, I pulled up my slacks and put myself back together before following her into the bathroom. She stood there in her bra, putting on makeup. I smirked, turned from her, and went into the toy closet.

I grabbed a vibrating egg and put the remote in my pocket. Emi was still putting on her makeup when I entered the room. She fixed me with a curious gaze and cocked her eyebrow. "What are you up to?" She had one eye closed and her mouth open.

"I want to play with you at dinner. You be okay with that?"

She stopped putting on eyeliner and looked at me in the mirror. I chuckled and pressed her into the counter, which opened her up for me. Running my hand down her back, she shivered and then nodded, giving me permission.

I moved my hand down to Emi's pussy and pressed two fingers inside her. She was already wet, and my fingers moved in smoothly. Pulling out of her cunt, I grabbed the egg and placed the smaller end to her entrance. She jumped a little before she relaxed, and I pushed it in.

Emi moaned as it settled inside her. I wrapped my hand around the back of her neck and pulled her flush against my body. She was gorgeous, her eyes fluttering and her thighs clenching. I reached into my pocket and turned on the egg, and her body shuddered. "Fuck, *dolcezza* you look so gorgeous right now. It's a shame that I have to cover up this body to go out. But the need to take you out and show you off is even greater."

Turning the egg off, I let go of Emi and smiled at her through the mirror. Emi resumed finishing up her makeup, and I walked out to allow her to get ready. Dinner was going to be great.

We walked down the stairs to the car, the remote to the toy still in my pocket. The thought of her trying it out made me hard as I opened the car door. Emi slipped into the car, and I shut the door. Emi sat quietly in the passenger seat. She didn't look upset, just deep in thought. I couldn't believe that there was a chance that she would be my wife. I just needed to get the timing right. I had every intention to ask her when the entire family was there.

I placed my hand on Emi's thigh and continued on to the restaurant. Her hand came to rest on mine and I grinned.

As I pulled up to the curb, I stopped the vehicle and got out. I rounded the car and opened her door to help her out. The valet came up to us and took the keys from me. They acted like this every time I came with my parents or TC.

The fucker never came with me anymore. Which I could understand now since he was crazy about his wife after all this time with her. It wouldn't have taken so long if the ass would have just let her in.

Emi and I entered the doors, and a hostess brought us to my usual table. It was toward the back of the room but not far enough that we were by ourselves. I liked being able to watch people as I ate, playing with Emi while everyone was in this room was going to be the next best thing.

I pulled out her chair and helped her to the table, then sat in front of her. I smiled and turned my attention to the male server, who was staring a little too long at Emi's cleavage. Clearing my throat, he brought his attention over to me.

He was definitely new because they all knew who I was. "We would like a bottle of your best champagne."

He nodded and left us as I reached into my pocket and turned on the vibrating egg. Emi moaned and slapped her hand over her mouth. Her eyes wide as she stared back at me. Faint whimpers were still coming behind her hand. Smirking, I turned the toy off just as the server brought the champagne.

He poured the champagne and then stepped back, pulling out his pen and notepad. "What would you like to order?"

"I'd like the filet mignon with a loaded baked potato," I answered him, and he glanced over to Emi.

"And for you, ma'am."

Just as she went to tell him, I turned the egg on and she had to close her mouth before she could speak. "The... chicken... ca... prese... with broccoli and a house salad."

I changed it to pulsing and she tried to order an appetizer. The server didn't flinch before he left to put in our order. Emi glanced over at me as she tried to keep from jumping up from her seat.

"I told you I was going to play with you, *dolcezza*."

Chapter Twenty-Four

EMI

During dinner, Drake turned on the egg eighteen times. Each time he did it was when a server came by or when I was taking a bite. He had me so turned on by the time we got the check that I could have moved from my chair and sat in his lap.

Every time he switched it on, I had to clench my legs to stop them shaking. Drake sat on the opposite side and smirked while he ate his steak. While I, on the other hand, had to keep myself from moaning each time I took a bite of my meal.

The look in his eyes whenever he had me just about there and then shut it off told me that he was enjoying himself. If he wanted to play this game, then I would play it, too. He better hope that he was going to make me come because I had been a good girl.

Drake stood from the chair and held out his hand. I took his hand and allowed him to lead us out of the restaurant, the egg still vibrating inside me. My legs were shaking as I walked beside him, but I used him to help me. He pulled me in closer when others started to stare at us.

"You did such a good job tonight *dolcezza*. I think I could whip up something to reward you with." His lips brushed the shell of my ear, causing a shiver to run through my body.

"Umm, I'd love that. Think that could happen in the car?" I grinned up at him, and the corner of his lip lifted.

"I will see what I can do."

The valet brought the car around, and Drake helped me into the passenger side. As much as he tried to make people think he was happy go lucky, most of the time, he was pretending. Because if you looked hard enough, you could see that there was something darker underneath.

Drake was quiet as we made our way back through the city to the house. I glanced over and noticed he was looking in his rearview mirror more often than normal.

"Is everything okay?" I tried to remain calm as I turned to face him.

"No, not really. Someone is following us," Drake answered and then reached into his suit jacket and pulled out his Glock, placing it on his lap.

He took the next left, and I noticed that the car did too. My heart began to race as he continued at an easy pace. I knew that he was trying not to bring attention to himself. We took another left, and the car followed. Now I knew that it wasn't a fluke, the car was tailing us.

"I need you to stay calm, okay? Whatever happens, I want you to stay in the car."

"What are you going to do?"

"You need to trust me. DO NOT GET OUT OF THE CAR." I stared at him and nodded. If there was one person I trusted more than my brother, it was the man sitting next to me.

The next thing I knew, Drake slammed on the brakes, and the person following us rammed into the back of the expensive sports car. I lurched forward, but the seatbelt held me firmly in place.

As soon as we stopped, Drake jumped out of the mangled

vehicle with the gun in his hand. I didn't mean to look in the passenger-side mirror, but I did anyway. Drake walked up to the car and shot the driver before he calmly went to the passenger side, dragging a man out of the beat-up station wagon. He slammed the man into the mangled metal, the gun pressed at the man's temple.

I tried not to watch what was happening but I couldn't pull my eyes from the scene in the side mirror. The man I saw was someone completely different than the one I had come to know. Was I scared that he might turn that person on me. No. But I was scared that I wasn't all that afraid of what he was doing.

Drake shot the other man and then holstered his gun. He pulled out his phone and placed it to his ear. A few minutes later, a man appeared on a motorcycle. They talked for a while before Drake made his way to my side of the car.

Drake knocked on my window and opened the door. "Come on. I have a car waiting for us. The kid is going to clean this up."

I nodded and gave him my hand. My eyes checked over Drake, and I didn't miss the spots of blood on his clothes. I should want to run away from him—the killing and how easy it was for him. Like, I should be scared of this man. I witnessed him murder two people, and now he was having someone clean it up.

Glancing back at the vehicle we were in, it was destroyed. There was no repairing this beautiful car, which was devastating. Before my attention landed on the dead bodies, Drake was pulling me over to the corner, and I realized that there was a black SUV idling there.

As we got to the SUV, I glanced back and noticed that the person that Drake called *the kid* wasn't really a kid. He was older than me, but he couldn't be the same age as Drake. The man caught me staring at him, and I didn't miss the glare he sent my way. Wow, I didn't even know this person, and he already hated me.

Drake opened the SUV's back door and helped me in. I slid over, and he entered after me. There was a divider between the back and the front, and once Drake closed the door, the driver pulled off. There had never been a moment when I wouldn't have asked him what was going on, but given the tense situation, I didn't say anything. I would wait until we got home.

After arriving home, Drake got on the phone and walked away to his office. I stood in the foyer and watched him until I could no longer see him anymore. Sighing I turned and crossed the foyer to the kitchen. I didn't want to bother him at the moment, so killing time in the kitchen with something to snack on was calling my name.

Entering the room I walked up to the fridge and opened the freezer door. I searched for my favorite ice cream, spotting it toward the back of the freezer. With a smile on my face from the label, I grabbed the pint of ice cream. The first time I had ice cream with TC, I figured out that we both liked the same flavor. Pistachio.

The ice cream was one of my first memories with TC.

I had walked into the kitchen one night and saw TC sitting at the bar with a spoon and a pint of ice cream in front of him. He hadn't noticed that I was in there yet. The look on his shadowed face worried me.

We had just gone to bed after the introduction party. TC seemed to have been having a good time, but now it looked like something had happened. In my eight-year-old mind, I couldn't think of anything that could have made him sad.

I padded further in, which was when he saw me. He watched me as I walked around the bar and climbed onto the barstool beside him with the spoon in my mouth.

"What are you doing up, Emi?"

"I was hungry. Is that your favorite ice cream, too?" I smiled after taking the spoon out of my mouth.

"Yes," He grinned briefly before his face fell back into a frown.

"Can I have some?" TC looked at me and nodded.

I bounced in my seat as I stuck my spoon into the ice cream. I grinned and shoved the big bite of the frozen yellow-green ice cream in my mouth.

TC laughed at me before wiping some of it off my cheek. Even though he had only been here a few weeks, I already considered him my brother. When my parents told me we were going to adopt a brother, I was excited. "Why are you up?" I asked after I swallowed my bite.

"I couldn't sleep." He sighed and shook his head before putting the ice cream on the bar in front of me.

"What are you thinking about?" I was never one to stop when I should.

"Grown-up things." He got up and walked over, and dropped his spoon inside the sink.

"You're not a grown-up."

"To you, maybe not. But I didn't grow up in a place like this. At your age, I had to find a way to eat by myself. I didn't have a mom or a dad to help me," TC snapped at me.

Being eight, I didn't really get why everyone wanted to keep things away from me. Just because I was young didn't mean I didn't understand.

"You don't have to be such a meanie." I watched him as he stood by

the sink. My mother had bought TC a whole new wardrobe for everyday wear, as well as a separate wardrobe for school. When he first came, he had long hair, and his clothes looked like he hadn't washed them. He was being very nice to me tonight. I didn't know why.

He did make a butt of himself with Dad's friend's daughter at his party. She had always been my favorite person when my dad took me to her house. Aurora was kind and pure, but never backed down when it came to a person she loved.

"I'm sorry, Emi. I shouldn't have done that. Matt told me I had to apologize to the Emersons' daughter. I just don't know how to do it." TC ran his hand through his hair and then leaned against the counter.

"It's okay. It's easy to say sorry. Just say 'I'm sorry.'" I climbed down with the spoon and placed it in the sink.

TC went to the bar and grabbed the now-empty ice cream, and placed it in the trash. When he looked back at me, his eyes were like ice-blue glaciers. Sort of like my dad's.

"It's not always that simple, Emi."

That memory was one of the saddest I had with TC, but also the only one that had brought us closer. He was the best big brother I had, and no one ever messed with me because of him. My family had what people thought was royalty status. But it never felt like that when we were with the other wealthy families.

Which was how I met Drake before he started college with TC. He was handsome in his suit with his mom and dad, but he didn't see me.

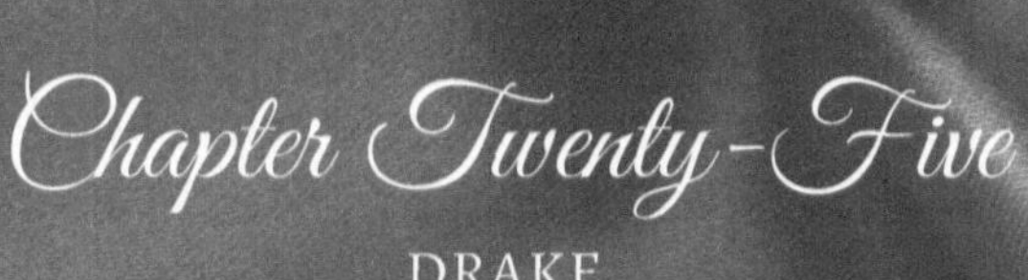

Chapter Twenty-Five

DRAKE

I sat at my desk, staring at my phone. My uncle had sent his threat about an hour ago. He was pissed I had sided with Jack and TC. Men who my uncle claimed wasn't fit for my loyalty. But my grandfather had been happy to do business with them.

Every time I saw him, I could tell it was eating at him. Not knowing if this man was going to kill him or his family kept him from being fully present. Standing, I pocketed the phone and walked out to Tiffany.

"Tiffany, what does my calendar say for the rest of this month?" The elevator dinged, bringing my attention to the long hallway.

Emi was at home today doing God knew what. So I didn't think it would be her coming to see me. When the door opened, I saw Sam and then Aurora. She looked like she was back to herself. The bruising was gone, and she was fuller in the face.

Sam and Aurora walked past Lindsey and Tiffany's assistants. Both TC and I knew the stress that we put on these wonderful ladies, so we got them help. Tiffany was combing through my calendar as Aurora and Sam stopped at TC's door.

Lindsey's desk was empty, meaning she was in the office with TC. If people looked at them, they would think that they were more than boss and employee. Lindsey didn't swing TC's way. At one time, I thought she and Tiffany were a thing.

"Tiffany, send me the calendar to the phone. I'll be right back." I went to the office door and barged in like I always did.

TC kissing the one woman he swore he wouldn't made me laugh internally. "Never thought I'd see this."

They both looked at me as I strolled across the room and sat on the couch. I watched them both walk over to the small seating area with me. They both tried to stop this happening by staying away from each other.

"Drake, is there something that I can help you with?" TC sat and guided Aurora beside him. Aurora crossed her legs and squirmed; she was hiding something. TC's hand went to the edge of the dress, just above her knee, and I smirked.

"I was wondering if you had heard back from your boss?" I leaned into the couch and rested my arms on its back. It was like he was on eggshells, waiting for the call.

"Not yet, but I'm sure I'll hear from him soon. What have you found out on your side? Didn't you say that you have ties to them?"

Aurora glanced between us; she either didn't know or she wanted more information about what we were saying. TC didn't move his gaze from me.

"Still working on that. My father is supposed to be setting up a meeting for me and him to discuss things. Once I know something, you will too." I sat still for a moment, watching them.

They deserved to have a long life after the bad shit that they had been through in the beginning. My father was trying to get his brother to stop his shit before something occurred where I had to finish Riccardo once and for all, putting my father where he belonged.

Taking a deep breath, I rose just as the knock came from the door, and Lindsey's face appeared.

"Mr. Churchhill, your lunch is here."

"Tell them to bring it in."

"You ordered me food, too?" I clapped my hands as the delivery guy walked in with the bags.

"No, asshole. This is my lunch with my wife. I'm sure you can make it back before I'm finished." TC stood, leading me to the door.

"What do you want me to do?" The smell of the food made my stomach growl.

"What have you heard from your uncle?"

"He sent me a threat this morning. My father is still trying to get him to stop this. If he doesn't, we may have to take him out of the equation." I held his gaze as he stared back at me.

"You would kill your family over me?"

"*You* are my family. When I marry Emi, we will be brothers. This man came to me after I was grown. He wanted nothing to do with me before now." I grabbed his shoulder and squeezed.

TC nodded and turned from me to go back to his wife. They looked good together, just like they always had. I remember watching them dance at his introduction party. My family was late getting there, which was partly my fault. I didn't want to meet the kid the Churchhills had taken under their wing.

I left the office and went back to Tiffany. She looked up and smiled at me. "Yes, Mr. DeLuca?"

"Field all my calls. I will be back in a few hours."

"Yes, sir." She went back to work as if I hadn't even stopped by her desk. Sometimes, I wondered why Tiffany had this job when she was much more intelligent than any other secretary. And could have been anything she wanted to be.

I had to figure out how to ask Emi to marry me without her figuring out what I was doing. I needed to go and see if old man Gabe, who made unique jewelry, had anything that screamed at me.

Chapter Twenty-Six

EMI

This morning, I had left Drake's house to meet up with my parents. Drake had told me that Aurora and TC were coming over for dinner tonight. TC hadn't been to Drake's since the wedding, so I wasn't sure why they were coming. Not only were the newly weds coming but my parents would be there as well, along with Drake's parents.

I sat outside with my parents while they argued over something meaningless as I ran through the reasons for this dinner. Drake normally never kept anything from me anymore.

"Emi, have you heard from your brother recently?" My mother's voice brought me into the present.

"No, but Drake has. Hence, dinner tonight," I answered her as I took a sip of my OJ.

"Those two have been thick as thieves since they met in college." My father chuckled, making my mother smile. I used to think I would never find something like this with a guy. But then Drake appeared in my life.

"What would you think about me dating Drake?" The grin on

my father's face faltered. But my mother's grew bigger, and she squealed.

"Oh, my Emi! Are you and Drake together?" Her hands came to my face, forcing my lips to pucker out.

I didn't appreciate that my father wasn't excited about me being with Drake. Why was he able to let him help run his company but didn't want him to date me? I pulled away from my mother and looked at my father.

"Daddy, is there something wrong with me dating Drake?"

My mother turned her attention to my father as he stared at me. Was there something I didn't know? That maybe the man that came up to me in the farmers' market was someone I shouldn't have met?

"There's nothing I would welcome more than our families merging." He smiled and finished the rest of his drink.

"Good because I've been living with him for a while now. I didn't think it would be a good idea to let you know since you would have told TC." I sat back and watched him. If TC had found out from someone other than Drake, we might have been in trouble.

But at this moment, I wanted to know if what I had just told my father would bring out that face that I saw when I asked about dating Drake. But he didn't budge. My father smiled and glanced away to the street. Like he didn't have a care in the world. From the side of his profile, he looked like the man who had come up to me.

"We need to get going. We need to talk with Gretchen. She did such an amazing job with TC and Aurora's cakes." My mother stood, and I followed her. I didn't mind Gretchen making the cakes. She was the best in town, but Drake hadn't even asked me to marry him yet.

"Mother, there's no point in going to see Gretchen right now. Drake hasn't even asked me anything yet. Drake needs us at the house in the next few hours." I linked my arm through hers and led her to the car.

My father followed behind us after he paid the check. He was hiding something from me, and by the end of the night, I was going to find out what it was.

We spent most of the day looking in shops and buying things that my mother thought would be good for the wedding that hadn't been thought of yet. I mean, if Drake asked me, would I say yes? Most definitely. But as much as he said that he loved me, there was still a doubt that it was true.

It was nice to shop with my mother. Lucky for us, the car was always close by to put the items in that we bought. I remembered when we would go shopping in my childhood, my father would carry most of my mother's items.

As we made our way down the sidewalk. Cars went past us, and a motorcycle engine brought my attention to a burger joint that I hadn't been to in years. The bright red Ducati was beautiful. It stopped at the curb and the rider sat there before dismounting the bike. He placed his helmet on the seat and entered the restaurant.

I shook my head and didn't think much more about the man and the bike. My thoughts were on the man who was waiting for me at home. I wanted to be wrapped in his arms, whether it was sex or just being in them in a hug. We made our way back to the car, our shopping spree over.

The car ride back to my home wasn't too quiet. My mother was talking non-stop about the potential of me marrying Drake.

Father was pretending to be as excited for her. She always got her way because he loved her.

We pulled up to the stairs behind TC's car, which Jake and Sam were standing next to. Benton came down to open my door. His smile made me feel like I was home. Everyone who worked here always wanted to stop and talk with me, which was fine because that meant I got to know them on a personal level.

Jake and Sam turned their attention to me just as the mahogany doors opened and my brother walked out. He didn't look over at us even though my mother called his name. TC never ignored her. Even though she wasn't his biological mother, she was the closest person to him.

I walked up to the doors and entered, looking for Drake to find out why TC would be leaving when we were about to have dinner. When I stepped into the foyer, I felt like I could breathe. This place gave me life. More than any place that I had ever been before.

My eyes landed on Drake, talking with Heath and one of his security personnel. I headed up to them and slipped my arm into the crook of Drake's. His gun pressed into my shoulder, reminding me that he was still worried about safety. That meant that he was still on the lookout for someone. Or something else was going on, because when I met his uncle in his office, he didn't like that I was there.

When he announced me as his fiancé, I didn't think much of it since he was talking with his uncle. But when he told me that he would be asking me to marry him, it solidified it in my mind. And it also made me wonder if he had ulterior motives.

Then again, I was in love with the idea of being Mrs. DeLuca and being in his arms for the rest of my life. Drake glanced down at me and smiled. He pulled his arm away from my grip and pulled me in close to him as he continued talking with his men.

Benton came in with my parents behind him. Drake looked over at them and all the bags on the floor. His lips brushed my ear when he whispered, "Did you get anything new to play with, *dolcezza?*"

"My parents were with me." I smacked him in the chest with the back of my hand, and he nodded to the two men in front of him before strolling over to my parents.

"Mr. and Mrs. Churchhill. Thank you for coming to my home. My chef is thrilled to be able to show off her talents." He and my father shook hands, and my mother brought him into a hug like always.

"We love that you finally invited us. Since it took our daughter living here to get an invitation." She giggled before she pulled away from him.

"Well, I didn't know if you would ever want to be in my house. Aurora is here, TC will be back before too long. Why don't we go to the sitting room? My parents are waiting for us, too." My father nodded, and more staff came out to grab the bags. Drake ushered me in front of my parents to lead them into the room.

I sat on one of the loveseats, and my parents took the other. Drake walked over to the bar and poured himself and my father a glass of bourbon. He handed the glass to my father and then sat beside me. "It's been a long time since everyone has been in the same room."

"Marlene, it's been a little bit since we've seen each other. How have you been?" my mother asked Drake's mother, smiling. They were good friends long before she was friends with Aurora's mom.

"Been doing great. I'm so glad that we were invited to the weekly dinner. And be able to make it," Drake's mother answered.

Drake placed an arm behind me and pulled me closer to him as he crossed his legs. I felt safe in his arms. My gaze went to

Aurora, who looked as though she was worried. I didn't like that TC wasn't here.

"Yeah, well, you should have come to ours. We would have loved to have you."

"We have been very busy. But you know, when your only son never invites you to things, you can only hope it will happen one day." Marlene laughed, making my mom giggle as well.

"This is true. Ever since TC moved out, it has been hard to get him to come see us."

"Yes, because we both know that Drake has always been a momma's boy." Marlene slapped her knee and laughed at the expression on Mr. DeLuca's face. "What? It's true."

Drake's booming laugh brought my attention back to him. His laughter lines made him that much more handsome. I always loved it when he laughed during our weekly dinners.

Two weeks before TC's wedding, we had our weekly dinner, and I was pulling some wine from the wine rack when I felt him behind me. I turned around and came face to face with him. My heart was racing as our eyes locked together. Drake's hand was above my head, just like in all those romance movies. When his eyes left mine to travel down my body, I just knew that he could hear my heart. His tongue whipped out and moistened his lips.

If I had wanted, I could have met his lips with mine. But I was too scared at the time to think that he would have anything to do with me. I was his best friend's little sister, and he wasn't going to ruin that with me. Besides, the women he was always dating were older and more beautiful than me.

"Be careful; you may just end up being someone's meal."

I had never been that wet before as he turned from me and took the bottles of wine into the dining room. That was when I knew that there wouldn't be any man who would measure up to the man who just walked away from me.

The rest of the dinner, I had to keep myself from staring at Drake. Even though I had caught him staring at me once or twice. The thought of those lips of his on mine made me squirm. It had been a long time since I had, and I knew that the man sitting across from me wouldn't be on the menu.

Benton let TC and Aurora in and came up to me as I stood in the foyer, waiting for Heath and James to come to talk to me. I pulled Aurora into a hug and then released her. My eyes searched for Jake and Sam. They were never far behind. If they weren't coming in, that meant TC wasn't staying long.

Aurora stepped back, and TC snuggled her into his side. He kissed her and then turned to me. I crossed my arms and smirked. "My parents are already here. Aurora, Benton can show you to the sitting room."

Benton came up to us and ushered Aurora to the sitting room. I watched TC stare after her until she was out of sight. He was fucking in love with the woman he swore he wouldn't ever fall for. You could see it written all over his face.

"You will keep them all safe if anything happens to me today. Right?"

"You know I will. I think you will be fine, though. You need to get back here so I can ask your sister to marry me." I chuckled at the lift of his brow. I had only mentioned marrying her once before, and that was at the hospital with Aurora.

"Have you even asked my father?" He crossed his arms as we stood in front of the stairs.

"No, but I feel that since we have been as close to family for years, he wouldn't say no."

TC nodded and sighed. I knew he was nervous about this meeting, but I was sure he would be fine. Hopefully, he would be able to connect to the man that he didn't know existed.

"You better wait for me. If I send our code word, that means I won't be coming back."

"Are you carrying?" I didn't like that he was telling me that he might have to use the code word. It made me start thinking that I had done the wrong thing.

"Yes, but I'm meeting him at the racetrack. I wouldn't put it past him to have a gunman up high." TC ran his hand down his face and opened his jacket. There sat the black Glock and his gold one.

"Have you ever met the man?" I was curious because he was under Marcus, and at one point, he had been Marcus's second-in-command.

"No, Marcus kept me away from him. Every time he met him, he had me doing something else."

I wondered if Marcus had known he had someone close to Jack? If that was why, he made sure to keep him away from him to use him later. TC grabbed hold of my shoulder, squeezing it. "I'm going to head out. I'll let you know when I'll be back."

"Stay safe, brother."

He nodded, and the corner of his lip ticked up in an almost smile. I had never seen that from him in years. Ever since I caught him stalking Aurora through her friends' social media. I nodded back to him and watched him walk out of my house.

Even though old man, Leo said he would be fine, I still thought he might not come back from this meeting. He was either going to accept that he was part of the LA mafia, or he was going to never come back to us.

Heath and James finally arrived just as the doors closed behind my best friend. I turned to the men who walked up to me. "Okay, guys. This is what is going to happen. Once Emi and Mr. and Mrs. Churchhill get here, the men on the posts need to ensure the gates are closed. TC will be letting me know when he is on his way back. I don't want anyone getting in who isn't invited. Do you understand me?"

They both nodded. James was always quiet. He had been with me for a very long time. I trusted him like I trusted TC. "Give me a run down of security. Anything happened over the past few days?"

"No, Sir. It's been quiet. We haven't seen nor heard from your uncle." I nodded, trying to figure out what he was doing and where he was. I hadn't heard from him or seen him since he told me I needed to kill my best friend.

I knew he was planning to kill them both. I was hoping that knowing I wasn't going to help him, he wouldn't try. But he had been quiet for too long, and that worried me even more. I was going to have to talk with my father about this at some point tonight.

From the corner of my eye, I watched as the doors reopened, and Emi came in first. Her parents and Benton were not that far behind her. I smiled internally. I had missed her. Fuck, I was becoming just like TC. What was up with these women making us act like morons?

Emi came up to me and slipped her arm into mine, leaning into my side. My gun pressed into my skin, reminded me that I was carrying it. The Glock had become second nature, and I no longer thought about it.

Benton carried tons of bags in and placed them in the foyer, and I smiled before whispering in Emi's ear, "Did you get anything new to play with, *dolcezza*?"

"My parents were with me." Emi scoffed and smacked me in my chest.

I stared around the room, my gaze landing on Aurora standing by the windows. She looked worried that TC wasn't here, and I didn't blame her. I was the only one who knew that he would be fine.

Tuning the conversation out, I went through my thoughts about my home security. All the windows were bulletproof. If anyone who wanted to hurt anyone in this house, they would have to send a rocket through it. The only person I was worried about storming this place was my uncle, and he didn't know where my house was.

"....Drake has always been a momma's boy." My gaze went to my father, and his face had me laughing. Technically, she was right, but I also knew that I wouldn't be the man I was today if not for my father. "What? It's true."

I nodded to her, and she sat back in her seat with a smile. She was one of the women in my life that I would kill for, and she knew that. Although, I was certain that my mother didn't know much about what my father and I did.

The woman beside me knew *everything*. I wasn't going to go behind her back like my father did with my mother. That was the only thing I didn't like about my father. He hadn't cheated on her. He knew if he did, I'd kill him.

I finished off my drink and went back to the bar to get

another. Part of me wished I was one of the men going with TC. My father grabbed the bourbon and poured himself another drink.

"You found out what the Churchhills are hiding. Didn't you, boy?" I glanced up and noticed that he wasn't looking at me but at the man and woman sitting on the loveseat beside the one Emi was in.

"What do you mean?" I stared at his profile, his right eye glancing over to me.

"I mean they are not the innocents that you think they are. You know that his father made a deal with your grandfather. They are more involved in the underground than you think they are." He finished the drink and poured another.

"I know that his dad and grandfather made a deal, you told me. But are you saying that Matt and Laura are in on this, too?"

"Why do you think your uncle wants Jack out of the picture? Why do you think he wants the heir out of the way? Do you think that when he gets those two out of the way he wouldn't come for Emi or them?" He pointed over to the woman I intended to ask to marry and then over to her mother and father.

"He won't dare touch them. If I marry her, they will be family," I growled at him.

"Ha. When you told him you wouldn't kill TC, you lost that protection."

"Do I need to worry about you, too? Are you going to kill your own son?" I snarled under my breath. I didn't like that he was threatening me.

"No, I got out of that life. My father made a deal with Jack. I won't go back on that deal." He sighed and then threw back his bourbon. "If you marry into the Churchhills, you may have a chance to protect them."

"You don't think TC could protect them?" I turned on him, "You think I wouldn't help him?"

"Drake, our family in Italy is a lot larger than us. The only reason they aren't coming over here is because of the issue with my sister-in-law. If that child isn't his, this family is yours. Which he knows."

Chapter Twenty-Eight

DRAKE

Before I could come back with anything, my phone rang. I had been fingering it ever since TC left.

"Hey, man. How'd things go?"

"I'm on my way back to your place. After dinner, we need to have a meeting with our fathers." I knew that this would be something he would want because he had just learned that he was the heir to the LA mafia. There was going to be hell to pay.

"Of course, man. You know I have your back. See you soon." My father tilted his head as I hung up the phone.

I walked to the middle of the room. "TC is on his way back. I'm pretty sure the food is ready."

Aurora turned her attention to me from the seat she had finally taken. Even though it had felt like a short time, it had really been hours since TC had left. I smiled when Benton came into the room.

"Sir, dinner is ready. Did you want to go ahead and start seating?"

"Yes, lead the way, Benton." My mother and the Churchhills stood and followed my butler, followed by my father.

Aurora and Emi came up to me and stood.

"Drake, I didn't ask this before, but is everything okay? Where was he going?" Emi crossed her arms over her chest and cocked her hip to the side.

"He was meeting with a man that he used to be associated with because of the shit that happened with Aurora. Once he is here and we have eaten, he wants to have a meeting with our fathers," I answered her.

"I want to be in there."

"You will have to ask your brother about that. Why don't we go to the dining room and sit? "

I knew Emi wouldn't leave this alone. She might just get her way about joining the meeting. She normally did when it came to TC; only part of me thought he might turn her down this time. I didn't know if he wanted her to know everything surrounding the family or that she could have been hurt at any point.

Aurora didn't say anything to me before she nodded and turned for the door. Emi finally turned too and walked with Aurora to the dining room. I was the last to leave the sitting room. If everything went well with TC and Jack, I figured we would be in a war with the Italian mafia.

My father and mother sat on one side, and then the Churchhills sat on the other side facing my parents. Emi sat down to my right at the head of the table. Aurora sat on the opposite side with the Churchhills at the end TC would sit at.

While everyone settled into their seats, I stood in front of the people I considered my family. The ones who gave my life meaning more. I smiled at them just as my best friend's steps sounded down the hall.

TC's hand clamped on my shoulder before he strolled down the left side of the table. He pulled Aurora into a brutal kiss before standing in front of his chair. I raised my glass to him and grinned.

He brought his up, too, and nodded. But what surprised me was the smirk on his face.

"Nice of you to finally join us, son." Mr. Churchhill spoke up as we sat down at the table.

"I had something that I had to take care of, and after dinner, the men need to have a meeting." He said it so matter of factly that I looked for people's reactions.

I turned my attention back to TC and stared at him. This was the man who was able to control a boardroom with just a look, and it did the same thing here at the dining room table.

"And why aren't Aurora and I invited to this meeting?" Emi leaned forward and turned to look at TC.

"Because it doesn't involve you or Aurora. Once we are finished, you can both come in and we will discuss things then." TC didn't bat an eye when Emi groaned and sat back with her arms crossed.

"How about we get some food in here? That way we get this meeting over with." I turned and nodded to Benton who left out of the room.

A few minutes later, a cart was pushed in and plates were placed in front of everyone. My chef had outdone herself yet again, and I knew it was because we had guests tonight. She hardly ever got to showcase her talents.

Just like that, everyone oohed and ahhed at the setup on their plates. Benton poured more drinks for everyone and then slipped out of the room. We all ate in silence. It felt nice that we were getting together to do this, because once we had this meeting, we would probably be at war.

After dinner, I led the men to my office. I'd had this room remodeled to make it soundproof. That way, none of my staff would know what was being said. I allowed the three men into the room and then shut the door, locking it for good measure. They sat around the coffee table. I took the empty one and turned my gaze to each one of them.

"So, TC, what did you find out from our friend?"

TC stood and ran his hand through his hair with a sigh. He placed his hands on his hips and turned. "Dad, I want you to tell me who Jack is."

Mr. Churchhill's face became ashen before he took a deep breath. He wrung his hands together before opening them palms out. "Jack is my older brother."

"And he's the reason you adopted me." The emotion he was trying to hold back almost made me think that he was about to cry. But that wasn't something I had seen from him.

"Yes, that, and we needed a direct male family member to take over the company. It has to stay in the family. Jack wasn't able to take the company since he had to run the more illegal side of our family. I took over the company. Your mom and sister don't know what goes on in Churchhill Logistics." Mr. Churchhill turned and glared at me. "Emi doesn't need to know any of this, do you understand? And neither does Aurora."

"We will get to them in a moment. But why didn't either of you tell me? Why did you keep me out of this?"

"I'm not sure whether Jack knew of you or not. Leo told me that you had gotten arrested. I had them move you to the children's home. We came to adopt you. Laura knew that you were my nephew; she didn't know that my brother was LA's most notorious crime boss. Emi thought you were just a regular kid. But I could see him in you, the younger him." I watched as he stood and walked up to TC.

That's when I really saw the resemblance between the two of

them. Fuck, that was the reason they were able to make people accept him as easily as they did. What I didn't understand was why Leo didn't tell Jack about TC.

He would have been taught about Jack's life, instead, he was able to change his life. Now Jack wanted his heir to take over. I stood and went over to them; they didn't move a muscle.

"So, what now?"

"Now you both have to make a decision. If you make the wrong one, this war with your uncle will get even worse," my father said from his seat.

"What do you mean?" I turned to him.

"I mean that your uncle doesn't know about the money-laundering. He thinks that this is just my way to keep my nose semi-clean." My old man sat back into the chair and sighed, "My father made this deal with Matt and Jack's father so we could combine the families. I never thought you would do this without me asking. I knew Emi was nine years younger than you. But people have married younger."

"You mean you want this to happen?" I was astonished by this information.

"Yes, we wanted to unify the three families. The Churchhills, us and the Emersons."

Both TC and I stared at our fathers. This was what they had wanted from the beginning. If Emi and I hadn't got together naturally, we would have been arranged, just like TC and Aurora. It was blowing my mind.

"We just didn't think that Laura would have a hard time conceiving.," Matt answered, bringing our attention back to him.

"How do you know Leo?" TC asked before I could.

"Leo has been in the Churchhill family for years. My brother was friends with him. You'd never know that he and Jack were the same age," Matt replied, running his hand over his face, "You see, Jack and Leo had always been tied at the hip. At one point, our father thought that they may have been a couple. When Jack took over the LA syndicate, Leo became Jack's eyes and ears. There was nothing that Leo didn't know that Jack wouldn't know shortly after. Other than you."

"What is going to happen now he knows I'm his son? You and he took over two different sides of the family business. How do I get to keep the company if I have to run a syndicate?"

"We will need to have another meeting with my brother. To find out what he wants to do." Matt walked over and sat back down in his seat, looking defeated.

"And my mother? Who was she to Jack?" My eyes went to Mr. Churchhill. I could only imagine what was going on inside of TC's head.

"Son, that would be something for you to ask Jack. I didn't know your mother. I didn't even know you existed until Leo called me." The way Mr. Churchhill answered that, I believed him. There were only so much that people tell their families.

TC nodded and sat down. I glanced around the room and leaned back. "So, why can't we allow Emi and Aurora to know what's going on?"

"If you allow them to know and they get kidnapped, they can say what is going on." In a way, I could see what he was talking about, but then I still thought that they wouldn't give up anything. I'd rather the girls be able to tell them and give them a fighting chance than hear about them being tortured for things they didn't know.

"I don't want to keep things from Aurora anymore. Even if I don't have your blessing, I will tell her anyway." I smirked at his answer. If there was one thing I knew best about TC, it was that he didn't take anything sitting down, and he always knew how much to push.

"Son, you will do more harm than good if you keep her in the

loop. This is why your mother and sister never knew about this."
Mr. Churchhill shook his head in disbelief.

"You really think Mother doesn't know? Then you are sadly mistaken. That woman knows more than you think." TC got up and walked to the door to my office. I knew that he was going to get Aurora and Emi. They had every right to know what kind of danger they were in.

I sat beside Aurora, waiting for one of them to come to get us. Aurora held my hand as we held our breath. Her engagement ring shone in the light beside her wedding band. I often wondered if TC would get her something different than the one he married her with.

As I flitted my gaze around the room, I didn't miss that I was starting to make changes to this house, and Drake hadn't said anything about it. My eyes landed on my mother and Mrs. DeLuca near the window, talking with each other. Part of me thought they knew something about what was going on.

When the door opened, I stood, bringing Aurora with me. My mother didn't move. TC walked in, his hair messed up, and scanned the room before his ice-blue eyes landed on us. From the way he looked at us, I knew that he was going against what Father had told him.

"Let's go." I knew he was holding something back.

We both nodded and moved forward. Aurora's hand slipped into his, and I turned to look back at my mother. She nodded to me, and I took TC's other hand. My heart hammered, and I could only think that Aurora's was too.

What were we going to learn? Was this something that we shouldn't know? Would this get us killed? I knew TC was in a gang before he came to live with us. But this seemed bigger.

We walked down the hall to Drake's office, even though TC had my hand I felt like I was in a dream. Whatever was going to happen in here was going to change my life one way or the other. I took a deep breath as TC opened the door I had been through multiple times. He held the door, allowing us in and the three men sitting in the room looked up.

My dad shook his head. Mr. DeLuca looked indifferent. Drake had the biggest smile on his face and motioned me to come to him. I half expected him to make me sit on his lap. He stood and gave me his chair, and Aurora sat in the other empty one.

TC stood next to Drake and placed his hands behind his back. Once we were all settled, TC started to tell us why we were here and what he had done before dinner. I went from astonished to upset that I had been kept in the dark about my family's affairs. Did my mom know? She had never shown me otherwise, other than the time she and my father were talking about adopting a brother. When I was a kid, I didn't think that much into it, but now it made sense.

I was walking past the family room after sneaking into the pantry for a late-night snack, when I heard my parents talking. Moving closer and being careful that I didn't bring attention to myself, I snuck up to the door. Their voices made my heart race at the mention of adopting a son. He was older than me and it took every-thing in me to keep my eight-year-old self quiet so that I could continue to listen to them.

My fingers tightened on the small table that held my mother's favorite vase. I couldn't believe this was happening. They had always thought about having another child, but for some reason, I never got a sibling. Now I would have a brother, he was older than me! He would be able to take me places, and I'd be the coolest girl in my school.

"Matt, how do you know he will be okay in this life? After all that he has been through?" The soft clink of glass hitting a table told me my father was drinking brandy tonight.

"I'm not sure. But I will be pulling Jake to be his bodyguard. Laura, I have to do something. If there was a way to pull him out of that life and give him a better one, wouldn't that be something to be proud of?"

"I understand where you are coming from, but do you really think this boy is his? You don't think that this man is lying to you to take this kid?"

"When you look at this picture, do you think that man is lying to me?" I had never heard my father yell at my mother.

"Okay. I trust you, Matt." My mother sighed, and I heard her heels getting closer to the door.

I scampered up the stairs as quickly as my little legs would take me. I slipped through my cracked door and into my bed. I stared up at my ceiling and smiled. I was already making plans for what we would do together.

That night, I was so excited that I was going to have a brother. I barely slept, tossing and turning. But it would be three weeks before we would even go and get him.

After TC stopped talking, everything was quiet as we took in all the information. The man I grew up with as my brother was my blood relation. Only, he was my cousin. Now, because he was the only male heir in our family, he would have to decide whether to continue with the company alone or take on both it and the syndicate.

I already knew that Drake's family had ties to the Italian mob.

But now, because Drake didn't want to kill my brother, he was involved in the war as well. But he was on our side. Which also put mine and Aurora's life in even more danger.

"So, is that why the man at the farmers' market didn't hurt me?" I asked everyone around me.

"What do you..." my father started before Drake interrupted him. I forgot that I hadn't told my parents about the chance meeting with Jack.

"Yes. He knew you were family and wouldn't have hurt you. I'm just glad he is the person he is now. That means if TC takes over, we have plenty of men to take on my uncle."

Drake glanced over at his father and then moved back to me before going on to look at TC, who stood there with his eyes closed and his arms around his chest. When he opened his eyes, they went to Aurora, and she nodded to him. He took a deep breath. "I'll be taking over Jack's side and keeping the company. I have the best COO I could ever ask for, so there's no reason why I can't take over both."

"You know I have your back, man. I'll be your ride or die." Drake turned to my brother, clapping him on the shoulder, and he nodded with a grin.

"Thank you. Because this is going to be like nothing we have ever taken on." TC playfully punched him in the arm. His smirk made me happy. They really did act like brothers in the rare times that TC let his guard down. I often wondered what he would have been like if my parents had found him earlier.

He was seventeen when he came to live with us. Would TC have been more playful? Been more of a kid without worrying about where he would get his next meal? I would never know, but I could see it every once in a while.

"That sounds like a challenge." He chuckled. I shook my head, my hand over my face, trying to keep my smile from him. I didn't need to encourage him because that would make it worse.

As much as he was a badass, he was a goofy guy sometimes, and that was what I loved about him. Drake walked up to me. He got down on a knee and took my hands. "Emi, I told you when our relationship started that I would always be honest with you. That is why TC brought you and Aurora in here. If you are not able to handle this, I won't make you stay and endure this."

I stared into his dark brown eyes. Those ever-knowing eyes. The ones that had seen more than I ever had. I nodded. "I will be by your side for as long as you will let me."

"That's my girl. You will always be mine, and like I told you before, I'm going to make you mine in every shape and form." Drake pulled my hand to his lips and kissed each knuckle before he placed a soft kiss on my lips.

I couldn't help the shiver that raced down my body as he stared at me. I squirmed a little in the seat, wishing that he would throw me over his shoulder and carry me out of the room.

Drake stood and leaned into the chair, his lips brushing against the shell of my ear, "I can see it in your eyes, but you are going to have to wait until our guests leave."

I nodded. Someone cleared their throat behind Drake, and a giggle beside me had me smiling. Drake stood to his full height and smiled at me with a wink. My heart was racing, and my panties were soaking, making me worry I was getting the seat below me wet as well.

"Now that you two have decided to come up for air, we have things to talk about. If Aurora and Emi are going to know what's going on with our lives, they need to be told about everything. You two can leave if you don't want to be involved in us letting Aurora and Emi know." TC looked between our father and Mr. DeLuca, "Since neither of you has moved, I'm going to assume you both are fine with them knowing. Now, start talking. I want to be up to speed with the past of this family."

We spent the rest of the afternoon in Drake's office. Discovering what my grandfather was really like and who my uncle was proved to be a little scary. What really scared me was when TC told me what he had done before he came to us. The thought of him having killed someone because he was told to brought back thoughts of what would have happened if he'd been adopted earlier.

After everyone left, I stood underneath the shower and allowed the water to pour over me. As much as the information scared me, it made me feel lighter that both Drake and TC trusted me with this. The door to the bathroom opened, and I heard Drake's footsteps on the tile floor. The glass door opened, and the cool air flowed around me.

I turned into his wall of muscle. He pushed me against the cool tile wall, causing goosebumps to rise across my skin. His fingers went under my chin, and his other arm rested above my head, the water dripping off his face onto mine.

"Emi, I will die before I let anything happen to you. Do you understand that? And I will make sure everyone in this world knows you are mine."

Chapter Thirty

DRAKE

I didn't get to ask Emi to marry me in front of our families. Besides I thought going to Mr. Churchhill and asking for her hand in marriage was a better idea. Even though she was supposed to be mine anyway. I didn't think that they thought through Mrs. Churchhill having issues conceiving when they made that decision.

Yet here I was walking up to the Churchhills' home. We would all be meeting here in about an hour. I arrived a little early to talk with Emi's dad. Emi was with her mother and Aurora.

Emi hadn't wanted to go at first. She had been very horny the past few weeks, and I was thinking about giving her everything that she ever wanted. But I needed to see her father before anyone else got here.

I knocked on the door, and the Churchhills' butler let me inside. He took my coat, and I headed down the hall to Mr. Churchhill's office. My heart was racing with the thought of him telling me that he didn't want me to marry her now. And yet, that wouldn't stop me from marrying her. I was doing this because TC said that it would make me look better.

His door was cracked open, and I knocked on it before entering the room. Mr. Churchhill was sitting at his desk, looking over some paperwork. He glanced up as I strolled closer.

"Drake, you're early. TC said that we weren't meeting for another hour." Mr. Churchhill put away the paperwork and leaned back in his chair, steepling his fingers while he stared at me.

"I know, sir, but I needed to speak with you alone. About Emi." I took a seat in the chair in front of him.

"What about my daughter?" His eyebrow lifted as he tilted his head.

I reached into my pocket, pulled out the box with Emi's engagement ring in it, and pushed it to her father. He snatched it off the desk and opened it.

"I want to ask you for Emerald's hand in marriage. You and my father had already wanted to join our families." I could tell that he was giving it some thought. He couldn't say that I didn't get her the ring that she deserved. "I will marry her with or without your blessing. She's mine and has been since you two decided to join our families."

"It's a nice ring. She will be happy with it. You can marry her as long as TC is okay with it." Mr. Churchhill pushed the box to me. Pocketing it, I grinned at him.

"Well, I guess we will find out when he gets here. My father is on his way as well." I sat back in the chair and stared back at my soon-to-be father-in-law. TC had already told me that he didn't mind me marrying Emi.

The door opened, and in came TC with my father. They must have gotten here around the same time. My father was chuckling at something TC must have said, but he hadn't been in a smiling mood for years. Mr. Churchhill stood, and we both joined him in the sitting room.

"Jack hasn't been here since before I married Laura. He is also strongly opposed to women being involved in men's business. So the girls will be out of this meeting and any future meetings with my brother." Mr. Churchhill looked between me and TC before he sat down. "He will be here in a few minutes."

"Dad, I don't care what this man says about Emi and Aurora. I will, however, allow it this time, and he will be told that they will be in future meetings." TC was authoritative. He always was when he wanted to get his point across.

"TC..."

"Ha, seems like he's a chip off the old block." We all turned to see the man I had been trailing these last few months. And then Leo came in behind him. "Matt, it has been a long time. You have done a great job with my son."

Matt went up to Jack and hugged him. Seeing them together, you could tell that they shared many similarities, but there were plenty of things that made them different. TC sat on the smaller couch with me. The way he looked at Jack made me wonder if he didn't like being in the same room as his biological father.

"TC does have some qualities that favor you. But I did get to make sure that he was able to lead a different path until now," Mr. Churchhill answered as he broke the embrace.

Matt definitely looked more like the father. Jack looked out of place in the house. Leo didn't look like he belonged here, either. Matt led them both to where the bigger couch sat and moved over to his original seat.

"DeLuca Sr., it's been a long time. Your boy looks just like you." Jack turned his sharp gaze to me before he continued, "So, did you find out anything while you were stalking me?"

TC glanced over at me. I had meant to discuss with him what my uncle had me doing at the beginning. He wasn't very impressed by the statement Jack had said out loud. I stared him in the eye and shrugged.

"TC, Drake was on an assignment from his uncle before he knew you were the heir to Jack's syndicate. My brother was trying to get him to take over the leadership of the Italian mafia," my father interjected before TC could say anything to me.

Yes, I had kept that away from him. Because I didn't know how much he knew about the inner workings of the deal his grandfather and mine had made. Fuck, I didn't know Mr. Churchhill was in on this too. Which made me wonder why he didn't say anything to TC.

"So Riccardo is here in my city? Hiding behind his family like always. No wonder the child in his home isn't his. Too worried about what I'm doing here in LA." Jack chuckled and glared over at me. "That was why you were tailing me? Doing your pussy of an uncle's bidding?"

"Yes, I was. But I told him that I wasn't going to off the one man I claimed as a brother. He has since disowned me. He does have a man in your outfit, which was how I was able to find you so quickly." I sat back, unbothered by his glare.

"Really? Do you know who he is?" Jack cocked an eyebrow at me as he continued to make it seem that it was just the two of us in the room.

"No, Riccardo didn't say. We did find a man named Harvey from your group," I divulged. If I was going to be honest, I needed to be honest about everything.

"Hmm," Jack looked over to Leo and then nodded to him.

Leo got up and left the room, bringing his cell to his ear as he went. TC turned back to the man that was his biological father and stared at him. "You knew where I was the whole time, didn't you? Leo was always around when I was in the gang."

"I didn't know about you until your mother died. At that time, you had run away. I had my men looking for you, but LA is a big city. When Leo found you, I told him to keep an eye on you. Marcus being what he was, I didn't want you to be killed, but you inherited my love of torture." The way Jack's eyes crinkled when he smiled threw me off. "After you did what you did, I'd have my men come clean it up. You were great."

"I did it to stay alive while you led a pampered life. You could have gotten me out of that life, but you didn't," TC snarled at him. I didn't think something like that would have happened. I mean, I knew it was a problem, but I wasn't going to put myself in this until TC asked me to.

"Yes, I couldn't have brought you into my house. It would have put a target on your back. I left you where you were because it kept you safer than being with me. That was why I left your mother. To protect you both. I sent her money to keep you both fed. When she started dating that underling, she signed her death warrant. The underling happened to be the man you killed." Jack's eyes turned back to me. "You see, he was another man your uncle was turning against me. He offered him money to kill your mother and you. But when you ran, and no one could find you, he told Riccardo he had taken you both out under my instruction. He was then killed because he was no longer useful since he wouldn't give anything else to your uncle."

"He was a double agent?"

"For a long time. Because to underlings, all you have to do is pay them double the amount they are getting from the other person, and they will roll over like the submissive dogs they are." I glanced over at TC and realized that he was looking at me.

"I didn't know he was a double agent. I've been more in the dark than I thought. I'm here to take my uncle out."

"There is no way I can trust a man that I just met." TC turned from me and stared back at his father. "If you want me to take over, you will step aside now and announce to your men that I'm the man in charge. Drake will be my second-in-command. They will swear loyalty to me and Drake. If they don't, they will be shot. They will then help us get rid of Drake's uncle."

Fuck, I couldn't even say that I was surprised by what TC had said to Jack. The way they stared at each other, Jack trying to figure TC out, and then TC asserting his will over a man who had killed more people than any of us put together.

The silence in the room was so thick I was sure that I was going to suffocate if it continued. Matt and my father sat there, waiting, as if they didn't know what to do at this point. Hell, I didn't either.

"Fine. But Leo will be your third until things settle down. At that time, he will do anything to help you. I can see that you want nothing to do with me, which I understand. When you have a child, you will know why I did what I did." After Jack answered him, the room came back to life.

"Sir, I think that when we announce this to the men. We will be able to find who has been in the fold." Leo's voice brought our attention to him in the doorway.

"Good because when I find him. He will be the last person to know what I can do." The way Jack's eyes lit up unnerved me, and I wasn't a pussy with torture. But what I saw in his eyes I had only seen once before—TC's.

Fuck my life.

Chapter Thirty-One

EMI

I sat in the kitchen of my childhood home with my mother and Aurora. The men were in my father's office with two other men. One of the visiting men I had met at the farmers' market.

My mother didn't like that the other two were here. Now she was in the kitchen making God only knew what. She did this when she was upset with my dad or if TC did something that made her mad like when he got caught doing drugs on a woman's stomach. When Mom got that picture from Aurora, at first, she cried in her room, and then she got mad.

That was when the whole house had smelled like a bakery. When she told my father, they decided to start the arrangement between TC and Aurora. I had seen what TC had thought of Aurora, but she didn't let him forget what he did to her.

Hell, I wouldn't have let him forget it either, but I could see what it did to him. It made him hard and cold. TC didn't date anyone. He had flings to take his mind off the one person that he had thought he wanted.

As much as we changed TC, he changed us too. It was something I didn't realize at first, but now I could see that our lives would never have been what they were today if he hadn't come into our home. I didn't want to know what my world would be like without him. He was always there when I was scared.

"Does anyone know who those two men are?" Aurora glanced between me and my mother.

"One of them is Matt's brother. We haven't seen him in years." my mother answered from the counter.

With each word, she sliced the apples a little more aggressively. She definitely didn't like my uncle. Other than seeing him at the farmers' market, I hadn't ever seen him before, much less knew that he existed.

"Why is this man here? Is he really TC's biological father?" Aurora stared at my mom's back as she continued to slice the fruit.

"According to Matt, yes. He would have kept it from me if he could have. TC looked too much like Matt to say he wasn't family." My mom slammed her hands onto the counter before she turned to us with a sigh. "When Matt talked to me about adopting TC, he said a man from his past told him that the boy needed to be with his family. I didn't believe him until I saw his picture. There was no denying he was his family."

"What picture did he show you?" I was curious.

"It was the jail who took the picture. It wasn't a very flattering one. He still had blood on his face, and he looked like he was older than he was. His eyes bore into mine in this picture; the coldness." The way my mom didn't look at us told me that she was mourning the child TC could have been.

Aurora stood and went over to my mom. She pulled her into a hug. I had never seen my mother like this. The way she melted into Aurora's arms was eye-opening. Aurora was the first to break away. "Mrs. Churchhill, even though you didn't have him until he was a teenager, almost an adult, you made him who he is today. I don't think a braver woman could have done what you did."

"Even if I wanted to have that title. You are braver than I could ever be by going through with the marriage. You changed him by being the woman that he needed to ground him." My mother placed a hand on Aurora's face and smiled.

"Well, we can only hope this new part of our lives doesn't make my job even harder. Since we will be growing our family in a few months." I glanced down at her hand before my mother did.

"Are you pregnant?" I stood from my seat and went over to them.

"Yes, I took a test this morning. I was hoping we would have a lot more time with each other, but it looks like we will be raising a little one." Aurora smiled, but I noticed that she was a little sad that they wouldn't have the time to make up for what they lost.

"This is so exciting! You are going to have to get a bigger place! I want hundreds of grandchildren." My mom was grinning from ear to ear with her hands on Aurora's shoulders.

"Well, I'm glad I'm not the first to start the next generation of Churchhills." I giggled, and my mom pulled me to her.

"You will be next." Aurora smiled and pulled me into a hug.

I couldn't think about starting a family now. Drake had told me plenty of times that he was going to marry me. He had yet to ask me, not that I thought he wouldn't. "Drake hasn't asked me to marry him yet."

"The way that man looks at you. He will be asking you. And soon." Aurora chuckled.

"Maybe." I laughed with her.

Aurora was already glowing, even if she wasn't showing yet. I wondered what TC thought of being a father. Would he be like his biological one, or would he be like mine? Only time would tell, but I believed that he would be more like mine.

The kitchen door opened, and my father came in, along with Mr. DeLuca. TC and Drake came in next, followed by my uncle and the other one who was with him. Both my mom and I stood in front of Aurora. I knew the four men in front of us would protect them. But it didn't stop me from trying to protect my little niece or nephew.

Drake came up to me, and TC took my place, wrapping his hand around Aurora's waist. My uncle looked between me and Aurora before smiling. He stopped at the other edge of the bar, keeping his distance from his son and his wife.

"She's very pretty. I guess the deal worked out for all three families, huh, Matt?" I didn't like the look that he gave us. It was like we were just something to be stared at and nothing more.

"Jack, I want you to know the women will be in the meetings. This is my wife Aurora, and you have already met Emi. Since Drake and I will be taking over both the company and the syndicate, they will be in every meeting. If any man under our command makes an attempt on their lives, we will make sure that they are no longer on this earth." I glanced over to Drake and then at TC. They both had stoic expressions, but the evil in their eyes made me believe their promise.

"Of course. The men will be at your command. They have been waiting for this day since you were born." He moved over to my dad and pulled him into a hug. "You did good with him. He is going to make us both proud."

"He has already made me proud, brother." He nodded and turned to the man with him, motioning him to follow. If the man had been younger, I would have thought he was his bodyguard, but he looked as if he was the same age as my father.

The air became lighter once they had left. Drake pulled me in close to his side. Being between them both, I felt safe. With them in charge, whoever else was born into this family would not be touched, that was for sure.

"Well, that was fun." Drake was the first to speak.

TC rolled his eyes and pulled Aurora over to the window seat;

Drake and I watching them. I was pleased that I wouldn't be kept in the dark.

"Did Aurora tell you the good news?" Drake whispered in my ear. I glanced up at him, and I didn't miss the excitement in his eyes.

"Yes." I giggled when he reached down and squeezed my ass.

"I think we are next. What do you think?" I held his stare, my mouth hanging open while my body flushed.

Drake knelt down while he held my hand. I couldn't help but stare at him as he smiled up at me.

"Emerald Marie Churchhill, you would make me the happiest man alive if you would be by my side forever. Will you marry me?" He pulled out a black velvet box, and in it was a rose gold princess cut dark blue almost black diamond with smaller diamonds around it. It had other diamonds around the curved part of it much like a crown sitting on a head.

"Drake... It's gorgeous." I was in awe of the ring.

"And your answer?" He chuckled while he continued to kneel in front of me.

"Yes, Absolutely yes." I felt the first few tears trail down my cheeks as I held out my left hand.

Drake stood and slipped the ring onto my finger. When the light hit it, the ring was more blue than black. This was the most gorgeous thing I had ever laid eyes on. After staring at it, I brought my gaze up to Drake's dark eyes and jumped into his strong arms.

His lips bruised mine in front of our families. I had to use every ounce of my will to keep myself from moaning from the kiss. Drake broke our kiss and pressed his forehead against mine. "I need you to be with me. I can't go through this life without you."

"I don't want to be without you either."

"God damn. Please get a room, and not this one." My eyes snapped over to TC as Drake allowed my body to slide down his.

"Don't worry, TC, I plan to." Drake's voice was husky, and

with the bulge in his pants, I knew that I wouldn't be sleeping much tonight once we got home.

I couldn't believe Drake would say something like that with our parents in the same room. But I was an adult, and they couldn't think that I was being abstinent. They used to be my age, so I wasn't embarrassed by his choice of words.

"I didn't need to know that," TC groaned as his hand ran through Aurora's hair. Her eyes fluttering closed each time that his fingers reached her scalp.

My parents left the room, not before congratulating us on the engagement. Mr. Deluca nodded and departed behind them, leaving only the four of us.

"Looks like you need to get one as well. I think the pregnancy hormones are kicking in." Drake chuckled at the expression on TC's face.

TC stood from his seat and left Aurora on the chair. He came up to Drake and clapped him on the shoulder before pulling him into an embrace. TC released him and came up to me. He ran his thumb over my cheek and hugged me tightly.

"If this asshole ever hurts you, make sure you tell your big brother."

Chapter Thirty-Two

DRAKE

sking Emi to marry me was probably the scariest thing I had ever done. She could have said no in front of everyone. Was the kitchen of her childhood home the place I wanted to propose? No, but it was the best I could do as they were all here.

It had been a week since I asked her to be mine. Now, I was riding in an armored SUV with TC, making our way to meet with the men we now commanded. Jack said that the men would follow TC because he was the heir, but I didn't know if they would be okay with me being at his side.

I was sure that they knew I had familial ties to the Italian mafia because it was my grandfather who made the deal with TC's. So, to say I wasn't nervous going into this foxhole would be a lie.

"When we get here, Jack is going to introduce us both. Today we take over. Are you okay with that?" TC asked me while he stared straight ahead.

"Of course, man. You know I got your back," I told him, waiting for him to relax.

He was just as nervous as I was, but to those who didn't know

him, it wasn't clear. TC was in business mode, and he wouldn't come out of it until he knew that he had their undivided loyalty. There was no way he wasn't going to get it.

"I haven't told Aurora yet, but I'm sponsoring a superbike racer. We will meet him today, too."

"After this meeting?" I turned to him, and he shook his head.

"No, he is one of the men in our ranks. He is one of Jack's best hitmen. When I went to the track to meet Jack, he was qualifying. He's good."

"Okay. I can get behind this. What made you want to get into racing?" I was curious about his decision.

"Well, I figured that if I'm sponsoring him and we need to pay him to take someone out, then it wouldn't look like anything." TC shrugged and continued to stare ahead.

I mean, he wasn't wrong. This was a good way to make sure that what we sent him looked legit. And if he made a name for himself on the track with our brand, it would bring more business to the company.

Even though TC grew up on the streets, he was a fucking mastermind with numbers and people. It didn't take me long to realize it when I first met him. He had only been with the Churchhills for a year when I met him. TC still had a little of that feral look in his eyes.

"What's this kid's name? The one we are sponsoring?" The men up front driving didn't even look at us as we talked.

"Riker. Riker Kidwell. The next time he practices, I'll take you with me and let you watch. He's fucking good."

"Young kid. Tall, built like a brick house?" TC nodded and smirked at me. "Dude you know the famous racers are small right? There's no way he will be able to make a name for you."

"You'll have to see him in action. I thought the same thing, but he was racing when I pulled up. When he came back in, I didn't believe that it was his time on the jumbotron."

"Sirs, we are here," the man in the passenger seat said before getting out and opening TC's door. I opened my own. I didn't need anyone to open the door for me.

Now that TC was taking over from Jack, he had an even bigger target on his head. We walked into a rundown warehouse, and as we turned the corner, we heard angry male voices. Not a good sign.

When we entered the room, everyone went quiet. Jack was in a chair on an elevated stage. Leo stood beside him, watching as we walked through the crowd. The men gave way to us as we made our way to Jack. Though I didn't miss some of them growling at us.

We climbed the stairs and headed to Jack, who stood and shook TC's hand and then mine. Jack turned from us and looked over the crowd. They all continued to be quiet. "Gentlemen, tonight will be your last night under my reign. From this point forward, TC and Drake will be taking over. I expect you to show them just as much loyalty as you have me over the years."

"Why should we follow an Italian?" one man shouted.

I knew they would have an issue with me being part of the commanding force. TC pushed forward and pulled his gun from his holster. He aimed it at the man, and those around him stepped away from him.

"Do you have an issue with the man standing beside me?"

"What if I do? You are a rich pussy with a gun. You don't have the balls to shoot me."

TC squeezed the trigger, catching the man in the left shoulder. He went down and screamed. TC brandished the weapon, and I was surprised when all of them kneeled in front of us. "If you think that because I'm the CEO of Churchhill Logistics I can't instill fear into you. You apparently didn't realize that I grew up in one of the gangs in the city, torturing people for the person I worked for. Does anyone have an issue with Drake being here? Because if they do, they will not be walking out of here."

Jack's laughter caused my attention to leave TC and turn back to him. Leo stood beside him with his arms crossed and a smirk on his face. They were both impressed with how TC was handling the situation.

I just hoped that being in command of this syndicate wouldn't make him go back into the shadows he had risen from. If I needed to, I would remind him that he was more than the street kid with blood on his face in a mugshot. Even more, now that he was going to have a family with Aurora.

"Now that we have established I am the don. I want to know what we know about the Italian boss who is here in LA."

TC could have easily asked me that question. He was trying to find out what these men knew. They each looked at the other before standing. One stepped forward and held his position until TC stared at him.

"Yes? Do you have information for me?" TC ground out to the blond man below him.

"I've heard from my captains that he is in a hotel close to the airport. I expect that he is trying to make a quick getaway once he is finished with his mission."

"I don't think that is the correct information." I glanced to the back and saw Riker. He was tall and broad-shouldered.

"And what is the correct information, Riker?"

"I've been following him. He's in a fancy schmancy hotel waiting. His underboss has been in and out, but he hasn't. If I had to guess, I think he is bringing in more people from his home country." Riker pressed forward and up to the stage.

"TC, I think that this is the real reason. My uncle isn't someone to fight fairly. I wouldn't put it past him to be calling more people over." I knew that mentioning my ties to him would make them uneasy.

They would get used to it. They would have to.

"Okay, Riker, take yourself and three others and keep an eye on him. Do not let him out of your sight. If you see anything, you call me."

Riker nodded and then left through the crowd with three men. The man who first answered seemed to have become nervous. His eyes were wide as he looked up at TC. I could only imagine the stare that he was giving the man who hadn't given the correct information.

"What is your name?" TC asked as he cocked his head to the left.

"Tyler."

"Tyler, did you think that giving me information like this would get you in my good graces?"

"I didn't mean to give that. The last time I saw him, he was in that hotel. I promise." His voice increased an octave with his distress.

TC jumped in front of him and put the muzzle of the Glock to the man's temple. Tyler froze in place. "If you provide incorrect information again, you will not leave my presence alive, do you hear me?"

"Yes, sir."

"Good. The same goes for any of you who decide to give me the wrong information intentionally. If I find anyone who is unloyal to this syndicate, that person will find themselves in an unmarked grave or a watery one." The coldness in his voice gave me goosebumps. Fuck, when he wanted to be evil, he most definitely could. "Now, get out there and find this fucking man."

TC and I went back to the SUV. Ted sat up front with Isacc. They had both pledged their loyalty to both us. Everyone in the warehouse did, some were more willing than others. I had doubts about some of them, but we would weed them out a little later. We had a lot going on and would until my uncle conceded or we killed him.

"So, what now, boss?" I asked as I pulled out my phone.

"We wait to see what Riker finds out. When he comes to us, this war will start. We need to make sure that Aurora and Emi are protected." TC took out his phone and began texting someone.

"Yes, we will need to make sure they have a least a few more guards." I figured he would be messaging Aurora, letting her know that he was leaving the meeting. It had taken longer to deal with as there were so many men in the syndicate. Most of the men were upper ranks , some were even hitmen like Riker.

For someone so young, I didn't think that he was as skilled. But I had learned from the other hitmen when we had our first meeting that he was one of the best. And I couldn't deny that he was big enough for it. Hell, when he stepped forward, he towered over most of the men.

I still had my doubts about him being able to race, but hell, if TC wanted to put some money into the sport so be it. It wasn't like he was going to be losing anything. He had the right mindset in paying him without it looking suspicious.

"Yes, it may take Riker a few days to get the information that we need. We will need to make sure we are always watching."

Chapter Thirty-Three

DRAKE

It had been two months since we had taken over the LA syndicate. My uncle had been keeping a low profile, jumping to different hotels to keep us on our toes. Riker had been stalking him for that time when he wasn't on his bike.

TC was right; he was damn good for his size. The way he let the bike practically lie on the ground as he rode it. I had never seen another racer get as low as he did. If we could get him into some big races, we just might be able to win.

I walked into the newly renovated warehouse. It was where we met with the high-ranked officers. We had weekly meetings with them to make sure everyone was doing as told, and then we would have a monthly meeting with all the men. When we started, most of the men didn't really like being here because Jack didn't meet with them at the end of his tenure.

The first floor held the monthly meetings, but the second floor had a boardroom where we used to meet with the territory officers. We also had a basement that we used for torture. Which allowed both TC's and my darker side out. It had been a few days since we last had the pleasure of releasing our dark side.

Tonight, it was just TC and me with the ranked officers. They had started to believe in us once we started taking down some of my uncle's forces. He did as I thought he would and had brought more of the family over from Italy.

"About time you got here. My sister keeping you away from your duties?" TC didn't glance up from the map that he was staring at. He had been working day and night, trying to make sure that my uncle didn't hurt his growing family.

Sometimes, I thought the man sitting beside me was a vampire, it seemed like he never slept. There were times when I would make him go home, but that was harder than finding my uncle. But once we eliminated the threat, he would be able to step back.

I pulled out the chair at the mahogany table and looked at the map. He had been expanding things on the illegal side, making it more legal. Or as legal as you could get it. There would never be anyway to make the syndicate completely legal.

TC was pissed that there was human trafficking and shut that shit down real quick. If the women and men wanted to be street workers, that was their choice. If they had been bought and made to do it, it didn't bode so well for their pimps. Some of them were now on missing flyers around the city.

"What land do you want to find and fix now?"

"I was thinking about taking that old warehouse that my father gave me and fixing it up. Is there anything that you need this building for?" TC answered, tapping his finger on the warehouse on the map. It would need some money put into it, but it wasn't like he didn't have it.

"Are you finally going to let me do something with it? I was thinking that I could use it to move some more of the laundering into it. Maybe we can build bikes?" Superbike racing had become one of his hobbies, and I made sure to mention it at least every day.

"I'm sure I could find some people to build them. Make our own brand of bike and then race it." He sat back in his chair, and I didn't miss the bags under his eyes. I shook my head, if he didn't get some sleep, he would be in the hospital, and that wasn't a good place for him to be. Especially not with my uncle trying to off him.

"We wouldn't be able to race them until we got the release form from the AMA. But it is something to see if we can. Then have Riker on it, showing people what it could do."

"That's not what we are here for, though. Drake, I need to know what you want to do when we kill your uncle, or he concedes?" TC looked me straight in the eyes as he waited for my answer.

I knew that he wanted to find out if I was going to take over the Italian syndicate. I had been thinking about it, but I didn't think I would be able to leave my brother to deal with this alone. And I for damn sure knew that Emi wouldn't leave her family.

"If there was a way to take over from here, I would to make sure all of you would be safe. But I can't leave. I won't leave," I told him, and it was the truth.

I hadn't been brought up in that life to die for something like that. I was family with the man who was sitting beside me, and I wasn't going to leave him.

TC nodded as the officers, who controlled their respective territories, walked into the room. This room had been constructed as a carbon copy of the boardroom at the office; only it had a lot more liquor and some other things. The lighting made it more inviting than the rest of the warehouse, but then again, we needed people to think that this was a business. TC and I had an office each on either side of the room. They looked identical to the ones at Churchhill Logistics, minus the view of the city.

The three men who walked in had served Jack for a long time and had continued to serve us when we took over. One of the men was grey-haired and in pretty good shape. The second was bald and could use less food and more gym time. The last one was younger but still older than TC and me. Like most of the officers in this business, he inherited his position, but he was damn good.

"Don, Drake. What do we owe the pleasure of this meeting tonight?" Craig asked as he plopped himself into the chair. Brandon and Terry sat on either side of him. The only one missing was Stan.

He had been absent at multiple meetings this month, and I wasn't one to miss that. TC wasn't either. Since we had been in this part of our new life, we had learned that there were five regions under our control.

With Stan missing and there being an opening for the fifth region, we were busier than we had ever been. Fucking Leo said he was retiring and letting us deal with it, which was why we had an opening. I hadn't seen anyone who was going to be better at taking over that spot, but we were going to have to decide and soon.

We had a lower-level soldier in charge at the moment, but we needed to find someone able to get these fucking assholes to do their jobs. Part of me wanted to murder Leo for just letting his post go. Yet the other part understood where he was coming from.

I still hadn't asked TC how he knew Leo and his connection to Jack before now. Jake had told me that Leo was there when they found Nick, and even that was bloody. Now I knew what kind of past TC had led, I could see why he was worried about maintaining order.

"Stan hasn't checked in at the last few meetings. Have any of you heard from him?" TC's eyes followed the last man to sit down.

The three of them shook their heads and glanced at each other. I watched them closely because someone was still feeding information to my uncle. We'd had a few of our safe houses ransacked. Guns had been stolen and other items. Some of them had even been burned to the ground.

"No, sirs. We have been watching out for the Italian boss, but we haven't seen him in our territories. The territory with the soldier and the empty one we have noticed have been the ones attacked the most," Brandon answered, his voice raspy from years of smoking.

"We are working on getting someone to be in charge of those territories. Riker is keeping an eye out for him. He has spotted him on multiple occasions. But we need everyone to be on the lookout. Understood?"

"Of course, Don...."

The door burst open, and Riker came in, blood all over his clothes and a bruising right eye. There was another man with him, underneath all the blood, it looked like Arlo. I stood from my seat, but I didn't move toward him. Riker threw him into the table, making it rattle. The man tried to catch himself, and Riker stepped back out of the way.

"Don, I found him sneaking around the warehouse on the dock. Seems like this little sheep has lost his shepherd." The sneer on Riker's face was a little unnerving. I hoped he knew he wouldn't be able to act like this in the public eye.

Arlo looked up at me and glared through his swollen eyes. I chuckled and sat back down. TC stared at him before looking up at Riker.

It looks like we have the second-in-command tonight, boys. What should we do with him?" TC ground out as he looked around the table.

"We should take him underground. See if he can withstand some of the things he used to do with other people," I answered him, bringing Arlo's eyes back to me. He knew what I could do. He had seen that firsthand.

I smirked at him and watched as he tried to get up from the

table. Riker was quick and stopped him. TC nodded to Riker, and the hitman pulled Arlo up and dragged him back out of the door. I didn't think he would be able to charm his way out of this.

"As I was saying before the interruption, I want to know if you think there is anyone you would recommend for those two positions from your own territories. If so, I want you to bring them to the next meeting with you." TC dismissed them, and they all got up except Terry. "Also, I need a headcount of your soldiers."

"Boss, what are we going to do about Stan? I know for a fact he was a loyal man to your father."

"I'll have Riker go to his territory and see if anyone knows his whereabouts."

"I do have to say, though, boss. I don't trust his second." TC and I stared at Terry before he continued, "I'm just going to say I wouldn't put it past him to do something stupid and side with the enemy."

"Okay, I'll check into it." TC answered him.

Terry nodded and left the room. I stared after the man as his silhouette disappeared in the frosted glass. He was very nervous to be in charge, but we never had any issues with his territory. At least it didn't get brought to us.

Turning back to TC, I didn't miss the glint in his eyes. He stood and straightened his jacket. "Let's go down and see if our guest has anything to say."

Chapter Thirty-Four

DRAKE

I followed TC to the first floor and into the elevator in the back. The trail of Arlo's blood made me smirk. I hoped he wouldn't talk so we could make him suffer. We could still make him suffer if he did talk though.

The elevator doors opened, and I could hear him yelling at Riker. That kid was something else. He didn't let his temper get the better of him, and I had never seen him get drunk before. It must be the way he lived, stalking the men we wanted to get a handle on and practicing as well.

Drake and I exited the elevator and walked down the hallway, coming to the first open door. We stepped inside, and my eyes landed on Arlo, already hanging from the ceiling, his toes barely touching the concrete floor. Riker was leaning over by the door and texting.

"He's been screaming already. I haven't even done anything to him." Riker's voice carried over to us as we approached the now silent Arlo.

"So, old man, do you want to suffer for longer? You see, I think you do. What do you think, TC?" I grinned at Arlo.

The ropes were so tight that they were already cutting into his wrists. Riker had left him in his bloody clothes.

"I think we could do longer. It's been a while since we allowed someone to suffer." There was that coldness in TC's voice again. Fuck, I never wanted to be on the wrong side of that voice.

Arlo hocked and spat at our feet, true to his Italian heritage. I never understood why anyone who was captured wanted to piss off their captors even more. Shaking my head, I walked past him and picked up a few things. Riker came over with a table to put the items on.

"Riker, lift him up some more. I don't want his feet touching the floor."

Riker went to the lever and hoisted Arlo up so his toes were no longer on the floor. This was probably the worst part of the torture since it used your body weight to pull your diaphragm longer, making it harder to take a breath. In hindsight, it was harder to get information from someone like this.

"Now that I have you where I want, how about you tell me where your boss is?"

"Fuck... You... Bastard... Child..." Arlo pushed out.

"That's what I thought you would say. Riker, put this bastard so the tips of his toes are touching but nothing more." TC walked over to the table and picked up a knife.

He loved to use knives. I did, too, for that matter, but he did crazy shit with a knife. For a kid with no medical knowledge, it was creepy that he knew where to cut, making sure that he wouldn't kill them too fast.

As soon as Riker had Arlo to his toes, he struggled to get his footing. TC walked up to him and cut his clothes off, leaving him naked. Riker made his way out before TC and I did too.

"You leave me in this room like this, Drake DeLuca, and I will make sure you never see the light of day. I will make that little

American whore mine and let every man in the mafia have her!" Arlo screamed.

I turned and walked up to him. TC was in the doorframe. Arlo wasn't going to be getting out of this place alive; this room was full of death.

"You see, that's where you're wrong, old man. You will never leave this place unless it is in a suitcase. I'm going to enjoy tomorrow because when I come back down here, I'm going to pull out each one of your teeth. So sleep tight." I winked and turned off the light behind me before shutting the door on his screaming.

TC grinned at me, and the three of us headed to the elevator. Fuck, after being up early and working at Churchhill Logistics and then here dealing with this bullshit, I was tired.

My phone began to ring just as the elevator doors opened. I pulled it out of my pocket and smiled. Emi was calling me as I hadn't answered the picture she sent me. "*Dolcezza,* are you missing me?"

"Drake, when are you going to be home?" she whined lustily.

"I'll be home in a few minutes. I'm finishing up at the warehouse with your brother, and then I'll be there." Just her voice was enough to make my body react.

"Okay, but don't stay long please?"

"I won't, *dolcezza*. I love you."

"I love you, too."

I hung up and noticed that both TC and Riker were watching me. Shrugging, I stepped between them and to the door, their footsteps followed me.

"Riker, I want you at the racetrack tomorrow. Monty will be waiting for you. He is older, but he knows his shit. He will show you what you need to do to make you better than you are now." TC turned to him as he stood face to face with Riker that was just a tad bit shorter than us both.

"Yes, sir, but what about Riccardo? If I'm not out there trying to find him, he could hurt any of you."

"We will be fine. I used to be like you before the Churchhills adopted me. Although, apparently, I've been a Churchhill my whole life. I'll be at the track with you tomorrow. If you don't start practicing, I won't be able to get you in on the next race. If you don't win this race, I will pull my sponsorship and all you will be is a hitman. You got that?" TC wanted Riker to believe that he would, but I knew that he wouldn't.

TC knew he was too good to let him not give one hundred and ten percent. Most of the time, TC did this to make the person push themselves harder, and I knew Riker was one to make that happen. Riker nodded before walking off to his bike.

"One of these days, you are going to say something like this and it's going to get someone hurt." I chuckled as the bike revved and then peeled away from the curb.

"Riker has it in him to be a great racer. I don't want him to be stuck in this life if he can find a way out."

"You think that getting him out of this life will be better for him? Because it worked for you, and now you want to do the same for someone else. But what you don't understand is that he is an adult; he isn't a kid like you were," I replied as I walked up to my car.

"I know he isn't, but he can still make a name for himself."

"Then you would lose your best hitman."

"I'm willing to do that." TC opened his door and got in without looking back. But that was him; once he made up his mind, that was what he was going to do.

Shaking my head, I got into my car and started it. I needed to get home to Emi. I didn't plan to make her wait any longer than she already had for me.

· · ·

After parking in the garage, I exited the car and headed for the door. Knowing Emi was upstairs, probably naked in our bed, was making me hard.

I took the steps two at a time and made my way to our room. When I looked through the paritally open door, Emi was where I knew she would be—her hand between her legs with that purple toy buzzing on her clit.

I undid my tie and belt and walked in. Emi's eyes cut to me, and a grin played on her lips. She closed her eyes and leaned her head back against the pillow.

"Are you making yourself feel good, *dolcezza*?"

"Yes." Her whimper was breathless.

I continued forward, shedding my shirt and pants. My cock was so fucking hard I was already leaking. When I got to the bed, I was completely naked. Fuck, just watching her play with that beautiful pussy had me gripping my cock to keep from busting my load.

"Does your pussy feel good with your fingers inside it?" I stood by the side of the bed, watching her play.

"Yes, Sir. But not as good as you." Her breathing started to become rapid, her chest rising and falling, pulling her babydoll taut each time.

I chuckled and walked into the toy closet, searching for the dildo that she liked being stretched with. After finding it, I headed back to the bed. Emi's eyes never left me as I knelt between her legs, showing her the toy.

"I want you to use this on yourself. Make yourself come all over it like it's my cock." Emi took the toy and replaced her fingers with it.

Her eyes never left mine as she slipped the silicone cock inside of her. I sat against the footboard, my legs wide as I watched her slip it in and out, her cream already at the base. My hand matched her urgency up and down my shaft.

"I'm coming!" Emi screamed as she arched her back, her whole body tense as she came undone.

"Fuck, *dolcezza*, do you see what you do to me?" Cum shot out, covering my hand and stomach.

Emi licked her lips. Getting to her knees, she crawled over to me, the still-buzzing vibe on the bed with the cum-soaked dildo. I cocked my brow, staring at her, as she licked up my cum from my stomach.

She glanced up at me, her eyes hooded while she ran her tongue over her lips. I released my cock and grabbed her face, crashing my lips to hers. The taste of my cum on her made me hard and searching for another release.

"I want to come all over your cock. Can I, Sir?" Emi's pupils were wide as she held my gaze.

"Fuck, asking like that will get you whatever you want, *dolcezza*." I moved my hands from her face to her hips, guiding her tight cunt over my cock.

Emi was still wet as she sheathed me with her warm, wet core. Her nails bit into my shoulders when I met her with a hard, deep thrust.

Chapter Thirty-Five

EMI

When Drake brought in the girthiest dildo I had ever seen for me to use on myself, I didn't know if I would be able to go through with it. It was something that I had never used before. The ones I had were smaller than this, but the dream of him watching as I came undone had come true.

His cock stretched me just like the dildo had done, but the way his hands ran up and down my body made me scorching hot. I met each of his thrusts with my own. The bars lining his shaft rubbed against the walls of my pussy. The way I wanted to come all over him pushed me to the edge.

"This pussy of mine feels great around this cock. When we set a date for the wedding, I want you off that birth control. I wasn't kidding when I told you I wanted to put DeLuca babies inside of you," Drake grunted against the skin of my throat.

"Whatever you want, I'll do it. I want to give you however many children you want." And I meant it because I wanted that with Drake, too.

Drake grinned at me before crashing his lips back to mine, taking my breath away as he continued to fuck me like this was our last time. His fingers pressed into the back of my hips, holding me on his lap. I continued to grind against him, my clit brushing against his groin, bringing me the release I wanted.

I leaned my head into the crook of his neck, taking deep breaths to compose myself. Drake's hands threaded into my tresses before pulling my head back, giving him access to my throat. "*Dolcezza,* we need to shower. Then I'm going to put you to bed so that you are well-rested for tomorrow."

"Why do I need to be well rested?" I giggled as Drake scooted us off the bed.

When Drake carried me, I felt like I was above the clouds. He kissed the tip of my nose as he slipped inside the shower door and turned on the water. He pivoted before the cold water could hit me. The water hit the tops of my feet, which were wrapped around Drake's waist, causing goosebumps to race up my legs.

"Because I plan to take you somewhere."

"And what about TC? Does he know?" Drake set me on my feet and stepped under the shower. The rivers of water ran through the creases of his muscles and down his muscular thighs. "He will when I get out of here. I meant to tell him tonight, but we had a surprise from Riker."

"What do you mean?" We switched, and he let me under the water to wash my hair.

"Riker found my uncle's second-in-command. He is waiting for me and TC to find out what he knows." I cut my eyes to him while I rinsed the shampoo from my hair.

Drake belly-laughed as he washed himself with the loofah. If I continued to stare at him, I would end up jumping him. I didn't think that he would concede on that because he wanted me to be rested in the morning.

"You promised to tell me everything." Sometimes, guilting him meant he'd tell me things, but other times he was steadfast with his decisions.

"I did if it was beneficial. This isn't, so I'm keeping my mouth shut." Drake zipped his lips with his hand.

Rolling my eyes, I moved out of the spray to wash myself. The way his eyes roamed my body had me smiling inside. I had never had a man make me squirm like he did. Drake finished his shower and stepped out, grabbing his towel.

By the time I got out, Drake was standing with the towel hung low around his waist. His happy trail marked the way to one of my favorite parts of him. The softness of my towel caressed my body, drying my skin.

"If you and TC are trying to get this man to talk, why are you taking me somewhere?" I wrapped the towel around my body and went to the sink.

"Because we have to let him stew for a few days." Drake came behind me, wrapping his strong arms around my body. "You smell amazing, *dolcezza*."

"Drake, if you want me to be well-rested, you can't get me wet again." His hands ran over my body, making my towel fall off.

"I know, but you look so gorgeous."

"Drake, let's go to bed." I held his gaze in the mirror. His five o'clock shadow tickled my neck.

"But I want to play now." Fuck me. I turned in his arms and gazed up at him.

"I want to play, too. But you said that we needed to rest so you can take me somewhere." I used my finger to run across his cheek and down to the corner of his lips.

"You are a tease, *dolcezza*." He sighed before kissing me. "Let's go to bed. I'm going to do some shit to you that you have never done before."

"You say that like you want to scare me," I answered as we walked back into the bedroom.

"You know I would never scare you. I'm just promising you a good time."

I crawled into the bed, and Drake followed me. Drake pulled me close, and I settled into his side. My cheek rested on his chest as I played with some of his chest hair while we fell asleep.

The alarm blared, startling me and bringing Drake up with me. My hand went to his arm and squeezed. I glanced over at him, and he shook his head, bringing his finger to his lips. His eyes were hard as he turned and reached for the gun, which was between the bed and the nightstand. "You stay right here, you got it?"

I nodded, and he walked out of the room, leaving me alone. The blaring finally ended, but the pop of shots had me running to the window.

Shadows of men were running around the grounds. I didn't know who was out there. There were mounds littering the grounds, which I could only assume were bodies. My thoughts went to Drake. Would he be okay? The gunshots faded, but not before a bullet hit the window of our room.

The round made me fall onto the wooden floor, bruising my butt. I turned on my hands and knees and got to my feet with the help of the footboard. Getting to my feet, I headed to the door, trying to shut it before running inside of our closet.

I didn't have anything to protect myself with. To say I was scared was an understatement. Hiding in the farthest corner of the closet, I pulled his suits around me to try to keep anyone from finding me quickly.

The muffled sound of the door crashing into the wall had me curling up into a ball until I heard his voice.

"Emi! Where are you!"

Life came back into my limbs, and I was able to climb out of my hiding spot. Drake entered the closet, and the sagging of his shoulders when his eyes landed on me made me run to him. He wrapped those strong arms around me and pulled me close.

"I was so worried that they had got you." I had never heard the tremble in his voice before.

Drake held me at arm's length and looked me over, which gave me time to check him over, too. Other than a few cuts and bruises forming, there wasn't anything life-threatening.

"How did they get in here? And didn't you leave naked?"

"Yeah, I did. Luckily, Benton had some sweats in the closet. If they had seen my fat cock they would have run screaming." Drake chuckled, and I shook my head.

I couldn't believe he was trying to make jokes. Staring at him, the grin slowly faded from his lips. "That isn't funny, Drake!"

"I know it isn't. I was just trying to lighten the mood. How they got in, I'm not sure yet, but we will find out. This is your haven, I won't allow this to happen again." Drake grabbed me by my upper arms, keeping my attention on his face.

"I believe you, Drake."

He nodded and led me back to the bed. "Go back to sleep. I'm going to meet up with the security personnel to see if they have anything to tell me. After that, I will be back."

"Do you really have to go now?"

"Yes, I need to know how this happened. We stopped them this time, but that won't keep them from coming back if I have a mole in my team."

I nodded and got into the bed. Drake kissed my forehead before heading out of the room. Just because he told me I needed to go to bed didn't mean that I would be able to sleep. The thought of something like that happening again without him here scared me.

When Drake came back in the room, I was halfway finished with my book. He cocked an eyebrow and sat beside me. "Why are you still up?"

"There was no way I was going to be able to sleep after all of that."

"And yet you could read that book with the things we do on the daily." Drake's hand landed on my thigh and squeezed.

"You need to get a couple of hours of sleep before our trip."

"Yeah, I think you're right. Wake me before ten o'clock..." I glanced at him from the corner of my eye. He was already asleep before he even finished his sentence.

Shaking my head, I returned to my book, getting lost in the world of shifters and vampires.

"Drake," I whispered, shaking his shoulder. He groaned and rolled over.

"Drake, it's ten. You said to wake you up." He turned again, trapping me under him.

"Just five more minutes."

I tried to push him up off me and then sighed, allowing him to lay on me since there was no way I was going to be able to get him off me. Drake laughed and pushed up to his hands and knees. "Okay, come on. Get dressed in something comfortable."

Drake got up and headed to the bathroom. I cocked my head while staring at the sway of his tight ass as he went across the room. Reaching the bathroom door, he turned and caught me staring at him.

"Chop chop, *dolcezza*. Get that beautiful ass moving. TC is going to be mad if we miss this." Drake clapped his hands before he shut the door.

"What do you mean that TC will be mad? Drake DeLuca, you come out of that bathroom this minute and tell me what you mean," I questioned him as I strolled to the door. I tried the handle, only to find that he had locked it .

Chapter Thirty-Six

DRAKE

I was a little late getting to the racetrack. TC would just have to deal with it since my uncle decided to raid my house at three o'clock in the morning. The motherfucker thought that he was going to get in and out without me knowing. Well, I proved him wrong.

The fucker was going to die. It might not be today or the next, but he would be having a watery grave before the month ended. I pulled into the parking space assigned to me, right next to TC. Shutting off the engine I glanced over to Emi and grinned as she pulled her gaze from her phone.

Exiting the car, I went to the other side and let Emi out of the vehicle before touching the hood of TC's car. It was just now getting cold so I wasn't too far behind. Emi and I walked in the main entrance of the track and down the hall to where TC said to meet him.

"A racetrack? Really?" I glanced down at her as she took in the pictures on the walls.

"What? This is your brother's venture, not mine," I told her, placing my hand on the small of her back.

I led her through the archway and along the sidewalk up to the main building behind the new grandstands. The nice new building had gone up quickly and another was being erected on the other side with more stands.

This place was a real stink-hole before TC decided to buy it. He said that it would be a nice tax write-off. But it was also good for Riker to practice on.

TC let others practice here, too, but not for free. Their owners paid for track time, and that was only when TC didn't have it for Riker. I was surprised the kid was able to deal with the strain of racing and working for us.

I opened the glass door and ushered Emi into the building. The tile sparkled in the sunlight that filtered through the open door and the white walls held pictures of previous racers that had been here and won. Black and white pictures of older superbikes racing on the older track were on there as well.

We came to the elevator and I pressed the button to allow us to go to the VIP floor and the box. I stepped in with Emi, pressing the VIP button for the floor. From the corner of my eye, I watched Emi as she stood there beside me. I didn't want to take my eyes off her.

The ping of the elevator alerted us we had reached our floor and the doors opened. TC didn't skimp on this floor either. The tan paint and bluish grey walls led us to the only door at the end of the hall.

Reaching the VIP box, I opened the door and ushered Emi inside. There were two reasons I let her walk in front of me: one, so that if anyone came up from behind me, I'd be the first line of defense, and second, so I could watch that plump ass sway in front of me. Fuck, it looked amazing, but it was gorgeous when she rode my cock in reverse cowgirl.

My eyes took in everything from the new floors to the paint on the walls. TC even had it stocked with his favorite liquor. When

Aurora was taken, he went downhill with his drinking, which was hard to see. Though he had been less of a drinker since Aurora was found.

Aurora wasn't at the track as she was on bed rest. TC had made sure that she hadn't lifted a finger. And he called me whipped. I shook my head when I spotted him in the balcony, which was a new feature.

"This is starting to look nice." TC turned to me and smiled.

As much as the man was hard and didn't show emotion, there were rare times when he did with me and his family. I walked up to him and looked down at the track below. That was the first thing that he'd had repaired.

"It is. I hope to have this place up and operational within the year. Right now, it's just a practice track. But I hope to have races here." The palm of his hand landed on my shoulder.

If this and that child with Aurora made him this happy I wasn't going to keep that from him. He had been without this type of love for a long time. TC turned and motioned for Emi to come to us.

"Come here, Emi, look at this place." Emi shook her head but stood between us.

"Wow. So, what happens here? Anyone going to explain?" Emi questioned while turning to her brother.

"This is where racers will practice and hopefully race at in the future. Plus, you will be the first to see Riker in action before his debut race." TC pointed to where a bike was parked.

Below us, two men were talking. One was in leathers with a helmet on, but I knew who he was. Riker was getting his shot to be a household name instead of one of the FBI's most wanted.

"Who is that?"

"He is the racer I'm sponsoring. If he wins his debut race, I will keep him as a racer; otherwise, I'll drop him, and he will become an independent."

Emi laughed and turned back to watch Riker get on the bike and set off. I smiled at her; she knew that her brother wouldn't drop him. We watched Riker speed past and then back away on the jumbotron. The kid was good. I could give him that.

"So, who is he?" Emi asked again, looking between both of us.

"His name is Riker Kidwell. If he races this well with competition, then he could very well be famous." TC finally answered her.

"Does he have a sister?"

We looked at each other. I didn't know whether Riker had a family. This was news to me, and it looked bad on us for not knowing.

"I don't know. I've never asked him."

"I think he does. His last name is the same as a girl I knew of. She was a year below me in high school."

It didn't take Riker long to finish his practice and come back into the pits. I could only imagine how hot it was in that suit with the helmet on. And then riding the bike and keeping it going at that speed.

"That is the fastest lap he has done."

"When do we actually get to meet him in person? I mean, if you are his sponsor, then why can't I go up to him?" Emi turned on her brother and crossed her arms over her chest.

"Because I don't want to distract him, which is why I don't allow the press in here. It's something I do for all the racers. That way, they can get on and off the track easily." Looking at her, TC held her gaze. She was one of the few to actually stare at him like this. He didn't like it when anyone else did it.

"Oh, well, it's good that you are protecting him. I want to let you know that I expect to be able to watch all his races."

I turned her to face me. "Do you like the racer, Emi?"

"No, but I'm family, and I like superbike races."

"So, do I need to buy a bike? Will that make you like me more?" I chuckled as she blushed.

I knew she loved me. I wasn't a jealous guy, but I knew her obsession with bikes and the men who rode them. TC laughed and went inside the VIP box.

Emi and I followed him in. He had sat in one of the new seats and I noticed that he didn't get a glass of liquor from the bar. I took the one beside him, and Emi sat next to me.

"So, Emi, have you been planning your wedding? You know that Mom will want to get that planned soon," TC asked eyeing how close she was to me.

"Yes, Mother and I are planning. But that doesn't mean that I'm getting married this year. I don't have to rush mine," Emi quipped and stuck out her tongue.

"Yeah, yeah. Keep that up and you will see if you get to keep anything." Even though his voice was dark, the glint of humor in his eyes told us that he was playing.

"So, what's on the agenda today, Drake?"

"Well, since my house was raided last night, I need to find out some information from our guest." TC leaned on his elbows to be able to look at both of us.

"What do you mean? Riccardo attacked your house?"

"Yes, it's time to visit our friend."

TC nodded and rose, straightening his jacket. He went to the door and turned back to us.

"Well, if you want to get answers. I will meet you there. Take Emi back to your house." He turned back and left the room.

"Are you going to take me back to the house?" The whimper in her voice hurt me because I knew she didn't feel as safe at the house after last night.

I stood from my seat and held out my hand for Emi. "Yes, just because he got in once doesn't mean that he will get in again."

I pulled up to the warehouse and went inside. Riker's bike was already here and so was TC's car, so I headed to the elevator. This man was going to give me what I wanted and that was that.

When the elevator stopped at the basement, I made my way to the room housing Arlo. The door was open, and I walked in just as TC stabbed him in the leg. He made sure that he didn't hit anything vital, but blood still squirted out from the wound.

After shedding my jacket, I hung it on the rack and rolled up my shirt-sleeves. It was good that I wore something more comfortable than my usual suit. I was planning to get dirty.

If my uncle wanted to come after my woman, I was going to make sure he felt it in his own ranks. I walked up to Arlo. Not only did he have multiple stab wounds, but he looked like he had been hit a time or two before I got here.

TC turned to me when I reached him. Arlo was breathing heavily. His glare made me laugh, because that was the only thing that he could do. "Has he answered anything?"

"I haven't started interrogating him. The thought that he and his boss came after my family pissed me off. I was letting off some steam." TC cut his eyes to me, a sadistic grin on his face.

"That's fine. He deserved it." Turning on my heel, I went to the tray that held the torture implements that we were going to use.

I had intentionally left it in front of him to make him think about what would happen to him. Grabbing the pliers, I glanced over at Riker, who was leaning against the wall.

"Hey, Riker, go grab some more rope. I need one of those legs tied behind him." Riker nodded and went into the storage closet.

Returning my gaze back to Arlo, I smirked up at him as he

started wiggling in the ropes, trying to get loose. Riker was good at knots, and that motherfucker wasn't going to be getting free anytime soon.

Riker came back out with the rope and went behind Arlo, grabbing him by the foot. He tucked it behind him, wrapping the cord around his ankle and then his upper thigh before tightening it. Arlo continued to thrash in his bindings as I stalked up to him.

"If you touch me with those, I'll make sure your woman gets the same thing!" Arlo shouted, trying to spin away from me.

I reached out my palm toward TC, and he slapped the hilt of his knife in my hand. The blood-covered hilt slipped in my hand so I flipped it to hold the blade and wiped the handle on my pants.

Turning my glare back to Arlo, I gritted my teeth. His eyes widened as much as they could, and he flexed his stomach and arms. In one swing, I buried the knife behind his kneecap.

Chapter Thirty-Seven

DRAKE

I felt the snap of ligaments and cartilage as the blade sliced through Arlo's knee. The first time that I did this, I didn't even notice the subtle stops the knife hung up on, but now I knew what it felt like going through. Arlo's screams made the dark part of my soul jump with joy. I left the blade in his leg where it hung, bleeding onto the cement floor. I grabbed a stool and put his foot on it.

"Fuck you, Drake!" His face paled with the pain.

"Naw, man. I don't swing that way. But just wait; I have more things planned for you. Like taking those nasty toenails off." I chuckled and kneeled. Taking the pinky toenail with pliers, I yanked. Blood trickled down the sides of his toe and onto the floor.

If he didn't talk, I would be taking all ten nails off. Then I'd take the bastard's cock off. I was going to get information from him one way or the other.

Arlo screamed again, and Riker smiled. "I didn't know you could be a freak like this Drake. You are my new best friend."

I winked at him and took the next toenail. Arlo screamed

again, his skin wet with sweat from the pain. I waited for him to say something before pulling the next one and glanced up.

"So, Arlo, where is Riccardo? If you want to keep the rest of your toenails, you'd better start talking."

"He is going to kill you. He knows about your house's defenses. Just because we never went there doesn't mean we don't have people there waiting." I reached down with the pliers, grabbing hold of the next toenail. "No, no, no, no! I'm not done! He wants to make sure we are who will be in charge of the company. Your grandfather made a deal and Riccardo feels like he has been cheated with how well the company is doing."

TC moved beside me and buried another blade in between the fifth and sixth rib. Arlo coughed up blood as it flooded his lungs. To me, it was too easy a death, but that company was just as much his baby as the one growing inside of Aurora.

"That company is mine. If he thinks he is going to take it from me, he is sorely mistaken. I will make sure when I get hold of him that I let him suffer a lot longer than you did," he snarled, as the blood ran down his hands and onto his sleeves.

"Riccardo is laying low at the hotel in the territory that doesn't have a leader. But you will never get rid of all of us. We will always have someone loyal in your ranks," he whispered, blood spraying with every breath.

"I will make sure that you don't. As long as I'm living, you won't hurt my family. They may not be blood, but they are more loyal than you fucks ever have been," I growled at him. The corner of his lip rose a little.

"You have your father's spirit. Too bad it won't be enough." Arlo coughed up more blood before he took his last breath.

I shook my head and signaled to Riker to cut him down. When his body dropped, the knife in his knee broke. I headed to the sink in the corner of the room and washed my hands, watching the blood turn a lighter pink as it ran down into the drain. Fuck, I needed to do that more. I was getting a little out of control.

"Drake, we know which territory he is in now. We need to act so that we can end this. He can't get to anyone in our family. He has to go." TC washed his hands beside me, hissing into my ear. It was nothing I didn't realize myself.

"I know, but we have to play it smart. He wouldn't have let his underboss be caught if he didn't have something else up his sleeves. Riccardo isn't someone to underestimate." I tore off some paper towels and dried my hands.

"I'm not going to underestimate him. But if he touches Emi, my parents, or Aurora and the baby, there won't be a corner on Earth he can hide in that I won't burn."

"You won't be alone, brother." TC nodded, slapping me on the back while we walked out of the room, Riker on our heels.

"So, are we going to find a bonfire and sing kumbaya?"

TC ignored him, but I turned on him in front of the elevator, getting in his face to make sure I had his attention. I liked the kid, but now that we had people's lives on the line, there wasn't time for jokes.

"Are you trying to be funny? Because it isn't the right time. You have to learn to read the room."

"My bad. Do you want me to get the clean-up crew down here?" Riker asked just as the elevator opened up.

"Yes, I need you for something else." TC ground out as he stepped to the back of the car.

"Do you have a sister?" I asked, taking my place beside TC. Riker was part of our business which made him family. I needed to know whether what Emi had said was true.

"Yes, and she's dating a douchebag that I'd like to put in an unmarked grave," Riker answered, the vein in his neck throbbing told me I had hit a nerve. His eyes had darkened.

"Well, you know that we have plenty of those." I egged him

on. Hell, I would love to find the guy so I could teach him a lesson. I may have been a player before Emi, but that changed when she and I got together.

"I would, but she claims she loves the fucker. If he disappears, she will know that it was me, and she will hate me forever. I mean, I think she already does because I wouldn't let him come to the house."

"All you can do is watch her back and be there when he hurts her," TC added just as we got back to the main floor. He wasn't wrong, but I wouldn't have given him that advice because I didn't have siblings.

"Riker, I want you to meet me at the estate. Okay?"

Riker nodded before he pulled his phone from his pocket and turned on his heel to call the clean-up crew. I went to walk to my car when TC stopped me. His hand gripped my shoulder.

"You need to get rid of those pants. There are extra clothes upstairs. Burn those." I glanced down and saw what he was talking about.

I hadn't even noticed that I had become covered in blood. Hell, I needed to change my shirt, too. "I think I need to get rid of this whole outfit. Do you need me at the estate?"

"No, you need to get back to Emi. Is Heath still with her?" TC looked at his clothing. The only speck of blood that he had on him was on his sleeves.

"Yes, along with more of my men. I decided that since she wanted to sneak away from her guard, she needed more than one." I chuckled and turned to walk away.

"Drake?" I turned back to TC and grinned, "Did she sneak off from him when she was at the company? Is that how long you two have been keeping this from me?"

I shrugged and continued to my office. I needed out of these bloody clothes.

The darkness of the night surrounded my sports car. I hadn't realized we had spent so much time with Arlo until I left the warehouse. The moon hung high in the sky, and the stars shone a little brighter here since there weren't many lights. Wind came around the building, bringing the smell of the Pacific Ocean to me.

I had texted Emi to say I was on my way home, but she hadn't replied back. It made me worried since my uncle's attempt at getting in. So I had the pedal to the floor, hoping that a cop didn't pull me over. But they wouldn't have been able to catch me anyway.

When I checked the cameras in the house, everything was quiet. The house was dark, and I didn't see anyone walking the halls. Men were patrolling the walls like I had instructed them. I probably put more than I needed, but my uncle wasn't going to get my girl if I could help it.

He didn't know it yet, but we were going to take him out. My uncle would be six feet under before the family across the pond even knew. The clean-up crew was already dealing with Arlo.

I rounded a curve a little too wide when lights came up behind me. It had either pulled out behind me or had been there for a while. The car came up on my tail, almost rear-ending me. If I weren't trying to get to Emi, I would have brake-checked the mother-fucker. Changing the gears, I stepped on the gas, surging forward. I watched as the car behind me became a dot in my rearview mirror.

Letting go of the gas, I slowed down. I didn't need to get pulled over when I needed to get home to Emi. The car jerked to the side, and I glanced over to see another car rubbing up against me. Hitting the brake, the other car flashed in front of me before crashing into the bank on the other side of the road.

The sky lit up as the vehicle exploded in flames. If it had been a few miles back, it would have been in the ocean. Not like drowning in a metal can was better than burning alive in one. I gunned the car again when I realized the other car was coming up behind me again. "Fuck, who the fuck are these assholes?"

Shifting down. I pushed the car to its limits. I sped down the curvy road, trying to keep away from the car behind me. My focus was divided. The only person I could think who could be doing this was my uncle. If he was behind this, I was going to have the time of my life when I got a hold of him.

I glanced to the passenger side just in time to see lights coming for me. The impact flung me and the car into the side of the mountain. My head hit the window, shattering the glass, and a searing pain ran down my arm. One gunshot rang out before another crash came from behind me. I reached over to try to find my gun to return fire but couldn't find it. It wasn't in its holster, and there was no sign of it in the car.

Hands were all over me, pulling me out of the wreckage. Metal crunching and caving onto itself was the last thing that I heard.

Chapter Thirty-Eight

EMI

I woke up and reached for Drake, the cool sheets waking me more when I realized that he hadn't come home. Sitting up in bed, I grabbed my phone from my nightstand. This wasn't the first time he had been out all night, but he normally texted to let me know that he wasn't going to be home.

Double-tapping the phone didn't wake it up; it stayed dark. I searched for my cord and plugged it in, and the phone flashed zero percent. Fuck. No wonder I didn't hear it go off.

Laying it back on the nightstand, I went to the bathroom. My bladder was screaming at me. I'd had a couple of glasses of wine to calm my nerves when I had been dropped off. Drake had kissed me and then sped off in his black sports car; the sun caught it just right to show off the iridescent purple shimmer in its paintwork.

Something was making me uneasy. It wasn't like me to be like this. I sat on the toilet, staring out of the window into the sky.

I finished up and washed my hands, hoping that I had given my phone enough time to charge to turn it on. Maybe he had texted me, and I didn't get it because it had died.

Sitting on the side of the bed, I grabbed my phone and turned it on. My heart skipped as I waited for the text that I was hoping would come through. After the phone turned on my notifications started popping up. I went into my messages, and my heart sank.

I'm on my way home, dolcezza.

If he was on his way home and he didn't get here, something must have happened. He wouldn't have told me that he was on his way and then not come home. That wasn't like him at all. Unplugging my phone, I ran down the stairs, hoping that he was home but had to deal with something.

I ran into Heath and Zach at the bottom of the stairs and grabbed Heath's shirt.

"Have you heard from Drake?"

"No, he didn't come in the gate last night," Zach answered my plea.

Letting Heath go, I pulled up TC's number. He was the last one Drake was with. It rang and then went to voicemail. I tried again, and he picked up. "TC! Have you heard from Drake?"

"No, I left before him at the warehouse. He said that he was going home. Is he not home?"

"No, he's not. Can you call someone to find him?" Tears were running down my face.

"I'll ping his phone and see if we can find him. Don't worry, Emi. I'll find him." TC hung up, and I sat on the bottom of the stairs to wait for any information my brother could find.

Heath and Zach stood in front of me, waiting for me to say something, but there was nothing to say. I mean, TC had a body-guard who knew where he was all the time. Did Jake do the same with Drake? Is that how TC was able to track him?

My ears were humming, and my heart was racing. I felt like I needed to throw up what I had to eat last night. The phone in my hand rang startling me as I had almost forgot that it was in my hand.

"Hello?" My voice trembled as I answered my phone. I didn't know what information that TC had.

"Emi, I'm on my way to where his phone last pinged." my brother's voice came across the speaker at my ear. My heart jumped into my throat at his answer.

"Come get me. I want to go, too!" I answered him as I rocked on the steps trying to calm myself.

"No, Emi...."

"TC! Don't treat me like I can't handle myself. Come get me right now!" I stood and brushed past the two men in front of me. Even though I was in a T-shirt and shorts, I was going. "I'm on the front porch you better get over here now."

The sigh from the other end of the phone told me he was doing as I had asked. I wasn't a child, and this was the man I wanted to spend the rest of my life with. "Fine, I'll be there in ten minutes. Jake turn around and head to Drake's. We need to get my stubborn sister."

The squeal of tires in the phone made me a little more happy. They were coming to get me.

We drove in silence down the back road to mine and Drake's home. This road was notorious for crashes and over half of it were cliffs, so people often went over the side and into the ocean, never to be seen again. Jake rounded the next curve and came to a sudden stop. A cop blocked our path, and I could see emergency lights a little further ahead. My hand tightened in TC's, and I glanced over to him.

"Is that where he is?"

"Emi, for the love of all things that we love. Stay. In. This. Car. Do you hear me?" The intensity of his blue eyes held me in place, and I nodded. I could see why so many people thought that he was mad all the time.

TC got out of the car and approached to the officer. I couldn't make out what they were saying, but the cop finally radioed someone. TC turned to the car and nodded, Jake got out and then opened my door. His hand tight on my upper arm.

"Thanks, Colt."

"No problem, Mr. Churchhill." The young blond cop lifted the tape, allowing us to move forward.

The sounds of people moving quickly ahead of us started to get louder. None of the sirens were on, but the flashing lights were beginning to hurt my eyes. As we turned the next corner, another cop came up to us and led us behind the fire truck.

My heart stopped when I saw the mangled wreck of the sports car that Drake loved. He'd had the car custom-made, and now it wasn't recognizable. Boulders rested on top of the car, and men were using a crane to lift them.

If Jake hadn't been holding my arm, I wouldn't be standing. There was no way that Drake was alive. The car was flat as a pancake. I couldn't hold back the sob any longer, and I broke down.

TC pulled me into his arms, my face in his chest as he continued to talk with the officer. I didn't hear a thing that they were saying. My whole life was in that car, and now I wouldn't be able to see him or talk to him ever again.

I sat in TC's living room, Aurora holding my hand as TC, Jake, Sam, and Riker talked in front of us. I didn't hear much of it as my thoughts were running a hundred miles per hour. What did Drake feel in his last moments? Was he scared?

The emergency crews wouldn't let us stay after they removed the boulders and started to pry the car apart. In my mind, I knew that he wouldn't have survived that. Even if he had gotten as low as he could in the floorboard, he would have been crushed.

"...did you see the tire marks? Someone T-boned him before those boulders hit." I heard Riker say over my rapid running thoughts.

"There were more tire marks from the back end of the car. He didn't crash into the side of the mountain. He was pushed into it," Jake answered, crossing his arms over his chest.

"The officer at the scene called me after they got the car apart. There was nobody in the car. Someone had to have pulled him out," TC carried on.

So, Drake wasn't dead? Could he still be alive? And if someone had pulled him out, why didn't they take him to the hospital? Why didn't they call the authorities to let them know that they had him?

"What are you thinking, sir? You think his uncle has him?" Riker asked the one question that I didn't even think about.

If Drake's uncle had him, he was probably hidden somewhere. We would never find him unless his uncle wanted him found. This was worse than thinking he was in all that rubble of the car. "What are you going to do now?"

All the men turned to me and stared. I hadn't talked much since I saw the car. Part of me thought why hadn't I stayed home?

"We are going to find him. If his uncle has him, he is going to contact someone to brag about having him. It's how these people work," TC answered, kneeling in front of me.

I nodded. TC was the best brother that any girl could ever ask for. I knew now that he was my cousin, but he would always be my brother. TC gave me that crooked smile that I had only seen him use with me, our mom, and Aurora. It was something that he reserved just for us.

"Now, has anyone spoken with Mr. and Mrs. DeLuca?" TC stood and gave me his back as he went up to the other three.

"No, I can call them if you want me to," Sam answered.

Gwen, TC's cook, came up to me and handed me and Aurora a mug. From the spicy apple scent, I could tell that it was apple cider. A few moments later, she brought a tray full of pastries and fruit. They all had me salivating since I hadn't eaten since I had woken up. I hadn't wanted to eat when the thought of Drake not being here was all I could think about.

"Yes, see if his uncle contacted them. If he has, we might be able to get a triangulation of where he might have him." TC's face was full of worry as he stood there waiting for the DeLucas to answer.

"Mr. DeLuca, it's Jake. I wanted to know if you had heard from Drake or your brother?" Jake nodded and answered with a lot of 'uh-huhs and yeahs' that I didn't like that one bit. "Thank you, Mr. DeLuca I will keep you informed."

Jake hung up the phone and glanced at everyone in the room. "He hasn't heard from them. But if he does, he will let us know."

My phone began to ring, and everyone stopped what they were doing and stared at it. I had forgotten it was charging on the table. No one moved. I didn't know the number on the screen. One of the things I didn't do was answer numbers I didn't know.

"Emi, answer your phone!" TC yelled.

I reached for the phone and slid to answer it. It was quiet on the other side, but I thought I heard water dripping. "Hello?"

"Why hello there, little Chuchhill. Do I have a surprise for you?"

Chapter Thirty-Nine

DRAKE

My whole body felt like I had been run over by a Mack Truck. I went to raise my hand, but something was keeping it from moving. Squinting my eyes, I tried to figure out where I was. The place was musty, and I thought I could hear water dripping somewhere from behind me.

The grinding of a door opening made me cringe, and whatever I was sitting on was making my ass numb. Steps slapped against the concrete toward me. I had to be in a basement of some sort. My vision was still blurry when I was finally able to open my eyes.

"About time you woke up. I thought we had actually killed you with that little stunt of ours. But you did kill two of my men, which I believe allows me to take the lives of two of your people." My uncle's voice came from my right side.

I tried to get up and realized that not only were my arms tied but also my legs. He came into my line of sight with a smile on his lips. I glared at him, and he laughed harder.

"Unfortunately, that comes with the territory—soldiers die," I growled and then smirked, "And so do underbosses."

"What do you mean?" My uncle grabbed me by my collar as he got in my face. "Where's Arlo!?"

"Let's just say he's taking a forever nap." I laughed at the look on his face when he worked out what I was saying.

"You think you are funny? Well, let's see what your little fiancé will say." He walked away from me and grabbed his phone, dialing a number. "Alex, get me Emerald Churchhill's number."

He turned to face me as the phone rang and then smirked when Emi picked up. "Why hello there, little Churchhill. Do I have a surprise for you?"

"Emi, don't do anything stupid. Whatever he says to you, make sure you tell TC! Don't worry about me!"

My uncle put his hand over the phone and spoke to me. "Drake, how can you tell her those things when you know you won't be okay?"

"Now, dear, this is what is going to happen. We are going to show my nephew just how much he means to you and the other Churchhill. The only way you will get him back alive is when TC gives me Churchhill Logistics, and, of course, the LA syndicate. If you don't, Drake dies."

"Emi! Don't do that! I'm not worth that, and TC won't do that!"

"Will someone gag that fucker!" Another man came from behind me and taped my mouth. I didn't need them to lose all of that because of me. I was sure that TC wouldn't because we had told each other that the company came first. "Right, now, that's better. So, what will it be, little lady?"

She must have told him something he wanted to hear because his grin widened. Fuck, if I could find a way out of this, then I could stop them. Riccardo hung up and came over to me, tearing off the tape.

"She's going to talk to her brother. I did this to show you that blood is thicker than the people that you have surrounded yourself with. Next, I will show you what happens when you turn your back on family." He nodded and went to sit by the door.

Two men came up to me, cracking their knuckles and wearing crooked smiles. I glared past them to my uncle, who sat there smiling. "The difference between me and you, Uncle, is I handle my own dirty work. I severed Arlo's knee, keeping him from being able to use it while I pulled out his toenails."

The taunt didn't seem to do much other than to have him turn a shade of red that I had never seen on a man before. I had gotten under his skin, and I would take whatever these two brutes could dish out. The first punch blurred my vision and made my ears ring.

"Is that all you have? You fuckers need a lesson on how to punch."

Asshole Two went for my midsection, snapping a lower rib in the process. Motherfucker wasn't just big but knew how to throw a punch. I didn't have time to egg them on anymore as they threw fist after fist.

A few more ribs broke as did my nose. They stopped after a few hours, leaving me in the chair. All I could think about was that Emi would hate me if I didn't make it back to marry her.

I spat out the blood that was pooling in my mouth from the cuts in my cheeks and gums. My tongue ran over my teeth, making sure that they were all there, which surprised me since they didn't hold back on their punches.

My vision was coming back to me again, and I was sure that I had a concussion, not only from the wreck but from their punches. If they thought this was bad, they didn't know the extent of how I tortured Arlo. The sharp pains every time I breathed in were worse when I took a deeper breath.

Taking sips of air to satisfy my body's need for oxygen, I sat there in pain from my ribs. It was going to be a long night as I tried to keep myself up because if I had a concussion, it wouldn't be a good idea to go to sleep. If I did, I might not wake up from it.

The lights came on, and I blinked as I glanced up. Asshole One and Asshole Two came in, bringing with them a few things that I would use to torture someone. Well, this was going to hurt. Hopefully they just want to get in my head, but I knew this shit.

"So, you knuckle-heads decided to get a little dirty." I tried to laugh, but the movement hurt my ribs.

"Not us pussy. We've got someone who is going to show you a thing or two." Asshole One guffawed before he and the other left the room.

It had to be the next day because my stomach was complaining that I hadn't fed it, and my head was killing me. It could either be because I hadn't had any water or the concussion. My ass was also still numb on this wooden chair I didn't even know if I had one anymore.

The door opened again, and a young woman came in with food and water. The way my mouth salivated at the thought of food had my stomach growling constantly. When she reached me, she placed the tray on the ground and opened the bottle.

It cracked before she was able to twist the cap off, but that didn't mean it hadn't been tampered with in other ways. I stared at her until she took a sip of the water and then she allowed me to take small sips.

"What's your name?"

She shook her head, making her red curly hair swing back and forth. I should have known that they would have briefed her that I would ask her questions. So, I decided to let her be for now. If they kept me here any longer, or if TC and the others didn't find me, I would try again.

That was if they sent her down here again. The girl went to the other side of the room and grabbed another rolling tray to sit the food on. Grabbing the spoon, she fed me some of the most awful mashed potatoes I had ever eaten. But it was something in my stomach, and I was grateful for that.

After she had fed me the rest of the food, she gave me more water. Letting me finish it off, she placed the water bottle on the empty tray and left me in the room. I just hoped that she wasn't here against her will. If she was, then I'd make sure I got her out of this hellhole.

It wasn't long before a man came in. He shed his jacket and grabbed the white apron with blood stains on it. I didn't know who this man was, so I could only assume he was from Italy. He was an older man, and I wasn't going to let his age deceive me.

"So, Uncle Riccardo is still being a baby and can't handle his own shit, huh?" I still couldn't laugh because of the broken ribs.

"Your uncle has more important things to do than what I'm about to do to you. We will see if that little Churchhill will still marry you if you aren't the pretty boy you are now." The old man grinned, showing me missing teeth.

My heart was racing as he turned to the table and tied the apron. He grabbed gloves from the bag he had brought in with him as he whistled. I was going to be in some fucking trouble if he decided to use that heating rod. He spent a few minutes at the table, tinkering with something.

"Are you going to start anytime soon, or are you just going to stand there?" I struggled with the long sentence since my ribs were broken.

"You're wanting to die quickly, huh?" He turned around with a knife in his hand.

"Well, I know I'm probably not going to get out of here alive, so." I tried to shrug but only ended up hurting myself.

He came up to me and ran the blade along my leg and up my chest, not getting too close to the bindings on my wrists. The blade cut my face from the bottom of my left eye to my jawline. Well, there went the wedding photos.

Blood ran down my face and into the five o'clock shadow I had been sporting for the last four days. I stared ahead of me, not looking at the old man whose knife was ready to rake down the other side of my face. The door opened, and in came my uncle with the two brutes.

"Your fiancé called. Said that her brother wants a meeting. Is there anything you want me to tell her since you won't be seeing her, and I will?" I didn't like the look on his face. There was no way TC would give this fucker the shit he asked for.

"You can go fuck yourself, Uncle. I don't know what you are playing at, but they would never meet with you." He had to be fucking with me to get me to speak.

"No? I think that they will. See the text? That right there is the time and place." Fuck, that was Emi's number, and the place they were meeting at was one of Jack's old haunts.

Were they really going to do this? They couldn't. What was their plan because they couldn't do what he thought? This had to be a way to get him out in the open. We never used that place to meet with people, even would-be officers.

Chapter Forty

EMI

I was nervous that this plan wouldn't work, but I was hopeful as well. My part was to keep Riccardo busy while TC and Mr. DeLuca went to rescue Drake. So here I was in this bright pink short-as-fuck dress. I kept telling myself that this was for Drake, and that was how I was going to get him back.

Turning from the mirror of my bathroom, I walked out to head downstairs. It had been weird being here without Drake, but it wouldn't be long before I had him back. Riker had found the abandoned building that he was being held in.

I just hoped that they hadn't hurt him too badly. If they had, I hoped TC made them hurt even worse. As I walked into the hall and to the stairs, the front doors opened. TC and Mr. DeLuca must be here. Riker was already in position.

TC was talking to Heath at the front door. He had made sure, since Drake wasn't here, that there were plenty of security patrolling the perimeter. I had refused to stay with him and Aurora. This place had become my home, even if it felt off because Drake wasn't here with me.

I walked down the stairs to my brother and Mr. DeLuca. They

were in jeans and a T-shirt, which I had never seen Mr. DeLuca in. It made him look like a normal person.

TC turned to me and raked his eyes over my outfit. I wasn't too thrilled with it either, but if I was to keep Riccardo busy, I needed it. He cocked an eyebrow at me, and it took everything in me to keep from laughing at him.

"Look, you said to distract him. How was I going to do that? I mean, I could have gone naked." I crossed my arms over my chest as I stared back at him.

"I wouldn't have let you go naked. This is bad enough. You don't let him touch you, do you understand? If he gets too handsy, you let Heath know, and we will pull you out of there." TC stood still until I nodded.

Would I let this man get handsy with me? Absolutely not. But would I do anything to keep him distracted enough to get Drake out of there? Yes, I would.

"Is that all you are going to tell me?" He hadn't told me anything other than we were going to one of Jack's old haunts and that I needed to keep Riccardo there.

"I'll explain more in the car. We need to get you there before Riccardo gets there. That way, you are already there when he walks in." I nodded, and TC took my hand, leading me out of the house. Mr. DeLuca was behind us. Heath went to get another car.

TC opened the door for me, allowing Mr. DeLuca and me to enter the car before him. I sat on the back seat along with TC. Mr. DeLuca sat in front of us.

"Emi, you need to be aware of your surroundings. My brother is not like me. He may have others there with him. I know you are not carrying a purse, but I would like if you carried this." Mr. DeLuca pulled a three-inch blade from his jacket along with a sheath to carry it with, "This was my grandmother's knife. When TC said that you would be distracting Riccardo, I figured that you would need something to protect yourself if he grabbed you."

He handed it over to me. I had never used a knife other than to cut my food with, and now I had a blade that could kill someone. "But I don't know how to use something like this. Where would I even put it?"

"This sheath is able to go around your thigh, but you will have to put the knife between your legs; otherwise, the dress you are wearing will give it away that you are carrying," TC answered me.

"What do you mean between my legs?" Was he insane?

"Like this." He grabbed the knife and showed me on his leg. The blade was facing his crotch, and the handle toward the ground, "Your dress will cover it. Just make sure you are quick enough to pull it. If he gets a hold of this, he could slice your throat in one swipe."

I nodded and took the knife back. When I got to the location, I would go to the restroom and strap this on. The sheath made sure that the blade wouldn't touch me.

If they thought he was going to hurt me, then why were they even doing this? I knew that Heath will be near me, but would Riccardo recognize him? I was starting to get scared, but I needed to get Drake back.

The car stopped in front of a bar, and I realized that Heath had gotten there before we had. That meant that he was already in there. He had probably staked it out as well to see if there were any people who were working with Riccardo.

I reached for the door, and TC grabbed my hand, shaking his head. He texted Heath's number, and we waited. TC got a text back, and he allowed me to get out. I tried to conceal the knife as best as I could.

Opening the door, I looked around and spotted Heath in a booth by the bathrooms. I walked over and went in so I could attach this to my thigh.

I sat at the bar with a glass of wine. Apparently, this place had to search for it because they never sold it. I didn't want to get anything to drink, but   it would look suspicious if I was drinkless.

The knife had me constantly moving in my seat, and I knew that I would need to stop that. Otherwise, Riccardo could get suspicious. If I hadn't come in the office when I did that day, a woman that had training to do this would have been able to take my place.

The door opened,, and a group of guys approached the booth beside Heath's. My heart was racing because all I could think was that they were here with Riccardo, and they were right on time. I glanced at the clock on the wall to make sure that it was that time. The next time the door opened, Riccardo stepped in.

He was in a suit, and his grey-peppered hair was slicked back. When he spotted me, I didn't like the smirk on his lips. Riccardo grabbed the seat beside me, and the bartender who had been cleaning glasses came up to us. "What can I get for you, sir?"

"Your best brandy," he answered without ever taking his gaze from me.

The man nodded and reached behind him to grab the bottle and a glass. Once he poured the amber liquid, he placed the bottle under the counter and walked away. I didn't want him to leave me even though he really didn't. He was just on the other side of the bar waiting.

A server walked around the floor, making sure everyone had what they needed. I didn't know how she was able to handle the whole place.

"Where is your brother?" If the man didn't have my fiancé held captive, I would have thought he was handsome.

"He's on his way. The other meeting ran over," I answered him, trying to keep my smile in place.

"Good, maybe we can get more acquainted than what Drake allowed in his office." His hand rested on mine, and it was hard not to immediately pull away from him.

I didn't like that he was touching me. I was sure that Drake would kill him and anyone else that tried. Slowly pulling my hand out from under his, I picked up my drink and took a sip. Riccardo watched me like a predator watched its prey.

"I don't see why we can't talk a little bit until my brother gets here. And when I marry Drake, we will be family, will we not?" I asked him, the wine giving me just a little more bravery than I had a few moments ago.

"Yeah, we could be family, but I don't think Drake will pick you after this. You see, as a male in the Italian mafia, we have to marry within the brotherhood. I hope you understand. He could always use a mistress, though." Riccardo smiled and tipped his drink back, draining it in one swallow.

Drake would never marry someone else. Hell, he didn't even know if he wanted to be the head of the Italian mafia. So I stared at him, trying to come up with something I could say but coming up blank.

"What, cat got your tongue?" Riccardo waved down the bartender and ordered another drink.

If I could keep him drinking, maybe I could get him drunk enough to be able to give TC and Mr. DeLuca time to get Drake. I took another drink of my wine and smiled.

"No, I was just wondering. If that happened, would that also mean that his wife would be able to have other men on the side? Or was that only for the male?" The way his face turned red told me I had hit a nerve.

Drake had told me that his wife had gotten pregnant and had a boy. But that boy, to his uncle's knowledge, wasn't his. That was what he had told Drake as to why he was there.

"No, the woman would only be there for her husband." His grip on his glass tightened, and if I continued this, I didn't think he would drink anymore.

He finally calmed down and then drank some more of his

brandy. Riccardo's other hand went to my thigh, and I tried to close them so that he wouldn't be able to get to the blade. From the corner of my eye, I noticed Heath getting up from his seat.

I grabbed his hand and placed it back on the counter, giggling. "Now, Riccardo. I don't think that your hand should be there."

Heath went to the restroom so as not to inform anyone who was there that he was with me. This was getting a little dangerous. I hadn't gotten any information on whether they had been able to get Drake out or not.

Heath came back out and approached the bartender. He didn't have a drink at his table other than the coke he had with his partially touched meal. The bartender nodded and then came over to us and poured me a whiskey on the rocks. That was my brother's favorite drink, but he didn't normally get it on the rocks.

"Looks like you have another admirer..." Riccardo's phone went off, and he answered it.

Riccardo's eyes snapped to me and then to behind me. I couldn't tell if he was staring at Heath or the men that had come in before him. The group of men stood and slowly walked up to us. They were with him.

Chapter Forty-One

TC

Jake drove away from the bar and onto the interstate to take us to where Drake was being held. Letting my sister face that man had my stomach in knots. Riker texted me, letting me know that he was ready and that there were no guards at the place. That bothered me even more. Even if I believed I had a person in a place where no one would find them, I would still have someone there to be a guard.

When we reached the house, I would never have thought that he would be in there. It blended in with its surroundings. No one would have thought something crazy was going on here. The house was a nice little place, but it was big enough to hold a lot of people.

Yes, Sir.

"Jake, find a place to hide the car. When I text you or if Riker texts, bring the car back around. If I know these people, we will need to take Drake to the hospital," I instructed as I exited the vehicle.

"Of course, sir." Jake nodded, and I shut the door after Mr. DeLuca got out.

We strolled up the path to the house. Even though Riker had told me that there was nobody on the grounds, that didn't mean that I wasn't going to keep my eyes peeled. Finally making it to the porch, I pulled my gun and turned to Mr. DeLuca.

He signaled for me to proceed, and I kicked in the door. A shrill scream rose, and boots ran down the hall. Raising my gun, I scanned the nearest man coming to me. He was huge and carrying an even bigger gun, spraying bullets at me and Drake's father.

I returned fire, putting a bullet in the guy's head and dropping the other man behind him. More shots rang out further in the house as I went into the living room, clearing it. Making my way back into the hallway, I opened doors, clearing them as I went through to get to Riker.

The kitchen was a blood bath there were at least four bodies on the ground, bullet holes everywhere. I spotted Riker over at the table with a red curly-haired woman. She was crying into his shirt,

"Anyone else here?" I questioned him.

"No, I got everyone in here. I found her hiding under the bar." Riker turned to me, a knot forming above his left eye.

"I don't see Drake anywhere. Are you sure you found the right house?" Mr. DeLuca asked as he holstered his weapon. He hadn't had to use it since I took out the only two who came to meet us.

"Do you mean the man who looks like you?" The girl's voice was raspy from all her crying. She couldn't be more than eighteen.

"Yes, is there someone else here?" I went to her and kneeled. She reminded me of Emi.

"Yes, he's in the basement. I was just about to take him food when he burst into the kitchen.

"Take us to him," I told her as I stood. She dried up her tears and led us to a door.

Opening it, she pointed down the stairs, and I glanced back at Riker.

"Stay with her; Mr. DeLuca and I will go down to get Drake. I want information from her by the time I get up here with Drake." Riker nodded and pulled the girl away from the opening.

"There's another man down there with him. He didn't look very friendly. And he looked at me weird." She shivered, and I could only guess why. He wasn't going to make it up from this basement.

I raised my gun and headed down the stairs. There was no way that he didn't already know we were here. If he didn't, that just meant we still had the element of surprise. Reaching the last step, the drip of water floated over to me, along with a copper smell.

That wasn't good for Drake. I took a deep breath and went further into the basement. Drake was tied to a chair, and he looked like he had been in that car when it was wrecked. Dried blood was on his hairline and a long scar ran from his eye to his chin. His eyes still held the fight I knew he would always have until the day that he died.

The old man behind him had a knife to his throat, a sadistic smile on his face. One of his eyes was clouded and he had multiple scars on his face and arms.

"Come any closer, and I will slit his throat." He pressed the blade tighter to Drake's throat, making his point.

What he didn't know was that I didn't need to go any closer to kill him. I scanned Drake for any other injuries. He looked fine, but I wouldn't really know until I got him to the hospital. After getting him there, I would go and kill that fucker who did this to him.

"Drake, are you hurt more than what you look?" I asked. I knew that he was hurt, there was no question about that, but I needed to know if he had any broken bones.

"I don't think so, but my whole body is numb from sitting here," Drake rasped, trying to keep the knife from cutting any more.

"Let him go and I might let you live," I yelled to the man with the knife to my friend's throat.

He shook his head and pulled the knife. I raised my gun and squeezed the trigger, putting a bullet right between his eyes.

Drake

When I heard the gunshots upstairs, I knew that my brother had found me. How was a different story. One I would ask when I got out of here. The fucker who had been torturing me came around behind me, the knife in his hand resting on my shoulder. The way I wanted to kill him for all the shit that he had done to me was strong.

But I knew that I wouldn't get to. There was no way I would be able to get out of these restraints. Heavy steps got closer, and he put the knife to my neck. Fucking scared bastard thought that hiding behind me would save him.

TC came in first, and then my dad. I didn't expect him, but I was glad to see him. Riker couldn't be too far behind.

"Come any closer and I will slit his throat." I didn't put it past him as the dull blade bit into my skin.

"Drake, are you hurt more than what you look?" TC questioned me, his eyes scanning me.

I knew I looked like shit. Hell, I felt like shit. "I don't think so, but my whole body is numb from sitting here."

"Let him go and I might let you live." I knew that if he did let him live, he would be in our basement at the warehouse, and I would be doing a whole lot worse to him.

I felt the pull of the blade. TC quickly raised his gun and squeezed the trigger, dropping the man behind me. My father came forward with a knife of his own. He started removing the rope from around my ankles and wrists. I didn't know if I would even be able to walk.

"Come on, man, let's get you out of here." TC put my arm around his shoulder and his arm around my back, hoisting me to a standing position.

We waited a moment, and the blood rushed back into my feet, the tingling sensation keeping me from moving. TC pulled his phone from his pocket and sent the code word to Jake. He must have been the one driving.

"If you are here, who's meeting with Riccardo?"

"Once I get you to the hospital, I'm going back for her. She has Heath there if anything goes sideways," TC answered me as we slowly made it to the steps. My father was behind us, making sure that we didn't fall backwards.

"You mean you sent your sister to meet with that man?"

"Yes, she had a knife on her. I needed her to distract him so that I could get you. If she hadn't already met him before, I would have used one of the women in the syndicate."

"I'm not going to the hospital until we get her. There is no way he doesn't know that you broke in here to get me. Did you see a youg woman upstairs?" I was worried about her. She needed to be brought with us; I had a nagging feeling that she was taken from her home.

"If you don't think you need to go to the hospital right now, I will let you go. And yes, she's in the kitchen with Riker."

I nodded. I didn't want her to be in this house any longer. Even though she wouldn't talk to me, I knew why. If they had caught her talking to me, she would have been dead. We got up to the kitchen, and Riker came over to help TC take me through the house.

The woman followed us, and my father brought up the rear. Jake was in the driveway when we got out. Riker and TC carried me down the stairs and into the car.

"I'll meet you at the hospital. I'm going to make sure we can't be traced," Riker said as he left the car.

TC and my father got in and shut the door. Fuck, these seats were soft. Jake backed out of the driveway and onto the road.

"Jake, take us to the bar. We need to get Emi before Drake will go to the hospital." He nodded and turned down another road.

If that man had touched one hair on her head, I was going to kill him. TC shoved a bottle of water into my hand, and I lifted it to my lips. I chugged the liquid down faster than I had ever drunk before.

We reached the bar, and Jake stopped, allowing us to get out. My limbs were no longer numb. After the water, I felt refreshed, but I also had a stabbing pain racing down my arm. My adrenaline made me do things I normally wouldn't. TC opened the door, and we walked in.

Heath was pointing his gun at Riccardo. Who in turn had two guns on him. The bartender had his shotgun pointed at one of the men near Heath. TC raised his gun, pointing it at my uncle. Emi's eyes landed on me, and she smiled.

Riccardo didn't have time to react when he spotted us, and I didn't see Emi's knife until she plunged it deep into his stomach. His eyes went wide, and the men he was with didn't see the bullets coming for them.

"That is for taking my fiancé away from me." I heard Emi say, and she pulled it back out before burying the blade into him again. "And thats for touching me and saying he wouldn't be able to marry me."

Fuck, she was beautiful when she was mad.

Chapter Forty-Two

DRAKE

When Emi stabbed Riccardo, my heart swelled. That woman, even though she had been raised away from the mafia life, knew how to handle herself. I fell back against the wall, my legs giving out on me, which brought everyone's attention to me.

Emi's eyes widened, and she ran over to me, pushing us further into the wall. We slid down to the floor, and she curled into my lap. She cried into my shirt as Riccardo's blood seeped from her dress. I pulled her close and held her as the others took care of the bodies.

"Come on. She's fine. Let's get you to the hospital." TC and Heath helped me up from the floor, throwing my arms over their shoulders.

"Yeah, I think it's time to go," I answered him weakly. When Emi had crashed into me, I was sure that she had broken the ribs even more. But I wasn't going to tell her that.

They helped me through the door and into the open car. Emi slid in with me, scanning me for anything that she thought was injured.

"Make sure to clean up those bodies. I don't want to see them found. Do you understand me?" TC growled out the orders to Heath and the bartender. Yancy had been under Jack for years, which was probably why he had my uncle meet here.

"Are you okay? What is going on?" Emi's hands ran over my body, causing a hiss to escape my lips.

"I'm alive, but the hospital will let me know if there's anything I should worry about." I smiled at her as I stroked her cheek. "Where did you get the knife?"

"Your dad gave it to me before I met with Riccardo." Emi pulled up her dress and showed me the sheath that was attached to that scrumptious thigh.

"Of course he did. My great-grandmother's?" I had seen that blade in my father's display case.

"Yes, I'm glad I had it." Emi pulled her dress back down when TC entered the vehicle.

"Is my dad staying?"

"Yes, he is going to help keep things under control. He will meet us at the hospital. They are getting your room ready and will be testing you to make sure you aren't bleeding internally," TC answered me, crossing his right foot over his leg and knocking on the window between us and Jake.

The car moved forward, taking us to the hospital.

My stay at the hospital was a long one. Ribs were broken, along with a shoulder that needed surgery to repair it. Internal bleeding because of the car crash and the assholes. After that surgery and recovery, I was allowed to leave.

My mother and Emi's were full steam ahead with wedding planning. I just wanted to make the woman my wife. My father had pulled the knife from Riccardo and cleaned it. Giving it back to Emi who said that it was now rightfully hers. Emi was proud of the weapon and had no problem showing it off to me.

I didn't mind her having it. It made her even more beautiful. I waited for her to meltdown after killing Riccardo, but she never did. She came and went from the hospital, bringing me things that the hospital didn't want me to have.

TC walked into the room his dress shoes clicking on the tile floor. Before he stopped beside me and grabbed my bag from the bed.

"You know I don't need help carrying that." I turned to him just in time for him to chuck it to me. Catching it with one hand, I dropped it back on the bed.

"Let's go. I'm ready to get out of this place. Between you and Aurora, I'd rather not be here any longer than I have to be. Okay?" TC crossed his arms and leaned against the wall, waiting for me to finish what I was doing.

"I thought Emi was coming to take me home?" I asked, grabbing the bag that I replaced on the bed and the paperwork that I was given.

"She was, but Mom and your mother decided that it would be a good time to go dress shopping. So, I came back to help you home."

"Well, then let's go then." I walked past him and out of the room.

Since I was on the VIP floor, there weren't many nurses and doctors at the nurses' station. This floor was now for TC and his family and friends. We also paid a few of the doctors out of our own pocket to stay on. They didn't ask any questions, and we didn't offer any answers.

We strolled down the hallway away from the room I had called my cell while I was here. TC walked beside me as I carried my duffle bag to the exit. We walked past the nurse station on our way to the elevator.

I pressed the button to take us to the ground floor. The great thing about TC was that we didn't always have to talk when we stood beside each other. Silence was comfortable with us.

While I had been here, the only thing I could do was watch TV. The news had covered the house that I was held in. Apparently, a gas leak caused an explosion. The bodies in the house were unrecognizable. I had to chuckle because that had Riker written all over it.

The woman had been brought here too and had been checked over. I didn't want to say that she was going to be fine because, hell, who would be after being trafficked? Just because she was physically fine didn't mean that her mind was still intact.

I had learned that her name was Chiara and that she had been taken from her family because the father had accumulated too much debt to my uncle. A few of the other girls had been sold to other wealthy people in Italy, but she had been kept by Riccardo. She was then brought over when he sent for reinforcements.

Chiara had promised me that no one had touched her, but she had a feeling that the man who was torturing me had wanted to. She had seen it in the way he looked at her. If TC hadn't killed him, I would have fucked his world up.

The elevator finally opened, and we stepped in. It was slow today, or I was just ready to get home and be with Emi. TC hit the button to take us down to the garage.

"So, what are you going to do about heading up the Italians?" TC broke the silence.

"I don't know. I may just let the kid take it over," I told him. I wasn't going to move to Italy. My place was here at TC and Emi's side.

"I think you need to go there for your honeymoon and make sure the kid is Riccardo's. If he isn't, appoint a person to handle that side of things. That's if you really don't want to stay over there."

"I'll see if Emi wants to go there for our honeymoon. If she does, we will, and I'll handle things over there. If not, I'll go after and deal with it."

After Emi had killed Riccardo, chaos had ensued. A man who had been loyal to my father had asked him to take his rightful place as Don. He refused. If the kid turned out to be Riccardo's son, I would have the man who had called my father in charge until the kid came of age. If not, I didn't know what to do.

I knew I wasn't moving there. Turning my head to the reflective wall of the elevator, I saw the work that had been done to my face. They wanted to try to fix the scar on my face, but I felt like it made me hotter. "Are you admiring the scar that we could have fixed?"

"Yeah, I think it makes me look more dashing. What do you think?" I chuckled,

"I think you look like an imbecile, but that's just me." TC had tried to convince me to get it fixed. Should I have fixed it because I was the COO of the largest logistics company in LA? Yeah, probably but other than getting it the way I did, I sort of liked it.

The doors opened to the garage, and TC exited before me, leading me to his car. I was devastated that mine had been totaled in the accident. I would have to buy a new one, again. Getting in the car, I threw my bag in the small space behind the seats and leaned into the leather.

"I'm not thinking about that today. Just take me home."

Today felt like deja-vu.

I now understood why TC was almost drunk at his wedding. My nerves were fucking shot as I stood at the altar, waiting for my girl. Aurora sat in the front with the baby in her arms. TC didn't have an issue walking with Emi's new maid of honor because he was able to keep an eye on her from the front. The little boy in her arms was quietly sleeping, but even if he was screaming, I wouldn't have cared.

The wedding party was already in position, and the only person I was looking for was my dolcezza. When the music changed, I stared at the doors, waiting. The doors opened, and there she was, just as beautiful as she was last night.

Her mother was adamant that she stay in her childhood home the night before. I didn't sleep well and decided to sneak in and see her.

Scaling the side of her home to her balcony last night wasn't as easy as I anticipated. I stayed with her until it was almost morning and then went down the side of the house before anyone was up. What I didn't expect was running into Jake, he just laughed and sent me on my way. The man was cool.

Now, though Emi was walking up to me on the arm of her father. She was fucking gorgeous, and I was ready to make her mine. The white strapless gown hugged her body and then fanned out at her knees. Lace ran down the top of the bodice and to the end of the dress.

Emi's flowers were bright and happy, just like she was. Her smile brightened my soul as she neared me. Mr. Churchhill handed her to me and went to sit with his wife and Aurora.

"If there is anyone in this room that objects to this marriage, speak now or forever hold your peace."

Then, Emi did something I never thought she would. She lifted her dress and showed the tip of the knife strapped to her thigh. Everyone laughed, including the priest.

DRAKE

We landed in Italy and checked into our hotel. The car I had requested was parked in the driveway, looking sleek and nice in the afternoon sun.

I had carried Emi over the threshold of our home before we left, so for good measure, I picked her up, threw her over my shoulder, and went inside.

The driver brought in our things and left after I tipped him. He was very excited about what I had given to him.

"So, Mrs. DeLuca, do want to go with me to meet more of the family? Or do you want to stay here?"

"I'll go with you. I think I've proven that I can take care of myself."

We took a little time to get our bags unpacked and then hit the road. I had already called Matteo, my father's loyal man, and told him that we would be there in the next ten minutes. He had told me that he would have the people who needed to be there waiting for me.

Before the wedding, I had him do a paternity test on the boy.

Luckily, they had blood from Riccardo to test it against the boy's. Matteo would have the results to give me when we reached them.

Emi and I drove along the countryside of Florence, making sure to stay away from the center. The expression on her face told me this was the right decision. Even though we were also here to deal with the shit my uncle wouldn't do.

I turned down a dirt road just before pulling into the drive, I killed the engine, and I went to the passenger side to get Emi. We walked in, and Matteo was the first to meet me.

"Your father could never deny you." Matteo pulled me into a quick hug.

"Yeah, that is for damn sure. This is my wife, Emerald."

Matteo pulled her into a hug before releasing her to arm's length and smiled. He pulled out the envelope and handed it to me.

"Have you looked at it?" He shook his head and led us to where everyone else was.

I went up to the front of them with Emi. I had briefed her on the plane about this, and she was okay with whatever I decided to do.

"As a lot of you know, I'm Giovanni DeLuca's son. Riccardo has been killed for coming after my family in the States. It has, however, come to my attention that Riccardo has a son that might not share our blood. I'm here to see if that is true."

None of the men in the room said anything, so I opened the envelope. Fuck.

"Ms. DeLuca, you and your son need to pack your bags and leave the DeLuca home. Riccardo isn't the father of your child."

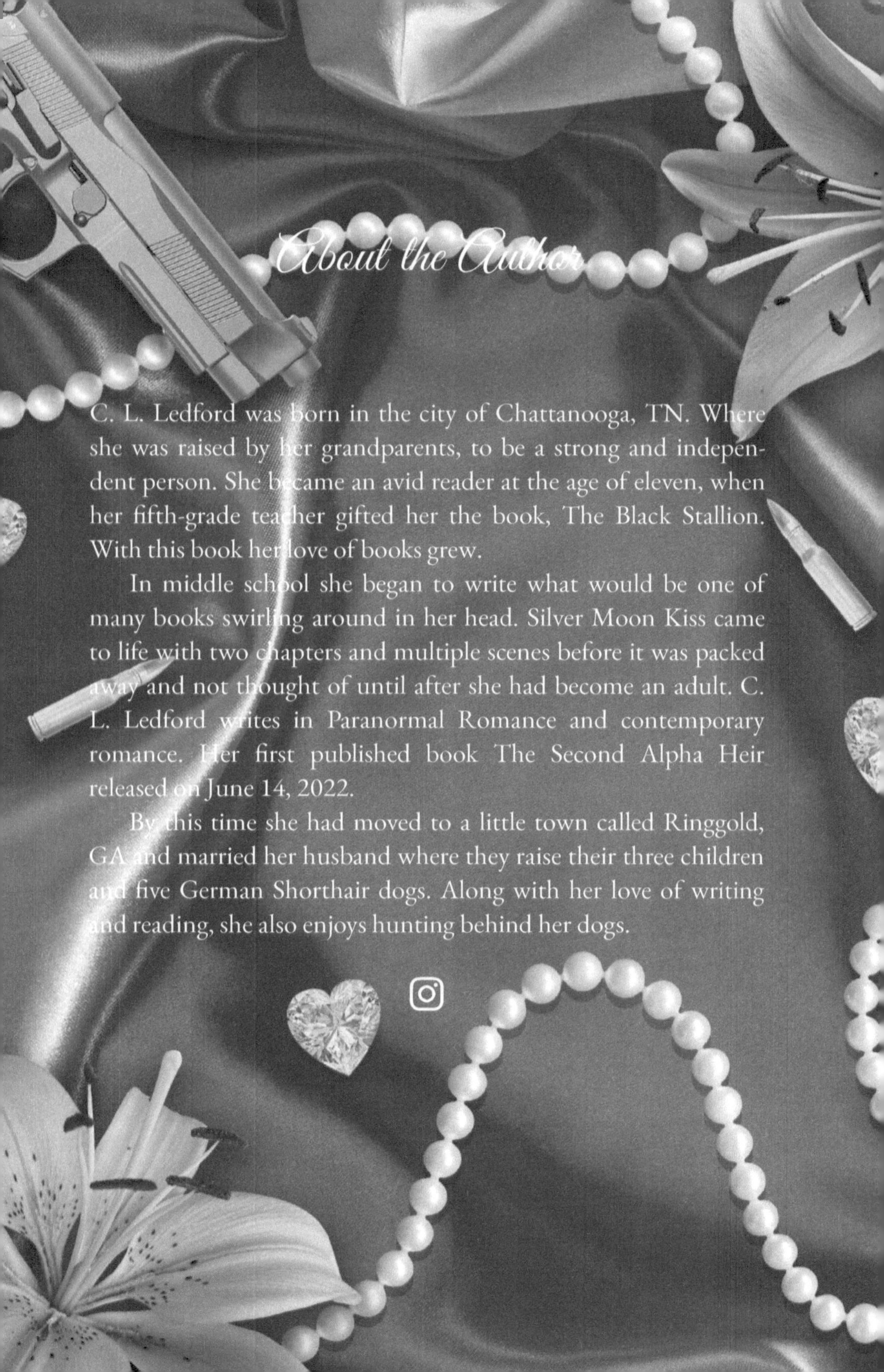

C. L. Ledford was born in the city of Chattanooga, TN. Where she was raised by her grandparents, to be a strong and independent person. She became an avid reader at the age of eleven, when her fifth-grade teacher gifted her the book, The Black Stallion. With this book her love of books grew.

In middle school she began to write what would be one of many books swirling around in her head. Silver Moon Kiss came to life with two chapters and multiple scenes before it was packed away and not thought of until after she had become an adult. C. L. Ledford writes in Paranormal Romance and contemporary romance. Her first published book The Second Alpha Heir released on June 14, 2022.

By this time she had moved to a little town called Ringgold, GA and married her husband where they raise their three children and five German Shorthair dogs. Along with her love of writing and reading, she also enjoys hunting behind her dogs.

Also by C. L. Ledford

Silver Moon Kiss

Silver Moon Kiss: Becoming Alpha

The Second Alpha Heir

The Fallen Alpha

Raising the Stakes

Haunted Love Co-write with J.L. Hinds